Maypole

Devon De'Ath

Copyright © 2019 Devon De'Ath

All rights reserved.

ISBN-13: 978-1-09985-180-3

This is a work of fiction. Names, characters, businesses, places, events, locales and incidents are either the products of the author's imagination or used in a fictitious manner. Any resemblance to actual persons, living or dead, or actual events is purely coincidental.

DEDICATION

In loving memory of Chris Chalk :

An outstanding craftsman and inspirational teacher.

The world is poorer without your gifts.

CONTENTS

1	Trouble in Paradise	7
2	Flying South	27
3	Bramley Cottage	47
4	The Woodsman	69
5	May Day	90
6	Shattered Peace	111
7	Vitruvian Vicar	132
8	A Head for Pastry	149
9	Intolerable Infamy	171
10	Shooting Stars	193
11	Lascivious Lines	213
12	Midnight Meanderings	233
13	Abduction	255
14	Old Flame, New Fire	277
15	Malice Striker	296
16	A Family Reunion	316
17	Just a Number	335

1

Trouble in Paradise

"Think you can play the field, do you? Nobody cheats on me." The man's voice might not have yet reached fever pitch, but his rage was clear. That and the stinging welt beneath Lisa Marston's eye, left the woman in little doubt about her boyfriend's emotional state. The round-faced thirty-year-old female lifted her pale green gaze. A stabbing pain shot up her spine from the tumble she took across the sofa. The dark wood laminate flooring of their living room was anything but comfortable. She didn't see the blow coming that had landed her in a heap on this spot. A cold grey stare locked onto her from beneath a pair of thick brows. Messy designer stubble - trying too hard to look cool - blended into shaved sideburns. These in turn led to a ragged mop of dark brown hair, swept to the left. The man thrust his oblong head forward. "Well?"

Lisa's tummy turned over, still in shock. She fought back a rising tremor that threatened to manifest as tears. The girl wiped the first hint away either side of her short, broad nose. "What are you talking about, Keith? The text was from Daryl. He's a new guy in the office." Her words came with difficulty in a heaving and broken voice. "It was only a message to thank me for helping him settle in."

"And you expect me to believe that?" Keith's jugular pulsed against the collar of his crisp work shirt. He threw his girlfriend's mobile smart phone onto the floor and ground the screen with one heel of his business shoes. The act looked like an interrupted smoker, putting out an unfinished cigarette with frustrated restlessness.

Lisa reached out a limp and hopeless hand as the device shattered. Her head sunk, causing the nut-brown hair that cascaded over her shoulders to flop forward.

Keith kicked the exposed crumpled circuit boards straight at her. "I don't want you going to work today. It's time you got another job."

Lisa blinked. "What the heck is wrong with you? Keith, have you been taking something you shouldn't? You sound like a madman. Of course I'm going to work. The rent won't pay itself. Your salary can't support us both; even in this little flat."

Her statement caused those cold male eyes to flash. A second later he bent forward and grabbed hold of her loose hair. A flat hand slapped across Lisa's face with a crisp and resounding report, amplified by the minimalist domestic chamber with its parallel wipe-clean surfaces. The woman let out an involuntary shriek. She dug her fingernails into the hairy wrist that tugged at her locks. Keith winced and walloped her again. "It's time you learnt your place, bitch."

Lisa tried to stand, without success. Her boyfriend pressed one foot across her folded ankles, pinning them to the spot. The frantic abuse victim scanned around with the limited range of head motion that restraining male hand allowed. Alongside the TV table to her right, stood a simple glass vase. Inside were some yellow freesias she'd bought on the way home from work yesterday. This morning the blooms were beginning to open. Her right hand flicked across and grabbed the container. Before Keith could respond, she tossed the contents at him and smashed the glass against the table. Lisa hammered the broken shards into his arm with as much force as she could muster. The furious man let go and recoiled, holding his blood-stained, lacerated arm with the other. Lisa didn't pause. Thick saliva clogged in her throat as coursing adrenaline delivered a sudden burst of energy to her limbs. She lunged for the hallway, pulled herself up against the door frame and tore at the handle with shaking fingers. Three seconds later she was into the communal stairwell and descending two flights to ground level.

The air was fresh and warm, even at seven-fifteen in the morning that early April Wednesday. Already it was light out, as the panicked female staggered onto the pavement of Back Silver Street. She caught hold of a cool, black bollard to steady herself and even out her breathing. Vertebrae still protesting, Lisa launched herself to the right and stumbled past an array of low, red brick craft businesses that squatted along the banks of the River Wear. The wharf-side residential building entrance door banged again. In the stillness of the early morning, the sound almost tapped the fleeing woman on the shoulder. She glanced back from ascending a southerly incline of the narrow thoroughfare. Keith appeared in the distance, a tea towel wrapped around his injured arm. His head whipped from side to side. Even at this distance, his quarry sensed that piercing gaze fall on her like a searchlight. And then he was coming for her; sprinting like a thing possessed. Lisa bit back a whimper and forced her legs to run. She rounded the corner into Fowlers Yard, grabbed hold of a chilly metal handrail and climbed a set of steps. Her panting breath reverberated off the close alley walls, until they opened onto the upward ascent of Silver Street to the marketplace. The streets of the old town in Durham lay deserted at this time of the morning. The spire of St. Nicholas Church caught the desperate woman's eye. Its door stood fast. She glanced across the open space, from the Victorian buildings to the mounted hussar statue.

"There you are." The growl of her boyfriend's voice burst out of the alley from Fowlers Yard. Keith was gaining on her.

Lisa ran around to the right up Saddler Street, desperate to break her pursuer's sight line. Could she give him the slip down one of the tiny passageways that criss-crossed the many-layered architecture of the ancient hill fort island? The only problem: he knew them as well as she. All those years at university in the city together, made her enraged partner a worthy adversary. *I've got to get help. But where?* Her thoughts turned back to earlier hopes at St. Nicholas. *What about the cathedral?* Her feet thundered against the paving stones, jarring her tender spine. She hurried on up the hill past tightly packed terraced Tudor, Regency and Victorian shops, pubs and cafes - all closed for business. Breathing became tough and laboured at the extra effort required to keep pace into Owengate. Above and to the woman's right, the ancient battlements of Durham Castle peered down. At that moment she wished for some ancient sentry to come back from the dead, observe her plight and stick an arrow in her foe. Her foe? Lisa risked a momentary glimpse across her shoulder. He was still gaining ground, clutching his injured arm in the makeshift bandage. Those grey eyes that once set her heart aflutter, burned with a fire of angry passion and vengeance. Durham Cathedral rose ahead in crowning glory above the city. The fleeing girl wanted to scream for sanctuary with the little air left in her lungs. At least the gradient was level now. Only another hundred yards or so to the entrance path. As with St. Nicholas, the doors stood fast. Lisa paused between two trees bordering the walkway. Should she run to the entrance and hammer for all she was worth? *There must be someone inside, this close to opening time.* Keith reached the level green that stretched out like a carpet before the breathtaking eleventh century house of worship. Lisa paused for a moment. *No time. Too risky. Got to reach busier roads.* A second wind rose at her momentary respite. The woman raced for the welcome downhill stretch of Dun Cow Lane. *If I can make our old*

Student Union, there will be traffic out front I can flag down for help. She doglegged around the edge of the museum. Her desperate steps followed the former church structure down Bow Lane, past elegant street lamps and a townhouse with Doric porch pillars. This fed into a tree-encased footpath towards Kingsgate Bridge. Behind, Keith roared down the hill, hurling obscenities after her like stones to drop his target. Lisa pounded across the high footbridge. Modern Student Union buildings overlooked the far bank, presenting a brusque facade like some eastern European Cold War era throwback. She kept on going to the New Elvet pedestrian crossing. A silver VW Golf emerged along Church Street to her right. The woman waved frantic arms, her dishevelled hair whipping about in all directions. Keith reached the side of the Union building.

"Come here!" he delivered the angry command with such force, the car driver jammed on his brakes. Strength sapped through physical exertion and emotional exhaustion, Lisa tried to reach for the passenger door of the vehicle. A large, bald man in his late thirties climbed out of the driver's seat. Steely blue eyes caught sight of the blood-soaked tea towel clamped to the pursuer's arm. He hurried around the rear of his car, fists clenched to stand between the adversary and his now trembling prey.

"Get out of my way," Keith bellowed.

The driver stood his ground and held up a warning hand. "Keep back, fella. I'm not going to let you hurt the lady. This isn't the way."

"You can fuck right off," Keith barked. He went for Lisa. The driver intercepted him. Both men fell to the pavement in a frenzy of windmilling arms and legs; the energy of their struggle matched only by the ferocity of unending profanity that accompanied it.

A police car cruising south along Hallgarth Street came to an abrupt halt. Seconds later its blue roof strobes flared to life. The engine gunned, and the occupants swept round to pull up in the opposite direction, beyond the Volkswagen.

"Thank God." Lisa couldn't hold the thought inside. She was squatting with her back against the Golf. Two burly male officers decamped from their patrol vehicle and rushed to break up the uncoordinated wild struggle between the bizarre combatants.

The woman sighed. She let her bruised face sink into quivering hands. At last the tears came like a flood. Sobs of shock, relief and heartache burst from her lungs in a relentless torrent of emotion. It was some time before Lisa managed to get hold of herself and calm down.

* * *

"Somebody's in trouble." The words came out in a hushed whisper from a pair of petite, pink lips. Janice Gange curled that tiny mouth into a sympathetic grimace. She glanced around with dark, furtive eyes and toyed with a loose strand of auburn hair that hadn't made it into her bun that morning. Lisa Marston plonked her handbag down at the desktop computer opposite and checked the large office wall clock. Two-ten in the afternoon. She sank into her seat.

"I've had a pretty shit day." They were the first words she had spoken to anyone since entering the building. The woman twisted her head to regard several new pieces of snail mail, sat in her in-tray. It was then Janice caught sight of the purple bruise peeking out from beneath make-up on her colleague's left cheek.

"Oh, my God. What happened to your face?"

"Keith happened to it. Repeatedly with his fists."

"F-u-c-k. Are you okay?"

"Bruised head. A jarred spine. Nothing terminal. Might be a different story if I hadn't stabbed the idiot and made a run for it."

Janice's eyes widened. She blew out her cheeks with a 'pah' noise. "Stabbed with a knife?"

"No. Some broken glass from a vase. All I could get my hands on while he grabbed me by the hair and stood on my ankles."

"Serious? Bloody hell, Lis'. Did you kill him?" She popped her head above the top of the VDU, like a meerkat on the lookout for danger. Might the police be kicking down the office door at 'Carlton Content Creative' any minute?

Lisa shook her head. "I cut his arm and got out of the flat as quick as poss."

"What happened then?" Janice gripped the black plastic arms of her chair.

An ice-cold, authoritarian tone cut across the retelling. "Lisa. A word if you please." Both women knew the sound before they turned. Jenny Duke, a fifty-year-old with a fat face and thick, black shoulder length hair stood rigid in a doorway. Lisa couldn't remember a time those thin eyebrows, hazel peepers, and constant grimace didn't give the Editorial Team Leader a face like a wet weekend. The boss smoothed down her grey power suit and span without another word to re-enter her office.

Janice wrinkled her nose, causing several pale freckles to become closer neighbours for a brief moment. "She's been on at me all morning, to find out where you were. I kept calling your mobile, but it went onto voicemail. No answer at the flat either."

"Keith smashed my smart phone. I've been busy with the cops most of the day." Lisa rose to her feet with a gulp. "I'd better get in there. I'll fill you in on the details later."

"Sure."

"Sit down, Lisa." Jenny Duke didn't look up from her computer screen as her subordinate entered the room. Lisa took her place at a hard, uncomfortable, static wooden-framed seat opposite the chunky desk. Jenny always sat with her executive leather chair pumped to the maximum height. From there she could look down at anyone unfortunate enough to occupy the place on which Lisa now sat. "So what on earth happened to you this morning? You had no leave booked. We didn't get a call. I've had Janice trying to get hold of you for hours."

Lisa fidgeted on the spot and angled her head to maximise the chances of Jenny catching sight of her bruise. The woman's face remained cold and miserable. If she noticed the injury, she wasn't about to make things easy. Once the silence had stretched out to ridiculous lengths, Lisa spoke again. "I got in a fight with my boyfriend. Or rather, my boyfriend lashed out and injured me."

"Your domestic disagreements don't concern this company, Lisa." The words came out in a flash, but she delivered them with deadpan emptiness. "Nor do they give you license to ignore the terms of your employment."

Lisa bit her lip. She wanted to lash out; to fight back. It had been an emotional roller coaster of a day. She took a deep breath, frightened that any outburst might see her dissolve into another puddle of tears. No way would she give Jenny Duke the satisfaction of causing or witnessing it. "I'll file a retrospective half-day leave request on the HR portal, once I'm back at my desk."

Jenny frowned. "I've already subtracted a full day from your allowance."

"A full day?" Lisa leaned forward.

"Of course. Core time in the afternoon starts at two PM sharp."

Lisa gripped her knees. "But I was only in ten minutes after."

"Perhaps you'll be more punctual in the future. I've recorded your unprofessional conduct in a file note. I'd watch it, if I were you. You're collecting quite a pile of those, ahead of your next performance review. I'll be writing it soon."

Lisa blinked. "File notes for what? Suggesting good ideas to senior management?"

Jenny cleared her throat. "There is a chain of command in any hierarchical structure. Best practices and correct channels for communication."

"The company set up a good ideas e-mail box for anyone to submit suggestions for improvements. I only sent one in. A workable solution, too."

"Yes, but you had already explained that idea to me."

"So?"

"So, as I made clear at the time, it caused considerable embarrassment when I presented it at a meeting. Mr Carlton pulled a printout of your suggestion from a file and told me you had already submitted the idea. Do you see why that is a problem?"

"It's only a problem for someone who took a great idea from one of their staff and tried to pass it off as their own." Lisa spoke through gritted teeth. The hackles were rising along with her temperature.

Jenny snorted. "That's quite enough from you, young lady. Your disdain for authority and lack of respect are about to land you in a world of trouble." She pointed a stiff finger at the door.

Lisa left in silence.

"Hard time with the Wicked Witch of the West?" Janice watched her colleague flop down into her chair and spin idly from side to side with a vacant expression.

"She docked me a full day's leave, you know."

"For a ten minute overrun? Cow. What are you still doing here then? She's taken the whole day. I'd bugger off, if I were you."

"I got a lecture about the file notes I'm accruing on my personnel record. She's got it in for me, Janice. My career is toast."

"That's because you've got spark, flair and talent. You're a bloody good editor and a decent staff writer when they need extra help. Duke got that position by default when the firm was a lot smaller. If they had based it on merit, the miserable slug would still be making tea for everyone."

"True."

Janice jerked her head towards the exit. "Go on, then. Off you pop."

"Don't you want to hear what happened this morning?"

"Yeah okay. But don't go doing any work afterwards. Jenny's taking the piss, as usual."

Lisa relayed the full sequence of events, beginning with Keith's discovery of an innocent text message from new office guy, Daryl; to the moment the police showed up. When she had finished, Janice whistled.

"Are you going home tonight? Will Keith be there?"

"After the hospital staff stitched his arm, the police took him in. I went along and spoke to a great Domestic Violence Liaison Officer. They've gained authority to serve a DVPN/DVPO on Keith."

"A what?"

"Domestic Violence Protection Notice/Order. It means they don't have enough to bang him up, but are concerned for my safety."

"So what does that do?"

"It means he can't return to the flat for now."

"How long does it last?"

"The notice is with immediate effect. Should keep him away until their application for an order has been actioned. That lasts between fourteen and twenty-eight days. It'll go before a Magistrate on Friday for a decision. If Keith breaches the order, he could be looking at prison. That would be terminal to his job. Don't think he's dumb enough to risk it."

"Gives you some breathing space, I suppose."

"That's the general idea. Thing is, if I leave Keith, pull out on renting the flat and get a cheaper studio cubbyhole somewhere; I'll be up the creek if Jenny torpedoes my work here."

"Not good. I thought you and Keith were the dream team. Soulmates. Has he done anything like this before?"

Lisa shrugged. "I've noticed him become more controlling of late. He always needs the last word in the relationship. He's become angrier, too. At first I thought it was stress from his Personnel Manager job."

"Has he ever hit you before today?"

"No. I got a shove out the way last week when he was in a mood. Put it down to *one of those things*. Crumbs, I'm starting to sound like some habitually beaten woman who makes excuses for her abuser."

"Don't think that's your style."

"This morning helped me understand them better. I never got it, before. I mean, why would you stay with someone like that for even five minutes? Now when I consider losing my home and think back to some good times Keith and I had at uni…"

"You're not going back to him are you? Shit Lis', you can do better than that."

"No. He's not getting the chance to do that to me again. Bastard's burned his bridges, as far as I'm concerned."

Janice wiped her brow with mock exaggeration. "That's a relief. Well, what you need is a quiet night in with my old friend, Mr Prosecco. He never disappoints. Though, I must confess he's made my head hurt once or twice."

Lisa grinned, stood and hitched her handbag across her shoulder. "Catch you later."

Janice nodded. "Have a good night. See you tomorrow."

* * *

It was three thirty when Lisa got back to the flat. She swept up the remains of her phone and was thankful to find the SIM card intact. *Thank God I always back up my contacts to the SIM.* She tipped the broken components into a bin and retraced the first part of her epic flight from earlier that morning, at a slower pace. A shiver pulsated her upper body, climbing the steps from Fowlers Yard to Silver Street. Once on the hill up from Framwellgate Bridge, she hung a right to the mobile phone shop at the bottom.

Back at home, the thirty-year-old sat down with a large wineglass, a bottle of Prosecco and a box containing a shiny new mobile phone. She eased the cork out of the bottle and poured herself a healthy dose of fizz. Relaxing hands reached round to unfasten the loose plait she usually put her hair in for life beyond the front door. Lisa took a sip of the drink and let the bubbles tease her palate. One of this world's simple but ecstatic pleasures. Eyes closed for a few moments, she felt the rise and fall of her diaphragm while taking some slow breaths. When the corded twist in her shoulders slackened, she allowed herself to focus on the room again. *Let's have a peek at this phone.* It was a newer model, but similar to her previous unit. She prized open the packaging, inserted her old SIM and got down to setting everything up.

The events of the day must have taken their toll. After fixing herself a mushroom risotto for tea, the woman collapsed on the sofa and drifted into unconsciousness. The television gabbled away to itself, until the new phone vibrated on a side table near Lisa's head. She lifted herself up from a cushion used as a makeshift pillow and picked up the device. No number on the screen. She pressed the answer button, held the phone to her ear and tried not to yawn. "Hello?"

"What have you done to my brother, you slag?"

Lisa gawped. It was the furious voice of Shelley Molloy, Keith's sister. "Shelley? What are you talking about? Do you know what he did?"

"Nothing more than you deserved, you trollop."

"What the fu-"

"This isn't over, Lisa. You're gonna rue the day you ever shat on a Molloy."

The phone disconnected. Lisa sat stunned, the phone slipping through her sweating palm. She let it fall and bounce on the sofa cushion beside her. The hallway landline warbled to life. The woman trudged over to answer it. "Yes?"

"Tarts should take what's coming to 'em." It was a rough male voice - gravelly from too many cigarettes.

"Excuse me?"

"You 'eard, slut. Take your beating and mend your ways. Then everything will be fine. Otherwise, someone might 'ave to do a proper job." The man hung up.

Lisa pondered dialling 1471, but thought better of it. First, because the number would have been withheld. Second, because the mouth-breathing rough speech of Keith's elder brother Jonathan was impossible to mistake.

She sat back on the living room sofa and picked up the mobile again. It was time for some moral support. She brought up Janice Gange's number and rang it.

"Janice?"

"Hey you. What's up?"

"Have you got a minute?"

"Yeah. Problems?"

Lisa relayed the content of the calls. "How did I ever get mixed up with a family like that?"

"Both his siblings sound delightful. Keith isn't roughly spoken though."

"No. He's always been a charmer. The smart one of the family, or so I used to think. Jonathan didn't even finish school. He dropped out. Only got employed by that cowboy building firm he works for, because Shelley was sleeping with one of the owners. Both the owners, if memory serves."

"Well, you know how to pick them."

"Thanks. Didn't think they'd ever have much impact on Keith and I."

"Sorry. I'm not helping much, am I?"

"Yeah, you are. I needed someone to talk to."

"How's Mr Prosecco?"

"I drained him dry."

"Slut."

"Please Janice. I've heard enough of those terms for one evening."

"Oops. Kidding."

"At least the bottle is sturdy enough to wallop any of Keith's relatives, should they decide to call."

"Crap. Do you think they will?"

"I hope not."

"Put the chain on the door, love."

"I will. Thanks for the chat."

"Stay safe. See you at work."

When the alarm went off next morning, Lisa had

barely managed a couple of hours rest. The bruise on her cheek throbbed like a calling card from the man she usually woke up next to. Somehow his presence was still in the bed, even though his body remained absent. Her morning routine was zombie-like that Thursday. No quips or discussions with another human soul. It was only the first day, yet Lisa's stomach felt like a bottomless pit of loneliness. Even a decent bowl of porridge and honey couldn't fill that void.

Lisa unlocked her dark blue Renault Clio and rested her bag in the passenger foot well. Seatbelt caressing her into the driver's seat, she fired up the engine. The car rolled forward a few inches, then jostled and shook. The woman applied the brake and got out to check the vehicle. "Bugger." The front offside tyre was flat as a pancake. She walked around to check the others. "No way." All four tyres sagged and twisted on their respective wheel rims.

"There you go. All nice and safe again." A plump, middle-aged mechanic lowered the Clio back down to the floor of his garage. "Bloomin' vandals are getting organised these days. I've seen a screwdriver put through the wall of a tyre before. But, I've never had a recovery lorry bring in somebody who's had all four tyres done with a nail gun at the same time."

Lisa wanted to say *'You've never dealt with Jonathan Molloy'* but kept the thought to herself. There was no

CCTV in the car park near the flat. It was pointless to hope for any retribution or justice for the attack on her vehicle. She followed the blue overall wearing man into his dirty, ramshackle office. It occupied one partitioned corner of an industrial estate lock-up. The room sat awash with loose papers, a dusty computer and printer, plus various oily car parts in various stages of assembly. He scratched his head and looked at a topless blonde model on a calendar fixed to the wall.

"Where are we today? Ah yes." He typed up an invoice on the keyboard with two hesitant fingers.

Lisa wasn't sure whether he didn't know to find the date and time in the bottom corner of his computer screen, or if he just preferred staring at a nice pair of tits. She smiled and half closed her eyes. A piece of paper emerged from the chugging printer.

The man coughed and passed it to his customer. "There we go. Four new tyres plus balancing and fitting."

Lisa blew out her chubby cheeks in dismay. Her mother always said they made her look like a squirrel concealing nuts in its mouth. Okay, she *was* only six at the time, but enough modesty resided within her to know the prominent facial feature still existed.

"VAT man takes his share, eh?" The mechanic grimaced.

"Shame you couldn't repair them."

"Yes. If you had run over the nails, that might have been possible. But not in the tyre wall. Those were deliberately put in."

Lisa pulled out her credit card and passed it across. "That much is certain."

Driving into work, Lisa heard the ten AM news announcer on the radio. *I'm still two miles from the office. This is no day to be late. Not after yesterday.* That familiar sensation of butterflies returned to her digestive system with a vengeance. As she pulled into a parking space at the office and turned down the latest chart hits, the woman got ready to face music of a different kind. The far less pleasant variety, courtesy of Jenny Duke. Like that psychotic woman needed more ammunition for the gun she was loading. The gun she planned to aim at the Marston girl's career.

2
Flying South

Lisa slowed down and indicated right. She turned her Clio through a narrow gate in a low stone wall surrounding the parish church of St. John, Silverdale. The car radio remained off. Somehow it seemed disrespectful attending a funeral with music blaring out of your stereo. She had driven in silence the entire way from County Durham, across the Pennines to the picturesque, spread-out Lancashire village. Memories were her only accompaniment on that journey. Happy, rose-tinted images of a great aunt who had taken a frightened fourteen-year-old girl in after the death of her parents. A rotund, jolly lady with not a penny to her name, but more love than all the money in the world could buy. She had transformed a weeping, terrified little girl into a strong, confident and independent young woman.

A fresh breeze blowing up from Morecambe Bay, ruffled Lisa's hair and clothes as she climbed out of the driver's seat. It buffeted the vehicle door, whose scored paintwork she had discovered first thing that morning. Most likely another form of intimidation from the Molloy family. The work of someone with a key in their hand and a chip on their shoulder. What were they hoping to achieve? Scare her into staying in what had become an abusive relationship with Keith, for fear of something they might do? If they were trying to wear down her resolve, they'd chosen the wrong target. Lisa was no stranger to tough situations. But the combination of abuse, threats of losing her job and home, nasty phone calls, repeated costly damage to her car (and now the death of Auntie Joan), provided an unwelcome emotional confluence that wasn't helping her remain buoyant.

Lisa locked her car and gazed up at the tall, grey, three stage limestone church tower, with its two-light bell openings on each side. This was brought into relief by buff sandstone dressings and contrasted with an attractive, red tile roof. It was a characterful and elegant building, much younger than it appeared. She'd arrived early. While not religious, Lisa had often found herself wandering into the church to sit and reflect on difficult situations during her youth. It was a habit carried over into the ecclesiastical buildings of Durham, when she left Lancashire to attend university and live in the city. The sound of her clipping shoes became muffled as she entered the church and strode onto the plush, red aisle carpet. St. John's was one of those immovable anchors in her life. A rock of certainty that would always be there and never change. Observing the familiar sandstone interior with its elegant carvings, brought a delicious moment of pause to her soul. The first she had known in over a fortnight. At least the Magistrate approved the DVPO and granted the full, twenty-eight days. The woman still had two weeks before Keith could return to the flat. Now she needed some direction. Was this the place to find it?

Lisa deposited herself in a pew midway down the left side. She glanced back over her shoulder to admire a beautiful, twenty foot glass installation. It was a piece called 'Revelation,' added between the tower and main body of the church to reduce drafts. The work of a local artist, the panel demonstrated a gorgeous blend of form and function. She lost all concept of the passage of time as her mind wandered. There were no flashes of insight. No sudden rapturous certainties about the course her life might take or what she should do. The arrival of funeral attendees from the village cut her pondering short. If visiting the church had served up a tonic, the beaming faces and hugs of welcome from locals amplified it. Those familiar characters formed a patchwork in her mind. They were common figures in the Bayeux Tapestry of her own life's story. Friends come to wish a fond farewell to one of their own: Joan Tanner.

The service was over all too soon. Lisa didn't want those pall bearers to remove Auntie Joan's coffin from pride of place atop trestles before the altar. In that moment the young woman felt a pang of loss she hadn't known since the car accident that claimed her parents. Her previous sense of comfort and certainty faded with the smoke of extinguished candles.

"Lisa?" A soft, weathered female hand rested on her

right shoulder. "Are you coming to the crematorium?"

Lisa twisted to meet a thin face and moist, blue eyes blinking from behind a pair of horn-rimmed spectacles. They belonged to an elderly woman, of similar age to her great aunt.

"Yes Martha. I'll be along soon. Are you going too? Do you need a lift?"

Martha blew her nose on a delicate silk handkerchief with floral edging. "No, that's alright dear. Harry Preston is driving a couple of us in his estate car. I only asked, because Joan left a box with a few keepsakes for you. Harry's got them in the boot. I'll fetch it after we're all finished up the road."

"Oh. Thank you." Lisa rose to accompany the old lady out of the church. "What happened to the bungalow?"

Martha steadied herself against the edge of the main doorway. "The owners have already rented it out. Joan never had much. You know that. Her savings about stretched to cover the funeral. Nothing else. The box is all that's left. Shortly before she died, I promised I'd make sure you got it if I didn't go first."

Lisa's brow creased. "It was so sudden. I used to phone her once a week. Things have been up in the air lately. I hadn't managed to call since the end of March. Then I received word she'd passed away. Thank you for getting in touch about that."

"You're welcome. Joan and I were neighbours for over half a century. I'm going to miss her."

"I remember. Crumbs, you watched me grow up through most of my difficult teenage years. What a time I gave her."

Martha's wan face broke into a tiny smile. "She loved you so much."

Lisa helped her into the front passenger seat of a large Subaru estate. She closed the door with gentle hands once the woman was in place, like a precious cargo.

Having a second, shorter service at the crematorium gave Lisa another chance to postpone the inevitable: that moment when her great aunt's coffin would roll forward through the final curtain. Pleasantries and greetings exchanged outside, Martha asked Harry Preston to retrieve the box. It was a sturdy, open-topped cardboard affair. The contents lay covered in an old, pictorial 'Silverdale' tea towel. One Joan Tanner had kept for decorative rather than practical purposes.

Lisa put both arms underneath the box to support it. "Thank you, Martha. I'll wait until I get home to have a look through."

"Are you coming to collect the ashes?"

"Yes. In a week or so. That's one thing Auntie Joan and I had well planned. There are two places she wanted them scattered: by the old chimney at Jenny Brown's Point, and along the woodland paths around Silverdale where the wild garlic grows in abundance. They were always our favourite local walking spots." She lowered her head to study the container in her arms. "It's odd. The contents of this box are almost the only remaining tangible evidence that Auntie Joan ever lived. She espoused the idea of a simple, low-impact lifestyle, decades before it ever became a trendy concept."

Martha's eyes sparkled. "But the intangibles remain."

One corner of Lisa's mouth raised. Her onetime neighbour was no confused old biddy. Sharp and neat as a new pin, despite her considerable years. "You mean the love and good feeling she left behind?"

"Yes. And the character she instilled in you. I know you weren't her daughter, but I can sense Joan's spirit in the way you carry yourself. She's a part of you, Lisa. She always will be."

Lisa wiped the faintest hint of a tear from one eye and kissed the old woman on the cheek. "Look after yourself, Martha. It was lovely to see you again."

The trip back to Durham was also conducted in silence. Lisa was in no mood for music. Her mind and emotions were too swamped with processing the sensory input of the day.

In the flat, she placed the box on the living room coffee table. The woman curled her legs up on the sofa, whipped off the tea towel and studied the few simple artefacts of Joan Tanner's life. On top sat a china ornament wrapped in white tissue paper. Lisa recognised the object before it was even undone: a cat clutching a fishing rod. It lay asleep by a stream with a hat covering its face. Lisa remembered the story associated with it. Joan had been eighteen when she fell in love with a young soldier called Mike. He'd shipped out to fight in Korea and never returned. Before he left, the couple took a day trip to Blackpool. It was there he'd won the cheap figure for his sweetheart, as a prize on a coconut shy. To Auntie Joan - who never loved again - it was like a priceless statue. Small wonder it formed one of her few remaining treasures. Lisa re-wrapped the figure for safekeeping. Below the ornament sat two worn leather photo albums and what appeared to be a rectangular jewellery box of some description. Lisa opened the box. Two shiny silver hair combs were secured inside, neat as new. These had only been worn on special occasions like Christmas, Easter or celebration days. Joan would also put them in if watching a royal wedding on telly. Lisa stroked the items with delicate fingers, careful not to tarnish the silver. Last of all she fished out the photograph albums and thumbed through the pages. The first contained pictures taken throughout Joan's earlier life. The other featured various images of friends, family and a few characters she didn't remember. One shot pictured her mother and father holding baby Lisa, during a flying visit to Silverdale in the late eighties. The girl was too young to remember that trip. She'd seen the first album before but never this one. Had Auntie Joan been trying to spare her further anguish, or was it because the book was still a work in progress? Near the end came a photo of Lisa's graduation day at Durham University. Smooth and handsome, Keith Molloy also occupied the shot with one arm clamped about her waist. They both looked ecstatic.

The living room window shuddered. Lisa snapped out of her curious reverie in time to notice egg yolk sliding down the glass exterior. From the street below came a female shout of "Slag!" She eased herself off the sofa and went to look out. No-one in sight now. *Shelley, if I had to guess.* Back at the coffee table, Keith's face grinned at her from the photograph. She grimaced, closed the book, placed everything back in the box and re-covered it with the tea towel.

* * *

"How was the funeral?" Janice Gange scratched her slender neck with idle fingers as Lisa poured herself into the office chair opposite. "Are you okay?"

Lisa played with her blouse. "Yeah. Yeah, I'm okay. It was beautiful as funerals go. Great turnout from the locals, too. No surprise, she was well loved. Auntie Joan would have approved. That's what matters."

"Something good at least. Any more trouble? You know, from Keith's family?"

"My car got keyed the morning of the funeral. Could be them. None of the other vehicles nearby were done. My little old Clio is hardly a standout target to make people jealous. Glad they didn't do the tyres again when I needed to drive over to Lancashire. Oh yeah, someone chucked an egg at the living room window and shouted. No more nasty calls though."

"Bet they're mixing things up to avoid trouble with the law."

"That's what I thought. How did I get in this mess and not see it coming?"

Janice delivered what could paradoxically be described as a sympathetic smirk. "Love is blind?"

"Damn near myopic in my case."

Jenny Duke appeared at her office door. "Lisa. A moment of your time, please."

Lisa spoke under her breath, loud enough for Janice to hear. "Here we go again." She lifted her torso from the desk with reluctant arms.

"I've been reviewing your performance and thinking about ways to safeguard your future." Those words were out of her boss's mouth before Lisa had even closed the door. The matter-of-fact tone with which Jenny delivered them, did little to inspire confidence.

"Safeguard my future? What's wrong with my work? The company intranet news mag have cited me for it several times this year alone?"

"You don't report to the intranet news mag, you report to me. The court of popular opinion holds no sway over your performance review."

Lisa ground her teeth and sat down on the stiff, low chair in front of Jenny's desk. "So what's *your* problem?"

Jenny scowled. "You can't even ask a legitimate question without resorting to your obvious disdain for my position, can you?"

Lisa remained silent.

Jenny went on. "I like to cultivate a positive team ethic, where we all receive credit as a group for the performance of the unit."

"You mean, those too lazy or lacking in talent to produce anything worthwhile get carried along. Lifted by staff working here on the basis of actual skill, hard work and merit?"

Jenny's eyes narrowed to slits. She clasped her fingers together on the desk. "You are less than a fortnight from your performance review. At which point, if you don't evidence behavioural changes to satisfy me, you will be leaving Carlton Content Creative."

Lisa sucked air into her nostrils while her mouth remained clamped shut. Jenny was waiting for some sort of response. "Okay. And which behavioural changes exactly are you looking for?"

"Apart from some manners and due deference, you will take on editing for the Harris account."

"Isn't that one of yours? I thought the Harris account was a key part of our core business."

"Precisely why it will give me some breathing space and offer you a chance to shine. A way to evidence your abilities that I can document."

Lisa fidgeted. This didn't sound too bad. That's what made her suspicious. "Which of my own accounts are going on hold?"

"None of them."

"None of them? You mean I'm getting some compulsory overtime?"

"No. How you find the time to do your work is up to you and your much-trumpeted skill set. There won't be any extra pay."

Lisa spat. "So you're dumping your work on me."

Jenny studied her with cool disdain. "Since Nathan Coombs has gone on long-term sick, you will also perform the daily internal post run to the Newcastle office until he returns."

"What?" Lisa half rose off the seat. "That's more than thirteen miles each way. I'm an editor and staff writer, not a delivery driver."

"You're all the above for at least the next two weeks. That is, unless you care to seek other employment?"

Lisa's mouth became dry. Her tongue rasped against the roof of her mouth like sandpaper. She trembled with anger but her legs were weak enough that she took her seat again.

Jenny typed on her keyboard. "I'll give you access to the Harris files in a moment. There's a release that needs drafting by lunchtime, plus a few web articles by close of play tomorrow. Some research required." She looked from her computer screen back to the young woman sitting before her like a rabbit frozen in a set of headlights. "Are you still here?"

Lisa trudged to the door and let herself out.

"Should I even ask?" Janice peeled open a chocolate bar wrapper and took a bite.

"She's given me the Harris account along with my current workload. Plus, I've got to do Nathan's Newcastle post run until he gets back."

"What?" Janice shouted. She covered her mouth as groups of people in the large, open plan office looked round. The woman lowered the volume of her voice. "What? So she's dumping her work on you and solving the problem of Nathan's sickness by giving you his job too. I hope you told her to poke it."

Lisa shook her head. "She put it to me as an offer I couldn't refuse. Either I do this and kiss her arse, or she'll sack me at my APR in a couple of weeks."

Janice slammed her chocolate bar on the desk and shook her head. "Well, I'd say your first course of action is to look for another job."

"I've been looking. Couldn't take the chance of leaving it. There's nothing much around. Not in our line, anyway."

"What about freelance?"

"Do you know, I've had a few clients say they'd take me on if I ever did that. But I've got rent to pay, and it takes time to build a portfolio of freelance clients. Hard to get enough work to keep the wolf from the door, when you're getting started. I've no nest egg of savings to fall back on. Best suck it up for now. This is all I need, on top of everything else."

"Gather round, everyone." Mr Carlton the company director paid a rare visit down to the editorial office a week later.

Janice leaned back in her chair and shrugged at Lisa. "Is the golf course shut today, do you think?"

Lisa lifted her head to show she was listening.

Mr Carlton clapped his hands together as Jenny

Duke emerged from her office into the larger workspace. "Here she is: our star of the moment." He swept his gaze around the assembled staff. "I know Jenny cultivates a strong team approach with regard to glory, but today we should give credit where it's due."

Janice whispered across her computer. "Has she won first place in the national office sleaze-bag awards?"

Lisa snorted and agitated a half-empty Styrofoam cup of coffee with a wooden stirrer.

Mr Carlton paused for dramatic effect. "Harris are so impressed with Jenny's recent web articles, they've decided to transfer all content work from their sister company to us as well. This is a significant business win."

There was a polite ripple of nervous applause, slower than one might expect from a delighted crowd.

Carlton continued. "You'll find a nice little something extra in your pay packet this month, Jenny. Well done. And congratulations on leading by example to your team." He shook the falsely modest woman by the hand with a series of vigorous jerks.

Lisa's face turned ashen. She pulled up a web browser and typed in the URL for Harris.

Janice fixed her with bulging eyes. "Please tell me she hasn't."

Lisa froze. All the web articles she'd written in the last few days were published with one author credit: *Jenny Duke*. Her head nodded in ponderous agreement.

Janice gritted her teeth and scowled at their boss, still lapping up praise. "Lis', check the original file documents on our system while Carlton's here. They should have you on the meta tags as author. Quick, you need to show him before he disappears, or she'll get away with it."

Lisa opened the file system. "Shit. She's already removed my access to the Harris account. I'm stuffed."

"Have you got a local backup?"

"You know we can't do that."

"No notes anywhere?"

"Not enough to convince Carlton of anything other than I'm a troublemaker. I'm sure he's already had a heads-up from Jenny on that score." Lisa put her head in her hands.

One corner of Jenny Duke's mouth rose in a sneer. She slithered back into her office, casting one last triumphant glance at her crestfallen employee across the room.

* * *

"Sorry I'm late, Lis'. But, you're gonna be pleased I was when you hear." Janice sat down on a barstool alongside her colleague. Outside, the street lamps of Durham cast an atmospheric wash of light across the ancient city. The trendy wine bar remained quiet, this early on a midweek evening.

Lisa sipped from a large, thin-stemmed glass of Chardonnay. "Go on. I could use some good news."

Janice smiled at the barman. "I'll have the same." The chap hooked out an identical glass and filled it. Janice shifted on the stool. "So. You've got about a week until they allow Keith back to the flat. He and his family are likely to keep hassling you, wherever you go in Durham. Your boss is a monster who takes credit for your work, and will kick you out if you don't continue to crawl around her. You need to find a new place to live, but if you lose your job, you'll be on the street. You've got some leads on freelance work, but it might not be enough to cover your bills - for now."

Lisa was about to place the glass down, but took a large gulp instead. "If you're trying to cheer me up, Hun, you're doing a lousy job. Tell me something I don't know."

"Okay, I will." She pulled out her purse and paid the barman. "Thanks."

Lisa watched; a hopeless, faraway stare painted on her face. It was the look of someone resigned to their fate.

Janice retrieved a folded piece of paper from her handbag and placed it on the bar next to her colleague.

"What's this?" Lisa put her drink down.

"Open it and see."

Lisa unfolded the paper and read aloud. "Anne Weaver. Plus a phone number I don't recognise. That's not a familiar prefix: 01227. Where is that?"

"Kent. I believe it's a Canterbury dialling code."

"So, who's Anne Weaver and what's in Canterbury?"

"Not Canterbury itself. A village somewhere south of there."

Lisa raised upturned palms and stuck out her bottom lip. "Are we playing twenty questions?"

"Sorry. You want to know what's there? Your future.

Or one possible future."

"Huh?"

"A friend of my Mum's got an e-mail from some old lady she knows in Kent called Anne Weaver. A retired primary school teacher, if I heard right. So, Anne's getting on a bit and looking for a live-in helper. Sort of mutual benefit arrangement, rather than heavy, all day labour."

Lisa's face brightened a little. "Go on, I'm listening."

"Well, Anne is willing to offer room and board at her house in exchange for a little day to day help. That and some company, I imagine. Don't know if she's widowed, but the woman lives alone. There's no money involved. A place to sleep with a roof over your head and food on the table. That's the deal. Plus time to yourself to pursue other avenues."

"Like freelance writing and editing work?"

"Exactly. You've got a laptop and some contacts. You can work from anywhere. How often does our job need a face-to-face?"

"True."

"You might pick up new clients down south as well. The point is, it gets you out of Carlton, away from the Molloys at the other end of the country. Also solves your housing dilemma and gives you a shot at doing your own thing. By all accounts this Anne is a sweetheart. Some sort of local treasure."

"Bit like Auntie Joan." Lisa lowered her eyes.

Janice pursed her lips and reached for the paper. "Of course, if you don't want it I can pop this back in my bag."

"Bugger off." Lisa swiped her hand away with a grin. She picked up her wine again. "Auntie Joan always said that whenever a door closed on me, somewhere another would open. This could be it."

"Why don't you give Anne a call? What have you got to lose? Ring her when you get home."

"And find someone else has already got the position? Screw that, Janice, I'm calling her now." She fished out her smart phone and keyed in the number.

* * *

A montage of memories both recent and distant stole Lisa's focus away on her drive back to Silverdale. At least two angry drivers sounded their horns to avoid a near miss from the dreamy thirty-year-old. Replaying her dramatic departure from Carlton Content Creative was so delicious, it had run on a near constant mental loop ever since that fateful day. No *'one month required notice period'* for Lisa Marston. She had mere days at best to get away from Keith. Jenny Duke received a tongue lashing she would never forget. The image of tipping the office document shredder contents over her boss's head, never ceased to make Lisa laugh to herself. That incredulous, suit-wearing snake sat frozen in shock and disbelief. The escapee also sent an e-mail to Mr Carlton, explaining a few home truths. No doubt he would dismiss it out of hand. But, she was starting self-employment with clients who knew what she could do and cared nothing for her former office politics. The whistles, shouts and rapturous applause that accompanied Lisa on her final victorious exit from the hated building still echoed in the young woman's ears. She'd enjoyed one last evening drink with Janice Gange. It had been tough to say goodbye to her old colleague and friend. Would Jenny Duke leave the poor girl alone, or take out her spite on Janice instead? *Dear God, let it be the former.* It was easier than expected to leave the flat. Something about Keith's actions dismissed any sentimental aura the dwelling might have conjured under other circumstances. Keith could do what he liked with it. She was out of there and not coming back. Among the more distant memories were those of Auntie Joan. Here Lisa sat at the start of her flight south, making a stopover to collect and scatter the ashes of her beloved guardian. This was goodbye at last. The little car almost bulged with her clothes, laptop, the box of keepsakes from Silverdale and other assorted knick-knacks. Not many possessions for three decades on the planet. Martha might have a point about Joan Tanner's spirit upon her.

The Clio crunched to a halt alongside a dry stone wall on a single track road near Jenny Brown's Point. Lisa climbed from the car and lifted out a container from the crematorium. A fresh salt breeze filled her nostrils. She descended the bank and strolled close to the water's edge, scooping handfuls of ash into the air. This was a continuation from earlier rambles along nearby woodland paths. There she left parts of Joan at their favourite resting places among the wild garlic flowers. The last human remnants slipped through her fingers. Lisa cupped both hands beneath her chin and whispered. "I love you, Auntie Joan." With a gentle exhale she blew the remaining powder into a spring breeze and watched it sail away. She couldn't remember how long she sat there looking out to sea. There was still a considerable drive south to make before the day was done.

Even in the decade or so since she'd become a motorist, Lisa was aware how increased traffic and bad road manners made long journeys less enjoyable. It was something of a relief cresting the high QE2 bridge over the Thames estuary. Midway across the span, a sign announced that she had entered Kent. Not long now until the hassle of motorways lay behind. *So this is 'The Garden of England' then? Suppose I should reserve judgement until I hit the minor roads.* Dartford and the M2 might be less than thrilling, but once she left the A2 at Bishopsbourne, Lisa felt like an excited schoolgirl. There she found rolling hills, little rivers, ancient woodlands, timber-framed cottages and abundant oast houses - all the hallmarks of England's most south-easterly county. At every minor village and hamlet, she spied a black and white sign topped with the regional shield. Prior to her departure (and being no stranger to research) she discovered that the prancing white horse on a red background once belonged to Jute chieftain, Hengist. The slogan 'Invicta' beneath it - 'unconquered' in Latin - referred to the local inhabitants confronting William the Conqueror. They offered a treaty or to fight him. William chose the former and allowed them to keep their local ordinances, unlike the rest of England. Beyond that, she knew the word Kent came from an ancient tribe known as the Cantii. Also, if you lived east of the River Medway, you were a man or maid of Kent, but otherwise a Kentish man or maid. Interesting history and customs. "Oh crap." Her mobile phone lost its signal and the satnav application span the base-map in random directions. Next it went grey and froze. *Should have brought a paper map. Okay, I know it's somewhere between Bossingham, Stelling Minnis and Bladbean.* She slowed the car right down to squint at an approaching road sign. Trees arched over the tiny lanes like organic cathedral buttresses. The rough tarmac surfaces crumbled into potholes. A present courtesy of a storm known as *'The Beast from the East'* back in late February and early March. "Ah, here we go. Up that track to the left. Must be a pretty small village." It felt reassuring to say the words out loud. The Clio shifted down a gear and climbed a steep rise under minor protest. At the top, trees parted to reveal a large expanse of green meadow surrounded by chocolate box cottages and a square church tower. The church appeared older than St. John's in Silverdale, but shorter too. Another one of those village signs welcomed the northerner to her new abode: *Wrenham Green.*

3
Bramley Cottage

Lisa's car crawled through a twisting, narrow road lined with an assortment of cottages. A warm spring day gave way to a chillier evening. With the village green opening out on her right, she caught sight in the rear-view mirror of a cottage on the bend. Thoughts of Anne's instructions over the phone came flooding back. *That must be it.* She stomped on the brake, crunched the vehicle gears into reverse and performed a turn in the road.

Bramley Cottage was a two storey, three bedroom black and white. The Tudor, timber-framed house featured a high-pitched roof and chimneys at either end. Its wonky walls, beams and windows gave the appearance of a sprouting mushroom. Almost as though the place was built before the invention of the ruler. The structure stood hemmed in on three sides by a low brick wall, bordering the lane that fed into the village. Poky, leaded light windows peered out, while roses around the door welcomed visitors across the threshold. Three or four steps were all it took from the wrought-iron gate in the wall to the front door. Herbs and colourful cottage flowers filled every space of the scant, wraparound garden. To the right of the cottage lay a driveway big enough for two vehicles. An old, red Vauxhall Corsa already occupied the first spot. Lisa deposited her Clio in the second and switched off the engine. She got out, stretched and pinched her own backside to encourage circulation of blood after the long journey. It had been some time since the last break for petrol. A Friday afternoon jam at Grays on the Essex side of the Dartford River Crossing, kept her jammed into that seat for an uncomfortable spell. Life seeped back into stiffened limbs, chasing away the pins and needles. *Should I start unloading the stuff? Nah. Best introduce myself first, before I make a mess on the poor woman's driveway.* Lisa locked her fingers together, cracked the knuckles, then separated her hands and wiggled the digits to relax. Her neck clicked as she twisted it each way for blessed relief and wandered round the side of the building. The dark, wooden front door opened before she could raise a hand to ring an attractive, antique brass bell that hung alongside. Pale blue eyes either side of a long, broad nose peered from the dim interior. An elderly, female figure stepped out. The evening light fell across centre-parted white hair in a shoulder-length bob. That face inched forward, creased with the lines of age. But Lisa couldn't escape the intelligent alertness in her gaze. Tall and slim with good deportment, the woman stood dressed in an open-necked sky blue blouse and long, navy skirt. She fiddled with a chunky necklace of red, grey and aquamarine stones.

"Anne?" Lisa broke the initial awkward silence.

The elderly woman's face brightened. "You must be Lisa." She extended a thin bony arm. It was decorated with the involuntary tattoo ink of blue veins poking through.

The new arrival leaned across and gave her hand a warm shake. "Pleased to meet you."

"Welcome to Kent. Did you have a good journey?"

"It was long. Sunny though."

"Yes, it's been unseasonably warm of late. But here we are acting like two classic, polite English people and discussing the weather."

Lisa let go of the pensioner's hand and cracked a smile. It had been difficult to gauge what this woman might be like from their brief phone conversation. "Shall I fetch my things before it gets dark? I didn't want to land on your doorstep with a pile of luggage."

"Yes. Bring them in. Hang on a minute, I'll grab a shawl and give you a hand."

"Goodness no. I'll be fine."

Anne waved in dismissive annoyance, as if swatting a wasp away. "Nonsense. The old girl isn't as useless as all that." She unhitched a woollen shawl from a hook in the hallway and wrapped it around her shoulders.

Lisa blinked and turned on the spot. "O-k-a-y then."

"You found us alright?" Anne studied the young woman as they ambled round to the Renault.

"Yes. My phone lost its connection a short distance away, so the satnav app packed up. But by then I was close enough to rely on road signs for direction. Good job. All these overlapping wooded valleys might confuse a stranger."

"Have you been to Kent before?"

"No."

"We'll have to pop out and visit a few places."

"I'd like that. Thank you." Lisa opened the boot of the Clio.

Without hesitation, Anne reached over and lifted a large case.

Lisa winced. "That's a heavy one. Are you sure you're okay there?"

Anne hobbled back towards the front door, clutching the luggage by a handle. "Let's see who shifts the largest number of items."

Lisa stood open-mouthed on the spot. Then a horrid thought occurred: this situation - which appeared like an answer to prayer - might end in a flash if the old woman suffered a heart attack while carrying her bags. She hunted around for the next biggest item she could find, to avoid her host having a crack at it.

Before long, the hallway at Bramley Cottage filled with the contents of Lisa's car.

Anne closed the front door. "Now we have to get it all upstairs."

Lisa puffed out a tired sigh. A dark wooden grandfather clock ticked with deep, comforting regularity.

Anne hung up her shawl again. "A quick tour of the house and a spot of tea first. Have you eaten?"

"I grabbed a wrap at a motorway service station. I'm

more tired and thirsty than anything."

"Of course. A pot of tea and *then* the tour."

Lisa fidgeted. "Shouldn't *I* be making it?"

Anne's eyes closed for a moment with amused satisfaction. "You're not my maidservant, Lisa. What did you imagine our arrangement to be?"

"I'm not too sure." She flushed.

Anne nodded to herself. "You thought you'd have to help a confused old dear to the toilet, tuck her in at night and remind her what day of the week it is every five minutes. Am I wrong?"

Lisa bit her lip. "Embarrassingly close, actually."

"What day of the week is it, anyway?" Anne crossed her eyes and pulled a face. "When you don't have a schedule as such, it's easy to forget sometimes. Come on, I'll show you the kitchen."

Lisa followed her into a classic country kitchen with shaker units and a Belfast sink.

Anne filled a kettle from the taps and plugged it in. "The truth is, I *am* slowing down. I may need a little extra help before long, or if I have a fall - heaven forbid. My body is eighty, even if my mind still wants to be twenty-one. Wrenham Green isn't what it used to be either."

"It's beautiful, from what I've seen," Lisa offered.

"Thank you. Yes, I've no argument there. But its heart is dying like so many places out in the sticks. When I was a girl, we had a butcher, greengrocer, all manner of little shops and local businesses. The last shop here was a convenience store cum post office. That closed a couple of years back. Now there's the pub, church and primary school. That's it. Plus various houses, either owned by commuters who are never here or the odd retiree waiting for God."

"That's sad."

"Have you lived in the country before?"

"Yes. At fourteen I moved in with my great aunt in Silverdale. That's a small rural community on the coast near Lancaster."

Anne frowned, hesitant to enquire further.

Lisa sensed her discomfort. "My parents were killed in a car crash. Auntie Joan - as I called her - was my next of kin. Guess the extended family didn't have a good run of things, health-wise."

Anne's curious eyes softened. "I'm sorry to hear that. Is Auntie Joan-"

"She passed away recently. I scattered her ashes in Silverdale on my way here."

Anne warmed the teapot and spooned in some loose leaves. "A difficult time. I had no idea. And you were living in Durham until recently?"

"Yes. My boyfriend and I had a flat there."

"Anywhere near the old part?"

"Inside it. Do you know the city?"

"I visited for a teacher's conference once. Lovely. Tomorrow we'll have a wander round Canterbury if you feel like it. That's an ancient walled cathedral city with rivers and old streets. Not hilly like Durham. We lost a lot of historic buildings during the Blitz, but I imagine you'll enjoy it."

"I'm sure I will. Here, let me." Lisa lifted a tray bearing the teapot, cups, saucers, milk and strainer.

"Thank you. Let's get comfortable in the living room."

The pair entered a large, low beamed room with a broad inglenook. The open fireplace stood topped by a sweeping metal hood. Beside it rested a long-handled copper bed warming pan. Horse brasses dangled from the beam above and an impressive but faded floral rug filled most of the cosy chamber. Lisa set the tray down on a coffee table. At Anne's gesture, she deposited herself on one of a pair of two-seater sofas facing each other. Anne drew the curtains and settled down opposite.

"Have you lived here long?" Lisa felt the need to fill the sonic vacuum with something.

"All my life. I grew up here. Bramley Cottage belonged to my parents. I was born February 1938. Gosh that seems so long ago now."

"Did you ever marry?"

Anne shook her head. "It wasn't the done thing for female schoolteachers so much in those days. Oh, they abolished the 'Pledge' in 1951 when I was only thirteen. Long before my career began. Female teachers could get married, but culture took a while to adjust. I never had a desire for that sort of life, so it didn't affect me. I loved my job and cared for Mother and Father until the end." She leaned forward and poured out the tea.

Lisa looked around. "Were you an only child?"

Anne pointed to a faint, black-and-white photograph in a frame on the wall by the fire.

Lisa rose to examine it up close. There stood a proud

mum and dad with their arms around two fair-haired girls and a dark-haired boy. The image had been composed in the lane outside, with Bramley Cottage behind. The building hadn't changed much in the time since. Lisa cleared her throat. "You have a sister and brother? Is she your twin?"

Anne passed a cup and saucer to Lisa as she took her seat again. "I *had* a sister and brother. That picture was taken in 1944 when I was six, a year before we lost them. Father came home on leave from the fighting, so we grabbed the opportunity to have a family photograph done."

Lisa bit her lip. "Was it the war?"

Anne sipped her tea, pointing one elegant little finger aside like a refined lady of good breeding. "No. Daniel - my older brother - fell from an upstairs window at the cottage and broke his neck. My twin sister, Beth, disappeared shortly afterwards. We never saw her again."

"Oh how awful." Lisa's expression froze.

"May 1945. Four months before the end of hostilities. Father went off at the start of the war to fight, leaving three children. He came home to one. A cruel irony, considering the dangers he faced and got through unscathed."

Lisa drank some of her own tea.

Anne studied her. "It's Daniel's room you'll be sleeping in."

The younger woman tried not to choke on her drink in surprise.

Anne drew a thin smile. "Don't worry, I've never

known the cottage to be haunted. Sometimes I wish it were so. Life gets lonely these days, what with the village the way it is now. I'd give anything for a minute or two with either of my siblings - ghosts or otherwise."

Lisa regained her composure. "Is that why I'm here?"

"Partly. I could do with some stimulating conversation. I sometimes get an old pupil pop in for a visit with their children. That's always nice. But, the discussion only goes so deep before they have to leave or the youngsters get fractious."

"I'll do my best to be interesting."

"When you said you were a writer and editor, I knew we'd have some great chats." Her face darkened. "But you haven't told me why you're really here."

Lisa shifted in her seat. "How do you mean?"

"An intelligent, attractive young woman with a successful career and a flat in Durham? Why is she giving all that up to move in with an eighty-year-old spinster at the opposite end of the country? A spinster who isn't paying her."

"I wouldn't put it quite like that. Room and board for a bit of help and some conversation? Okay, I went through a major bust up with my boss. She had it in for me. Enough was enough, and I wanted to take up some offers of freelance work. Don't need to be in Durham for that. But I couldn't guarantee enough income to pay the rent. When I heard about your offer, it sounded ideal."

"Your boyfriend couldn't take up the slack while

you worked on your business plan?"

Lisa screwed up her nose. She'd been rumbled.

Anne nodded. "That's what I thought. Did he hurt you?"

Lisa swallowed hard. "Yes. Not the charmer he once was during university and our early working life. His family made my life hell too."

"I'm sure he's still a charmer. Manipulators usually are. It's one of their tactics. Well, don't you worry; you'll be safe here. Wrenham Green is in the back of beyond. We also have one of the most annoying retired police officers you're ever likely to meet. And meet him you will. I imagine he's already recorded your arrival in his pocket notebook."

Lisa relaxed and finished her drink. "This is the second time in my life I've felt like Anne Shirley."

The old teacher's face lit up. "You've read Lucy Maud Montgomery?"

Lisa's eyes widened. "I *adore* Lucy Maud Montgomery. Auntie Joan gave me *'Anne of Green Gables'* when I first came to live with her. I guess she realised I'd find solace reading about another orphan girl; even a fictitious one. I devoured that book and the rest of the series, right up to *'Rilla of Ingleside.'* It was those stories more than anything that got me interested in literature and writing."

"And I'm your new Marilla Cuthbert?"

Lisa's face reddened. "You wouldn't think I was thirty, to hear me prattle on."

Anne put down her cup and saucer. "Don't feel embarrassed. If you've placed me in a category with your late Auntie Joan, I'd say I'm in honoured company. But don't dye your hair green by mistake, like Anne Shirley did."

Lisa rested her hands together in her lap. "It's good to know I'm staying with someone who likes L M Montgomery."

The old woman moved to get up. "I read *'Anne of Green Gables'* to so many classes of children over the years, I lost track of the count. Some stories never age. Shall we take a look at your room now?"

* * *

With the nine-to-five treadmill behind her for now, Lisa wondered if Saturdays would still feel the same. Daniel Weaver's former bedroom was comfortable. A modest space but large enough to accommodate her belongings. She lay back against the plump, white pillow in a tall, metal framed single bed. Orange sunlight crept around the thick drapes of the deep-set casement, accompanied by a dawn chorus of birds from trees across the lane. The woman took a slow, relaxing breath and thought back to her arrival 'tour' the night before.

Upstairs the cottage consisted of three bedrooms, a family bathroom, several cupboards and a loft hatch. The first room they entered contained twin beds. Anne explained it had once belonged to her and her sister. Lisa's eye was drawn to an old but well-loved rag doll laying atop one of the mattresses. She wanted to question the old woman about the toy, but propriety halted her curiosity. The homeowner became misty-eyed the moment they entered the room. Despite many decades of elapsed time, pain from heartbreak and unresolved loss still shadowed her face. If the doll had belonged to Anne's sister Beth - as Lisa suspected - she didn't need to know. Certainly not at that moment. If the topic came up again, she might slip the question into their conversation. Anne slept in the master that had once accommodated her parents. The bathroom contained a sturdy old roll-top bath with brass mixer tap and shower attachment. Next to the loo by a white pedestal basin, sat a ramshackle pile of glossy country magazines. The pensioner wheezed at Lisa's quip: *'Don't you like the writing? Or are those next to the loo for when the going gets tough and you can't get going?'* If Anne looked like a frail old woman on the outside, that deceptive appearance belied obvious reserves of some deep inner strength. The kind people discover and draw upon when necessity comes to call too many times over the course of a lifetime. Whether by habit and muscle memory or sheer force of will, she nipped up and down the stairs faster than her new, thirty-year-old companion. Lisa struggled to keep up. She'd lost the *porter battle* to haul the most items of her luggage upstairs, by a country mile.

Light levels increased enough to lure Lisa from beneath the comfortable duvet. She drew back the heavy curtains and opened the window latch. The cool, thick walls of her bower were slippery to the touch.

Visions of young Daniel plummeting headlong to the tiny cottage garden below, caused her to stumble on the spot. A flash of panic stopped her leaning over too far. Fresh wafts of early spring air seeped through the gap into the room. The window was located at the upper front left of the building. It looked across that sweeping road bend to the expansive village green beyond. In the distance, Lisa could make out a tall, wooden pillar like a telephone pole. No wires were attached, though it featured some sort of ring attachment encircling the top like a horizontal halo. *Is that a Maypole? Haven't seen one of those since I was a kid.* Lisa twisted her head to the right along the northern periphery of the green. There stood a classic, weather-boarded pub with long, sweeping Kent peg tile roof like a shaggy fringe obscuring someone's eyes. A gold-lettered sign declared it to be *'The White Hart.'* Further to the west on the far corner nestled an old red K6 telephone box. Its domed roof and embossed crown were such an iconic symbol. The young woman wondered if the villagers had the kiosk listed to protect it from replacement. Across the far lane from that, rose the church tower she spied on her drive in.

A tentative knock on the door interrupted her cursory upstairs survey to get the lay of the land. Lisa smoothed down her night clothes and opened up. Anne Weaver clasped a round tin tray containing a steaming cup of tea. "I wondered if you were awake. Would you like a cuppa?"

Lisa fought down the urge to make another comment about her role in the domestic scheme of things. "Thank you." She accepted the drink. "I was taking a peek outside."

Anne nodded. "Bramley Cottage occupies a good spot for views of the green. If you're a cricket fan, you can sit in the garden and watch the local club play without even crossing the lane."

"Cricket's not my thing, although sitting in the garden sounds pleasant."

"Not a cricketer myself either. But it's a nice spot to enjoy on a summer's afternoon. So, did you fancy that trip into Canterbury?"

Lisa signalled left and climbed a slip road off the A2. Alongside her on the front passenger seat of the Clio, Anne glanced right to catch the outline of Canterbury Cathedral in the distance. The woman pointed beyond a set of traffic lights ahead. "Go right here. If you don't mind a leg stretch, we can park at Wincheap and walk into the city. It's a lot cheaper and the stroll from Castle Street through to the Buttermarket makes it worthwhile."

"Great. Tell me where to pull in."

Anne directed the driver through a nondescript industrial estate to a pay and display on Maynard Road. Minutes later the pair emerged on foot from an underpass on Rheims Way, to catch sight of the ruined Worthgate towering above them. Anne strode at an energetic pace. After all she had experienced of the curious woman so far, this no longer caught Lisa off guard. "I like the medieval walls. Reminds me of a trip down to York I took with some girlfriends at uni."

"Did you walk the entire circuit?"

"Eventually. We stopped at every pub in sight along the route, if memory serves. And by the time we got back to the beginning, memory wasn't *serving* too well."

Anne's eyes glittered, the edges creasing into laughter lines. "There isn't quite such a navigable stretch here. But, what there is makes a pleasant change from the hustle and bustle of the streets below."

They wandered on until the overhanging timber-framed eye candy of Mercery Lane opened out to reveal the Cathedral Gate. Lisa swept her gaze around The Old Buttermarket, taking in an elegant war memorial and the neat Burgate flagstones. "Reminds me a little of Durham Market Place," she shuddered.

Anne caught the involuntary spasm. "Bad memory?"

"Not of the market itself, that's lovely. Keith - my ex-boyfriend - chased me through it once. It was the day he took a hand to me. I've never felt so scared and alone."

Anne shuffled. "Would you like to see the cathedral?"

The cloud lifted from Lisa's brow. "It'd be rude not to. Then I should buy you lunch."

They took a pleasant turn around the ancient place of worship. A typical tour encompassing the shrine of St Thomas Becket and the tomb of the Black Prince. Afterwards, Anne led the northerner to a bridge on the

High Street over a narrow river. Lisa admired a multi-storey black and white structure with overhanging bay windows. One aspect faced onto the river where small boats took eager visitors on waterway excursions. She read a sign above the entrance to the fairy tale-like building aloud. "The Old Weavers House A.D. 1500. Weavers? Nothing to do with the family?"

Anne stepped forward to peer through some black railings that topped the bridge. "No connection other than the profession my ancestors once took their name from. But see here, we have our own ducking stool for husbands to dunk wilful wives and the like."

Lisa joined her to examine a wooden chair. It sat atop a thick black beam that jutted out across the water near a riverside patio. "Now I'm extra glad Keith's not about. He'd be strapping me into that thing. Don't reckon he'd lift it back up, either. Hey, is this a restaurant? Would you like to eat here?"

* * *

"I'm not that religious, but I used to go to the church of St. John in Silverdale whenever I had something on my mind." Lisa put one leg in front of another at a relaxed place as she and Anne approached St. Mary's, Wrenham Green that first Sunday morning.

Anne listened, but lost her focus amongst the gravestones surrounding the old church like sentries. Her voice was wistful. "I've come here every Sunday since I was a child. I don't know how much of it is tradition."

Lisa examined a set of gargoyles leering down from the parapets above. "After everything you've been through, I'm amazed you ever wanted to darken the door of a church again."

"It was so important to Mother and Father. They're buried here with my brother Daniel. I like to visit their graves after service. You don't have to come along-"

"Don't be silly," Lisa cut across. "Unless you want a private moment, I'd like to join you."

Anne swallowed. "Our latest vicar is an acquired taste. Either that or I haven't warmed to him. I'm sure you'll make up your own mind."

Lisa shrugged. "I'm starting to trust your judgment. I'll let you know after I meet him."

They stepped into the porch and joined a disproportionately aged communion of parishioners. Each one hopeful to hear an encouraging message from God, before they met Him in person.

Lisa had never been a cheerleader for fake emotion. Reverend Brendan Stokes was a mask wearer, she had no doubt. The fifty-five-year-old with salt and pepper hair must have held the office of a darling amongst some local, lonely widows. He liked to pause and let his voice ring out of that square head. One with dark eyes always half-closed in pretend laughter. His smile - that only revealed a top row of teeth - reminded Lisa more of a game show host than a serious man of the cloth. Every time the churchman delivered a saccharine coated scriptural interpretation, he adjusted his oblong, rimless glasses. By the time his sermon was over, the mere action caused a psychosomatic response in Lisa that forced her stomach to revolve in disgust. The only distraction from his cringe-worthy exegesis, came in the form of an uncomfortable hot sensation burrowing into the back of the woman's neck. Whenever that sensation became overwhelming, she shifted in her seat and glanced around. The *'scowl sniper'* appeared to be a man around sixty, with piercing grey eyes. White hair receded round his temples, leaving a point at the front. The feature echoed the style of some lead vampire in a classic, old-school Dracula flick. If Brendan stokes was the proud owner of a cuboid noggin, this guy must have epitomised the caricature of a classic ancient Goth or German soldier. He didn't smile once. His stare remained fixed on the new village arrival, until she hurried from her pew at the end of service. Of a meeker appearance was the quiet, friendly looking woman who accompanied him. Lisa guessed her to be some poor, long-suffering wife.

"Good morning, Anne." Brendan Stokes shook the retired schoolteacher's hand on her way out of the church. "And who is this with you?"

Anne looked at her companion. "Lisa Marston. She's come to stay with me for a while as a live-in helper."

Brendan's face beamed with overdone pretend joy. "Oh how marvellous. It's such a rarity to find selfless Christian charity toward the elderly on display in this day and age. Especially amongst the younger generation."

Lisa grimaced. "Thanks, but I wouldn't call it

selfless. Anne's providing me room and board in exchange for a few chores and some company. Rather think I'm getting the better end of the deal. No sainthood for Lisa today."

Brendan roared and clapped his hands together. The impact reverberated off the tiny medieval porch walls. "Well you are very welcome in our community, Lisa. I hope you'll join us for worship on a regular basis."

Lisa put on her best polite smile, strained though it felt. She was thankful to take Anne's lead, escaping from the minister's slimy clutches.

"So what do you think?" Anne smirked as they followed the churchyard path around to the eastern side of the building.

"Of Reverend Stokes?" Lisa shivered. "Not my cup of tea. You were right. If he stopped amping up all the overcooked sentiment, he might be half decent. Impossible to tell. Of course, given my recent history I may not be the most reliable judge of character."

"Hush now. Don't keep beating yourself up about it." Anne stopped dead and flushed. "Oh my, Lisa, I didn't mean to make light of your difficult situation." Her embarrassment proved short-lived. The brown-haired orphan couldn't stifle her roar of delight if she'd wanted to.

"Hello Anne." A male voice came clipped and business-like.

The pair swivelled and Lisa's face fell. It was the *'Scowl Sniper,'* although without wifey in tow this time. He almost marched, his limbs were so stiff and regimented.

"Good day, Martin." It was an unusual turn of phrase for Anne Weaver. She meant it as both 'hello and goodbye,' but the hint flew straight over the stern fellow's head.

"I heard this woman is staying with you." He locked that stare onto Lisa's pale green eyes.

"Yes." Anne kept her response to the polite minimum.

"I hadn't realised you were taking in a lodger." He pulled a black, leather bound pocket notebook from his jacket and clicked the button of a ballpoint pen.

"Lisa, this is Martin Coleman. A retired Detective Sergeant with the police." Anne motioned between them.

Lisa remained silent.

The man jotted down some notes and raised a curious expression back to the young woman. "Lisa-?"

"That's right. Lisa." She took her lead from Anne and kept her face blank.

"No, I mean, what was your surname?"

"Why do you want my surname?"

Martin sighed. "Because I like to keep abreast of what goes on in the village. A police officer is never off duty."

"Aren't you retired?"

Those grey eyes flashed for a moment. "I prefer to keep a lookout, anyway. Make sure everyone is safe. 'The Job' have their hands full enough with the cutbacks and escalating crime rates."

Lisa caught a shrug from Anne and rolled her eyes.

"Well, that's commendable. I'm Lisa Marston. And your name was Martin Coleman, is that correct?"

"Yes."

"Coleman - C-O-L-E," she spelt the first few letters as if to reassure herself mentally.

"That's right. Why?"

"Oh, nothing. I'm a freelance writer and editor for various outlets. One of my clients asked if I could do a pop psychology piece on retired control-freaks with self-esteem issues who can't let go of the past. I like to cite my sources, should I include them for publication." Lisa crossed her arms and tapped one foot.

Martin's nostrils flared. He closed his book, tucked it away and regarded the younger woman in stern silence. A moment later he walked off, leaving only a faint "Good day," hanging in the air behind.

Anne lifted one hand to cover her smile. "My goodness, Lisa. Making friends in Wrenham Green already?"

"I'm sorry. Can't abide busybodies. I'm sure he means well, but he's got a lot to learn about dealing with people. At least in a way that doesn't get their backs up. Once a cop always a cop, I suppose."

"Come on, I'll show you my f-a-m-i-l-y." The last word came out with a strain.

They proceeded a little further to where three gravestones stood side by side beneath a tall yew tree. Lisa mentally noted the names: *'William Weaver. Doris Weaver. Daniel Weaver.'* How it must torment the kind-hearted old spinster to reach such an advanced age without a place for Beth.

"Anne?"

"Yes?"

"Did you ever think of placing a memorial stone for your sister?"

Anne's eyes glazed over. "Many times. Something inside me can't let her go."

"It might be because you're twins."

The elderly woman reached a quivering old hand out to touch the top of each stone.

Lisa seized the moment with as much delicacy as she could summon. "I hope you don't mind me asking, but did that rag doll in your old room belong to Beth?"

Anne nodded. "She's called Molly. Beth didn't like to go far without her."

"And you kept her all these years as a memento?"

"Or in case Beth ever came home. I must seem like a daft old woman to you."

"Not at all. She is- *was* your sister and you love her. It's beautiful."

4
The Woodsman

"Okay world, what words can I compose or edit for you today?" Lisa sat back in a stiff wooden chair at a low table in Daniel's room. Even though Anne referred to it as 'your room' in discussions with her, that didn't feel right. She remained a guest of sorts. The room was on loan. Its former occupant departed this life long ago, and in tragic circumstances. But, it would be Daniel's bedroom as long as Anne Weaver lived at Bramley Cottage. It didn't matter who else occupied it. Lisa's laptop welcome screen flashed up. She keyed in her password and waited for the machine to finish its start-up procedures. This was the first day in her attempts to pull paying jobs out of the ether. What if those former clients from Carlton who offered freelance work, had been blowing smoke up her backside? If the pennies didn't start rolling in by late summer, she'd go broke. Thank goodness bills were limited to the basics and no household utilities or food costs. Except buying Anne lunch in Canterbury and paying for parking. This first Monday morning felt more like fear than freedom. "Change can be uncomfortable." She uttered the attempt at self-reassurance aloud and pulled up her e-mail application: A few marketing messages and one from *janice.gange@cccreative.co.uk*. She opened the digital envelope and stroked her chin as she read:

'Hi Lion,

Hope you made it down to Kent okay. Thought I'd drop you a quick line from work this morning. It's all kicking off around here.

Seems your departure emboldened a few other folk in the office. Some of them have been collecting documented evidence of Jenny Duke's misconduct for a long time. Frustrations that she gets away with murder finally reached boiling point. That new guy, Daryl calls her 'Teflon.' When I asked him why, he said it's because nothing sticks. I like that a lot. Might use it myself.

Anyway, HR received a collated report of misdemeanours so large, they've launched an internal enquiry. You can cut the air with a knife whenever the Wicked Witch of the West comes in. But, there's revolution in the wind. I hope they crucify her.

In other news, I had a phone call on Friday afternoon from Gresham Associates. They were after one Lisa Marston, as you wrote a series of blogs for them a while back that boosted their revenue ten percent. I still remember the boss swanning about, claiming it as a team victory. Useless lazy cow. Didn't tell her about this call. I gave them your personal e-mail address instead and said you'd gone freelance. They sounded intrigued and mentioned they might be in touch.

Fingers crossed.

I haven't run into Keith yet. I'm hoping he'll steer clear of the office. The git will have to strangle me before I'll talk, don't worry. If he hasn't realised you've scarpered away from Durham yet, it's only a matter of time. Maybe we'll all get lucky and he'll move on with his life when he can't find you?

Don't be a stranger. If your messages to me bounce, you know I followed your shredder example and stapled Duke's hands to her desk.

Later Babes,
Janice.'

Lisa let out a faint but satisfied snort of air. She spent the next hour or so composing and sending a form letter to contacts in her address book. This introduced her as a freelance writer/editor available for work. She'd been smart enough to keep a personal copy of the contact list, when things went from bad to worse with her boss. Another perusal of her in-box revealed nothing new of interest. She stretched and rubbed the base of her spine. Either she'd have to invest in a proper office chair at some point, or confine her work to short and regular bursts. The second option sounded quite appealing. A bumble bee buzzed around the half-open window. Lisa watched its plump body bounce against the glass a couple of times and then zip off.

"How are you getting on?" Anne appeared from the living room with a folded newspaper as Lisa descended the stairs. It was late morning.

"Not too bad. I had a message from an old colleague.

She's pointed some possible work my way. I've also sent out introductions to a load of other places. In the meantime, I'll surf around. See if I can come up with any article ideas to pitch. My back is stiff, so I fancy a break. Shall I put the kettle on?"

"Please. It's so nice out. Why don't you take a walk in the sunshine?"

Lisa entered the kitchen and retrieved the kettle. "That's a good idea. Might find some inspiration in the great outdoors. Did you want me to take you shopping today? I'm happy driving."

"No, that's alright. I've everything in we need for now. If you don't mind doing some ironing later, I'll cook us dinner."

"Deal."

* * *

Wrenham Green lay still and tranquil that Monday lunchtime as Lisa set off on foot from Bramley Cottage. The weather was bright with a sharp chill in the air. Winter may have lost its fight, but the downed adversary still had a few gasps left. She passed by *'The White Hart'* and turned south between the phone box and church. Beyond a compact row of terraced cottages on the western edge of the green, she took a right-hand track signposted *'Public Footpath.'* Dense undergrowth enveloped the trail fifty yards beyond. The gradient ran uphill until thick bramble bushes thinned out to reveal the boughs of a dark, mature deciduous wood. This close to the start of May and with an overall pleasant spring, clumps of bluebells began to carpet the spaces between each trunk. It would be another week or two until they reached their best. The impressive, gnarled wooden Ash tree denizens deadened what sounds remained, apart from the odd bird call up above.

Something disturbed the greenery. "Shit," Lisa caught hold of her chest. A deer leapt deeper into the undergrowth further up the incline. Its tufted tail flicked and disappeared. A rustling of bushes rippled across the gloomy, canopy-shaded spot for a heartbeat or two. The woman let out a sigh of relief. *So I was being watched after all*. She allowed her fingers to brush against the tree bark, like some tourist seeking to connect with an ancient monument. Three minutes later the bank levelled out into a wide grove. The trees weren't packed as tight up here, allowing more light to filter through to the mossy floor. Lisa perched on an upturned stump. It rested at a jaunty angle, caked with white decay. She closed her eyes and listened to a soft, wistful breeze swish through the newer branches way above. An odd sensation of dizziness clouded her mind, as if the world were spinning. From far into the woods, a twig snapped like a firecracker. Lisa's eyes flashed open at the sudden report. A series of dull thuds followed it. Someone or something was lumbering through the undergrowth. She lifted herself up and moved to investigate with befuddled limbs. Until she knew who or what it was, the woman thought it best to make as little noise as possible. Only trouble was, this proved easier said than done.

"Oh, a woman. Thought it was a bloody elephant escaped from the zoo for a minute there." The gruff male tone sounded almost as annoyed as Lisa felt when she heard the statement. Stumbling off the path and batting thorny twigs away from her face, had done more to announce her presence than conceal it. She detached some clingy stems from around her ankles and straightened. Before her stood a stocky man around her own age or older. A diamond shaped head with blond-tinted fair hair was adorned with sideburns leading to neat designer stubble. Lisa's first thought was that he had achieved the look Keith always aimed for but missed. He was also taller and broader with watery blue eyes. The man wore a heavy, protective jacket and soft leather boots. An old green wheelbarrow rested alongside him, filled with fresh cut firewood. On top rested a chainsaw and safety visor.

"Are you allowed to take fuel from a public wood?" Lisa was desperate to even the score.

"This part isn't public. I own it. The firewood's from my coppice."

"Oh." For the writer, her linguistic well had run dry of creative comebacks.

The man pointed in the direction his intruder had come. "Over there by the grove, the woods are public. If you'd stayed on the path, it would have led you round the hill to the south."

"I came this way because I heard the noise of you and your wheelbarrow. Thought I'd see what it was."

"Well now you know."

"Am I trespassing here?"

"I suppose. Doesn't bother me too much, as long as you're not planning to start a blaze or anything."

"Says the man with a barrow full of firewood."

The woodsman frowned. "I'm not going to burn it here, you daft bint. This is for my stove."

Lisa scowled. "How rude. Excuse me for being a concerned citizen."

The fellow shook his head and lifted the wheelbarrow handles. "If you head back the way you came, I'm sure you'll find the path again." With that, he stomped northward downhill.

Lisa watched him for a moment, grinding her teeth. Two seconds later she stormed after him. If her sleeveless top had featured arm coverings, she would have rolled them up. "Hey. You can't chuck insults around at people and walk off."

From the bushes ahead, a caustic tone replied. "I can when I find someone stumbling around on my land."

"So that gives you the right to behave like a nasty prat, does it?"

No reply.

The trees gave way to a gentle hillock covered in tufts of grass. It led down to a small field, sheltered from a narrow lane by a wall of bushy, thick hedgerows. Scattered about the field stood several shed-like wooden structures. They were the architectural equivalent of patchwork quilts, hammered together from all manner of unrelated timber offcuts and assorted light industrial junk. Each featured a corrugated metal roof. The largest was adorned with solar panels and included more windows than its neighbours. A grey stovepipe poked out one side of the hovel, allowing puffs of white smoke to escape into the spring air. The woodsman reached the base of the hill and deposited his barrow outside one of the smaller buildings. He looked up as Lisa approached.

"Are you still here? I thought I told you to go back the way you'd come." He began unloading the wheelbarrow into a store.

"I'm waiting for my apology." The girl harrumphed and stopped dead.

"Your what?" A chunk of firewood fell from the man's startled fingers and landed on his foot. "Ow! Fuck me that hurt. See what you've done?" He bent down and rubbed his toes through the boot.

"Serves you right."

The pale blue eyes rose to study her with more care than before. "Are you always this annoying?"

"You mean, calling people out for their unreasonable behaviour? When I need to be."

"Is it a natural talent or did you do a degree?"

"I did a degree. What is this place, anyway?"

"What is it?" He stood straight and examined the loose collection of makeshift huts. "It's my home of course."

"Your what? You mean you actually live in this dump?" Lisa attempted to peer through one of the murky windows.

The man wobbled his head and impersonated her

sarcastic feminine tone. "Yes, I actually live in this dump."

"What are you, some kind of hermit?"

"If you mean: Do I like to be left alone? Then, I guess we're getting somewhere at last."

Lisa stopped still. "Fine."

The man flushed and paused from his manual task. "Okay, maybe I was a little harsh. If it makes you feel better, I regret what I said or the way I said it. Sorry."

"Lisa."

"Pardon me?"

"Lisa. That's my name: Lisa Marston." She stepped closer and extended her right hand.

"Jeremy Lewis." He shook it. "Are you a rambler? Where are your walking boots?"

Lisa's tone softened. "No, I'm not a rambler. That should answer your second question, too. I was out for a short stroll."

"Are you local? We've never met before."

"I only moved in Friday night. I'm staying at Bramley Cottage."

"With Anne?" Jeremy cocked his head and adopted a friendlier posture.

"You know Anne?" Lisa tried to hide a growing smile.

"Everyone in Wrenham Green knows Anne. She's a nice lady."

"Glad to see we agree on something. How's your foot?"

Jeremy unloaded the last of the wood. "I think my big toe is swelling."

"Whoops. So, were you one of Anne's pupils?"

"No. I'm a Kent lad, but I grew up in Ashford. Not around here."

"Is that far?"

"Not especially. Getting nearer all the time."

"Huh?"

"Housing developments. Most of the surrounding farms were bought up and built upon. The conurbation is spreading like a bloodstain across the map. I couldn't wait to leave when I was old enough. It was never much to look at. No place for a country bumpkin. Or one at heart, like me."

"I see. Whereas now you live in this exquisite paradise?" Lisa raised one curious eyebrow as she glanced from hut to hut.

Jeremy put away his chainsaw and safety visor. "I suppose that's a fair comment. Not much to delight the eye, is it? So how did you come to be with Anne, Lisa Marston? I didn't think she had any surviving relatives."

"Lisa Marston," the woman repeated his reserved term with a hint of mockery. "She advertised for a live-in helper. I was looking for a change of location and a reasonable place to stay while I start my own venture."

"Doing?"

"I'm a freelance writer/editor. At least, I'm hoping to be. Used to perform that role in the corporate world for an employer."

"Haven't you come in the wrong direction if you're looking for a reasonable place to stay? That *is* a northern accent, isn't it?"

"Lancashire. I was born in Preston. Lived in Silverdale during my teens and then moved to County Durham. You recognised the accent?"

"Not exactly. I just knew it originated at a higher latitude than the Watford Gap, that's all."

"So it's expensive down south then?"

"Yeah."

"Is that why you live in a shed? What do you do anyway, sell firewood?"

"After a fashion, once I'm done with it."

"You're a charcoal burner?"

Jeremy smirked. "No. Let me show you. He opened the second largest hut and indicated towards the interior with his head. A pleasant aroma of sawdust and wood shavings escaped from captivity.

Lisa poked her nose around the frame and drew in a gulp of air. "Oh my goodness. How cool is that?" Her eyes widened. Beyond the doorway stood a collection of large, wooden sculptures and bespoke, carved garden furniture. There was a freshly oiled six foot Barn Owl, a three foot Kingfisher perched on a branch and a two-seater bench with flowing sides shaped like bunches of hanging grapes. "Do you do this with a chisel?"

"Chainsaw for the most part. Angle grinder and power sander too."

"Jeremy, they're amazing. Have you got a gallery?"

"No. I tend to work on a commission basis when I can get them. Only been doing it a couple of years, but things are picking up."

"And you love your work so much you sleep next

door?"

Jeremy laughed. "I bought the land from savings I'd accrued for a house deposit. That wiped me out."

"I see. Couldn't you have got a house nearby and rented a workshop?"

"Live in Wrenham Green? Hang on while I pull half a million quid out of my arse, would you?"

Lisa nodded. "Yeah, I know the score. So you got planning permission to live here?"

Jeremy shifted and closed his workshop doors. "I'm sure Anne will explain things to you. She knows all about my situation."

Lisa's face fell. "Why don't *you* explain it to me?"

Jeremy studied her like someone gauging the trustworthiness of a person to whom they might divulge a great secret. "Would you like to come inside?"

"Okay. Why not?"

The longest shed was comfortable and toasty warm. A log burner crackled in one corner. Lisa wandered around studying bookcases, sofas and other up-cycled furniture. The home lay subdivided into ordinary rooms like a small bungalow. It demonstrated the perfect blend of ingenious thrift and practical taste. Jeremy removed his boots and let the toes of his injured foot splay across the wooden boards.

"That's better. Should help the circulation."

"What should?" Lisa scratched her head.

"Underfloor heating."

"In a shed? Be serious."

"See for yourself."

Lisa crouched and placed the palm of one hand on the floorboards. "Oh my goodness, you're not kidding. Freaky. So how did you get the council to sign off on this? Aren't building plots expensive?"

"Yeah, I couldn't do that. I was after some wooded land I could use to coppice for fuel and provide a source of timber for my business. Since the plot is hilly and with little agricultural value, I managed to find a landowner interested in the sum I could pay. There's an artesian well for water and I've got a reed filtration bed for organic waste. Solar panels for electricity, as you might have noticed."

"So the council gave you some sort of eco pass?"

Jeremy winced. "If only. It's a low impact dwelling, of course. Off grid and built of sustainable materials. But I'm living here on the quiet."

"You mean they don't know?" Lisa jabbed her head forward.

Jeremy coughed. "Can I offer you a drink?"

The woman kept her gaze pinned to his face while her right hand lifted to point at a barrel on a nearby table. "Is that beer?"

"Homebrew. Would you like some?"

"Yes please."

"Okay, hang on a sec." Jeremy retrieved two old pewter tankards and filled them from a spigot on the barrel. "Here you go. Have a seat."

Lisa lowered herself to a sheepskin covered sofa and lifted the tankard to sniff. "Strong aroma of hops."

Jeremy sat beside her. "That's one thing the county is

famous for."

"Ah yes, I saw the oast houses for drying them."

"Most have been converted into homes these days."

"Cheers."

They clanged the vessels together, and each took a hearty gulp.

Lisa wiped some foam from her mouth. "Hey, that's not half bad. Thanks. So, you were going to confess about living here illegally."

"Not illegally; unlawfully."

"Is there a difference?"

"A big one."

Lisa took another sip and let out an accidental belch. She flushed. "Oops. So tell me."

Jeremy rested his tankard on a rough coffee table made from a pair of old crates. "Illegal activity is criminal and gets the police involved. Unlawful activity is civil and only involves the courts. It's not illegal to buy some land and live on it without obtaining permission, just unlawful."

"What happens if or when the council find out, or somebody drops you in it?"

"If the structure is considered permanent - i.e. not a caravan or other movable dwelling - you fall under what's known as the *'Four Year Rule.'* It's longer for non-permanent ones."

"So you can live here for four years?"

"Not quite. As long as my home remains unhidden and nobody complains, after four years of living here I can apply for retrospective permanent residence status. I'm not advertising myself to the council. If they came along and required me to apply for permission before the time was up, they could refuse me."

"And then?"

"After unsuccessful appeals, it would become a different matter if I remained living here. Then you move into criminal law and the police get involved."

"I see. Sneaky, risky, but clever. I was about to suggest writing an article for on-line publication about your lifestyle. That sort of thing always has a market. But I imagine you're not too keen on the publicity right now."

"It wouldn't be my first choice, no. Give it another couple of years if you're still about. Are you planning to stay?"

Lisa shrugged. "It's only my third day here. I have no idea. If I'm honest, I'm also running away from a dreadful job, an abusive relationship and my ex-partner's nightmare family." She didn't know quite why those facts popped out of her mouth. Jeremy was easy on the eye and seemed to have a pleasant way once you found a chink in his armour. Could it be that part of her wanted to believe in life and romance beyond Keith Molloy? "So how do you go about banking and receiving letters?"

"I put up a post-box."

"That's it?"

"Yep. Decided what I wanted to call the place, made a post-box with a name on it and stuck it next to my five-bar gate."

"And it worked without any formal records?"

"You'd be surprised at how efficient the Post Office

can be. I looked up the local postcode and began sending myself test letters to this address with the property name."

"What is the property name?"

"Ashdene."

"And the letters arrived?"

"It took a couple of weeks at first, but yeah. Once they were delivered with regularity, I changed all my accounts and other records to here. It's another way to demonstrate permanent residency when I file for it."

"You've got a pair, I'll say that. Amazing."

Jeremy crossed his legs and necked the rest of his beer.

Lisa sipped hers in silence for a few more minutes. "So where did you learn about forestry and carving?"

"After school I spent some time studying in Norway. Great teachers. My mother's Norwegian, so I had a workable grasp of the language from a kid."

"I thought you had something of the Norseman about you. You'd better watch out for that retired police guy. If he discovers what you're up to…"

"Martin? He's alright. We have something of an understanding. I help out a few of the old folks around the village and make carvings to raise money for the church."

"I didn't see you there."

"Not an attender, as such."

"But Martin Coleman leaves you alone?"

"He's not vindictive."

"Just a nosey parker?"

Jeremy cracked a lopsided grin. "Yeah. If I was a

criminal breaking the law, it might be different. All the while I'm good neighbours with people, there's less chance of anyone shopping me to the council. Martin turns a blind eye. He's old school police. Believes in discretionary powers, or something along those lines."

Lisa caught sight of her watch. "I'd better get back." She got up and walked to the door. "Thanks for showing me your place. Sorry I didn't leave you much choice in the matter."

Jeremy stretched his feet out flat to warm them on the heated floor again. "See you around the village."

* * *

"I'll see you the same time next week for another lesson, Jimmy." Reverend Brendan Stokes placed a warm hand on the right shoulder of an eight-year-old boy. The lad faced away at the open porch door. A silent tear rolled down one of his rosy cheeks. The minister bent forward to whisper in his ear. "Remember, this is our secret. God punishes tattle tales. You must always obey His shepherds."

A compact silver Peugeot pulled up outside the churchyard. A woman waved from the driver's seat. The boy trudged down the path, an uncomfortable limp in his gait caused by tensed buttock cheeks.

"He's doing very well, Mrs Walter," Brendan called with great enthusiasm. He swung his hand back and forth in exaggerated greeting.

The rear car door closed, and the vehicle rolled away into the fading light of evening.

Brendan eased the sturdy wooden portal shut. As he turned to re-enter the main church building, a draft caught him by surprise. The vicar lowered his head to discover his fly undone. With a look of deep satisfaction, he drew up the zip and swaggered down the aisle.

* * *

"Then he said Martin Coleman didn't give him any problems. It surprised me." Lisa turned a blouse over and continued to iron.

Anne reached a lit match into a clump of paper and kindling in the living room fireplace. It caught the packaging of a wrapped firelighter, causing a thin orange tongue of flame to slither out of the pile. "You'll find Martin sets a lot of store by motive, for all his intrusive and sometimes overbearing ways." She put one hand on the chimney breast and used it to support herself getting up. "Some older folk around here like having Jeremy living life on his own terms. Not only does it remind them of happier days, when many people round here enjoyed a simple, earthy life. But his bravado also sticks two fingers up at the nanny state. Good luck to him. Sounds like you took a shine to our local woodsman." Her eyes glittered.

Lisa swallowed. "Does it? I wanted to thump him for the first ten minutes. You're not going to tease me about this, are you? I only just met the guy and I'm hardly ready to jump into a relationship."

"You don't strike me as somebody who *jumps* into

anything, Lisa. I reckon you've a sensible head on your shoulders. No, I'm not going to tease you. I know what that's like. Whenever we got a new, dishy male teacher here in the village, I used to suffer those comments. People nudging, winking and laughing behind their hands."

"What did you do?"

"What could I do? I got on with my life and ignored them. For me, spinsterhood was no burden. I didn't want to marry. Of course, that means I'm alone now. But who's to say my husband wouldn't have already passed away and left me like this, if I had one?"

"Did the jibes get any easier?"

"Once I reached a certain age they stopped."

Lisa gulped. "Oh God, I haven't reached that age, have I? That's not why you're intending to leave me alone about Jeremy?"

Anne sat down and slapped her hands against the tops of her legs. "Good heavens, no!" she laughed. "You have plenty more years. But I don't think you're destined to live a single life."

Lisa put the blouse on a hanger. "I saw a man treating the Maypole with creosote on my way back from Ashdene. It *is* a Maypole, isn't it?"

"That's correct. Something of a tradition in Wrenham Green. It's Mayday tomorrow, but they won't hold the festival on a Tuesday. It'll be Saturday instead. The busiest our little village gets all year. Quite an event."

"Do children from the school perform a dance?"

The pensioner gave a wistful sigh. "Ten of them. A boy and girl from each class, except reception. They consider five years old a tad young. But the reception class always enjoy the festival, watching their older peers."

"Did you ever dance round the pole?"

Anne's eyes watered. "I was chosen once, aged seven. At the last minute I caught chickenpox and had to stay home in bed. Beth had already gone through the sickness, so she took my place. Daniel stayed behind to nurse me that year, while Mother went to the display. It was 1945…" Her voice trailed away.

"Oh Anne, I'm sorry. I had no idea."

"It's alright. Believe it or not, that pole is the exact same one."

"And it's lasted this long? Is that why the man was creosoting the thing?"

"Yes. They perform a safety inspection each year, before the event. Were the pole to rot, it could snap in half like a matchstick." Anne lifted an unlit match between both hands and broke it for dramatic effect. She tossed the remnants into the fire. They flared and died down as wood in the grate hissed and glowed. "The result could be catastrophic for the children, so they don't take any chances. So far, it's remained sound. The telephone company should source their poles from our wood."

"It's local then?"

"Yes. The previous one broke a week before I was due to dance. They cut down a new tree that year."

"So where does the tradition come from? I saw a Maypole dance when I was a girl, but I didn't understand the symbolism."

Anne stretched. "There's still some debate going around. Many scholars agree people erected them to celebrate the return of warmth and plenty. Others insist they were part of a pre-Christian pagan tradition of worshipping sacred trees. Some argue this to be mere speculation without any evidential base."

"You seem very clued up on the subject."

"After a career as a schoolteacher in the village, what do you expect? I've had to field many a heated discussion from parents at odds. Every party convinced their own understanding is the right one."

"Maypole bigotry? Now I've heard it all. Some people need to get a life."

"I suppose you could say that a Maypole *is* a BIGGER TREE," Anne winked.

Lisa snorted and wrinkled her nose. "God what an awful pun. Can I use it if I write an article about them?"

The old woman nodded. "Did you have any replies on your computer when you got back?"

"Yes. That enquiry from Gresham Associates my old pal Janice mentioned. They've commissioned an opening post for a new blog series. If that takes off, there'll be more work coming down the pipe. I should start researching in the morning. Those guys are prompt with payment too. What a great result on my first day."

Anne stood. "Well, this calls for a celebration. I'll see what's lurking at the back of my booze cupboard after dinner."

5

May Day

When Lisa awoke early that Saturday morning and peeped out of the curtains, the green already thronged with activity. Stalls, marquees and bunting aplenty lay in various stages of assembly. An array of vans were strewn at rough angles along the periphery, disgorging their contents into the arms of cheery, volunteer work gangs. Sun gleamed off the polished ring atop the freshly treated Maypole. It now looked resplendent, adorned with ten pink and blue ribbons.

"Quite a transformation." Lisa crept into the bathroom so as not to disturb Anne. She needn't have bothered. When she returned to the bedroom and dressed, a gruff male voice down below called out, "Good morning, Anne. Lovely day for it." The young woman opened the window and glanced down to the dinky cottage garden. Her landlady sat in one of two pale green wooden chairs that had been set amongst the herbs and flowers. The old lady returned the greeting across the low boundary wall, a steaming cup of black coffee in her hands. A weathered-looking character with mutton-chop whiskers, ambled off across the bend to play his part in the work.

Lisa descended the stairs with a spring in her step. She passed by the slow, deep-noted ticking grandfather clock. The front door stood ajar, held open by a metal doorstop in the shape of a cockerel.

"Good morning, Anne." Lisa slipped through the gap. A delicious mix of freshly brewed coffee and warm pastry aromas returned her greeting before the lady even spoke.

"Good morning, Lisa. I fetched my outdoor table and chairs from the rear store. Thought we could watch the festival preparations over breakfast."

"Great idea. Are those croissants?"

"Yes. Decided to go continental today. Warm croissants, jam, coffee and orange juice. Unless you fancy something else?"

Lisa reclined into one of the seats and poured herself a cup of coffee from a sturdy cafetiere. "This is perfect. Thank you. I was admiring the Maypole from upstairs. They've attached the ribbons. I'm guessing it's five pink ribbons for the girls and five blue ones for the boys."

"That's the way we tend to do it round here. But it's a local tradition. Something an old headmaster developed in the late thirties, when folk came up with the idea of gender balanced class representatives."

"Quite forward thinking for the early twentieth century."

Anne shrugged. "It was a good way to portray the school. We didn't have politically correct nonsense or permanently offended weaklings back then. You took a boy and girl from every class but one, then gave each an alternating coloured ribbon. Logical, straightforward and it made for a nice display."

Lisa cut into a croissant and spread some strawberry jam across it. "I'll wager you wouldn't have to go far to find somebody who gets upset at the colour choices."

Anne grimaced. "I'll wager they wouldn't spout off for too long round here before someone told them where to shove it."

Lisa bit into her pastry as Anne spoke. She inhaled some flakes while attempting to stifle her amusement.

"Are you alright?" The old woman bashed the spluttering thirty-year-old between her shoulder blades with a flat palm.

Lisa composed herself. "Better now. Thanks."

The dense scent of wood smoke caught a shifting breeze and altered course to blow across the bend.

Lisa raised herself up in the seat. She shielded her eyes from the sun with one hand to get a better view. "Is there going to be a barbecue?"

"Yes. A hog roast. Jake Harrap the local pig farmer usually takes care of that. I can't see from here, but it'll be him. I guarantee it. Ah, here's something that might interest you."

A muddy white van burning a little oil chugged to a halt near the other vehicles. Jeremy Lewis climbed out of the driver's seat and walked round to open the rear doors.

Lisa sipped her coffee. "What's he doing here?"

"I imagine he's carved something or other to auction in the marquee later. The proceeds go to the festival committee."

Lisa put her cup down. "Do you think he needs a hand?"

Anne leaned forward. "He might like a coffee before setting up. Why don't you ask him over?"

Lisa regarded her companion for a moment, senses straining to gauge whether she was being ribbed. Anne looked blank. She brushed pastry crumbs from her fingers with a nonchalant disregard for the scrutiny. Lisa got up. "Alright then, I will."

"Hi Jeremy. Anne and I are having breakfast outside the cottage. Did you fancy a coffee before you get stuck in?" Lisa stopped about ten feet from the bent over rear end that wiggled as its owner fished around in the back of his vehicle. Jeremy hadn't heard her approach. His startled head crashed into the roof. Rubbing the top of it, he backed away from the doors and rotated to meet the cause of his pain. Lisa spoke again before he could reply. "I'm turning this into a habit aren't I?"

Jeremy's strained face softened. "That's both ends now."

Lisa tried to remain serious, but the situation was too delicious not to milk. "Anne's coffee is so strong, it's like a punch in the gut. So if you want the full set of injuries…"

Jeremy closed the van doors. "They say these things come in threes." He surveyed the green. "The gang haven't finished erecting the marquee yet. I can't do much with this for now. Okay, lead on."

Don't be too enthusiastic, fella. Lisa resisted the urge to blurt the sarcastic statement out loud. Instead she jerked one thumb back towards the van as they walked. "What did you bring?"

"That Kingfisher you saw in my workshop. I made it for the festival."

"Alcedo atthis ispida." The woman stressed each word.

Jeremy blinked. "Very good. Bird watcher are you?"

"No. I wrote a piece for a nature photography site once. They'd captured some amazing shots of Kingfishers diving for their prey. That's when I learnt the Latin name. It must have stuck in there." She tapped the side of her head with an index finger.

"I imagine you'll be popular on quiz night over at The White Hart. We've a few wicked trivia heads in these parts. About time they had some new competition."

"I'll look into that."

Anne caught sight of the pair as they neared the edge of the green. She waved to Jeremy.

"Good morning, Anne. Lisa's invited me over for coffee." The voice projected a rich tenor, full of warmth and laced with a hint of good humour.

The old schoolteacher struggled up from where she had been set in her chair.

"Please don't," Jeremy held up both hands.

Lisa indicated her own seat. "Here, you can have mine."

Jeremy hovered above the low brick boundary. "No no, you take it. I'll perch here on the wall, if that's okay with our host?"

"Of course." Anne sat back down. "So what have you brought us this time, Jeremy? I do so love your woodcarvings."

The man went to reply, but Lisa cut across.

"A Kingfisher sitting on a branch." She looked at the table. "I'll need to fetch a spare cup. Back in a jiff."

When the young woman returned, Anne and Jeremy were nattering away like old friends. She poured out a coffee and handed it to their guest. "Did I miss anything important?"

Jeremy shifted position. "Nothing of consequence. Thank you."

"Milk and sugar?"

"No, that's okay. I take it as it comes." He smiled at Anne. "Lisa reckons your coffee is a gut buster."

Lisa frowned. She'd rather he had kept that comment to himself.

Anne shrugged. "See for yourself."

The woodsman took a sip and fought to catch his breath.

Anne winked. "Could be she was right."

Lisa folded her arms. "Too strong for a big strapping lumberjack?"

Jeremy scrunched up his eyes. "Lumberjack? Err, okay."

Lisa sat down and finished the rest of her croissant.

Jeremy blew steam from the surface of his drink and observed her deliberate, distant disinterest. "So have you seen our Maypole, Lisa?"

"Yes. Anne's been telling me all about it."

Anne sat upright. "Did your mother teach you any Nordic traditions associated with them, Jeremy?"

Lisa raised an eyebrow. "Do they have them over there?"

Anne nodded. "In Scandinavia, Belgium, Italy, Germany, Austria, even Malta if I remember right. As you might expect, the tradition spread to parts of the United States and Canada as a result."

Jeremy gazed left across the village green to where the colourful pole stood. "In Scandinavia, people usually put them up around midsummer rather than May. Over the centuries they added a cross beam after the adoption of Christianity. Another example of pagan religious traditions being absorbed into church life, to ease the conversion of natives."

Lisa leaned closer, cupping an elbow with one hand and tapping her lips with the other. "Are they a celebration of new life there too?"

"For the most part. There are old Norse legends about the Axis Mundi, of course."

"The what-ee what-ee?"

"Axis Mundi: The world axis. Right across Europe there was once a Germanic belief in Thor's Oak. Norse mythology includes stories of Yggdrasil, the world tree that connects nine worlds. That's an immense Ash tree, also sometimes referred to as 'Odin's Horse.' There are all manner of fables about spirits travelling up and down Yggdrasil. Like an inter-dimensional elevator. Sacred trees were sometimes revered as having a connection to it."

Anne stretched. "I explained a little of that to Lisa

yesterday. It seems that if there ever was any association between Maypoles and pagan worship, it's long since disappeared into the vapours of unrecorded history."

Lisa glanced from one to the other. "More of an excuse for a jolly good knees up?"

Jeremy licked his lips. "It is in Wrenham Green. Kevin Laycock does record trade over at the pub whenever the May Day Festival comes around."

Lisa grunted. "That's my kind of tradition."

"It's time for the Maypole dance with the boys and girls of Wrenham Green County Primary." An announcer's voice echoed through a loudhailer across the lunchtime throng of revellers.

Lisa scowled and handed Anne a paper plate loaded with pulled pork, coleslaw, sweetcorn and barbecue sauce. "They might have given us more warning." Billowing smoke from the fire caused her eyes to smart.

The announcer spoke again. "Correction: The Maypole dance will commence in ten minutes. Please make your way over to enjoy their display."

"That's better." Lisa collected her own plate. She poked at the food with a plastic fork.

Anne tasted a sample of the meat. "Mmm. Delicious as always. Where did Jeremy run off to?"

"He's in the marquee with his carving."

"Ah yes. All that interest from visitors could be good for business. Let's hope he secures another commission or two."

They strolled past a crowd of Morris Dancers enjoying pints of beer alfresco from The White Hart. Their bells jangled at the slightest hint of movement.

Reverend Brendan Stokes stood near the pole, caressing the long blonde hair of a ten-year-old girl as if she were a favourite pony. He flashed that sickening smile at the girl's mother. "Helen has been getting on very well with her extra religious studies. It's so nice to find a parent who takes their child's spiritual education seriously."

The woman's cheeks glowed a satisfied shade of rose. "Not at all, vicar. My husband and I are delighted you're willing to help her. Same time this week?"

"That will be fine." He moved his head closer to the child. "Now then, I understand you're going to dance for us. I can't wait to see it."

Helen looked like a petrified animal frozen to the spot. Her mother gave her arm a tug. "Come on Helen, it's nothing to be afraid of. See how excited your younger schoolmates are."

"Is this the big climax?" Lisa jostled with the growing crowd alongside Anne.

"In a manner of speaking. Afterwards they'll hold the auction. Then it's an afternoon of eating, drinking and playing games."

The dancers assembled, girls wearing frilly new dresses, boys with smart shirts, ties and long trousers. Each grabbed hold of a ribbon as they formed a circle around the Maypole. A folk band struck up a merry ditty, and the dance began. In and out the children weaved, overlapping and twisting the ribbons as boy faced girl and rotated in opposing circles. Once back to their original classmate partner, all ten children performed a half rotation to reverse their actions. They unwound the colourful garlands in the opposite direction. In the crowd, heads bobbed and hands clapped in time with the tune. The Maypole held firm, flexing when the streamers went taught. Lisa caught a glint of sunlight flash off the metal ring, much like she had from a distance earlier on. A sharp intake of breath cut across the revelry.

A nine-year-old girl lay in a heap on the grass, still clutching onto her ribbon. Round about her the remaining dancers stood still as statues, faces watching their companion with rigid, lifeless eyes. A woman screamed in the crowd. The collapsed child shook like an epileptic, jerking in a continuous fit of wild motions. The band ceased playing.

"Clear a path. Coming through please ladies and gentlemen." An event organiser led two black uniformed staff from St. John's Ambulance, parting the throng like Moses at the Red Sea with his authoritarian voice. One of the ambulance crew knelt by the quivering girl. His colleague touched a frozen boy on the shoulder who held firm like a block of marble. The medic performed a gentle wave in front of his eyes and squeezed one hand. He remained unresponsive.

Jeremy appeared next to Lisa and Anne. "I only just managed to get away from a chatterbox. What happened?"

Lisa shook her head, eyes never leaving the spectacle. "I'm not sure. One of the girls collapsed and had a fit." She caught sight of the old woman next to her. Anne stood motionless and quiet. At her feet the plate of food lay in the grass, its contents scattered across the ground. She spoke with a soft rasp.

"Look at the other children."

The fitting girl stabilised. At the same moment the remaining nine dancers fell to the grass unconscious.

* * *

The brass bell jangled at Bramley Cottage. Lisa looked away from the laptop screen and strained to listen. From down in the hallway, Anne was greeting someone. An old acquaintance by the sound.

It had been an uneventful few days since Saturday's excitement. A minute or so passed before all the collapsed Maypole children came to, unaware of what had taken place. Each one received a check-up by the ambulance staff. With no obvious medical explanation forthcoming, it fell to the event organisers to calm the waters. In the crowd, onlookers batted around ideas. These ranged from it being a joint practical joke to collective sun stroke. Neither answer felt satisfactory to anyone present who'd witnessed the drama. The fit endured by the first girl to collapse went way beyond playacting. While the weather remained fine, the sun's rays shone in subdued, intermittent bursts from behind passing clouds. What were the chances of all ten children suffering ill effects from it in perfect synchronisation?

Lisa saved her work. She'd made good inroads into the Gresham Associates blog opener. One more quick self-edit and proofing session to go, first thing in the morning. Then she'd send it over for appraisal. The young woman shut down the computer and forced stiff joints to move. Her back grumbled. She'd been engrossed and not stopped for a break in several hours. Now aches and pains were the toll levied on her body for taking the metaphorical work express lane.

"Ah, Angela. I don't believe you've met my new live-in helper, Lisa Marston," Anne piped up as the freelancer entered the living room.

Lisa found a woman in her late thirties with back-length brown hair and straight fringe, sitting on the sofa opposite the retired schoolteacher. Alongside perched a girl around nine, the spitting image of her mother. The child sat still and silent.

Anne spoke again. "Lisa, this is Angela Hackman and her daughter Tessa. Angela was a former pupil of mine some years ago."

"Too many years," their guest half-grimaced at the mental arithmetic. She rose from the sofa to exchange a brief hand squeeze with the northerner.

Anne indicated to the child. "Tessa was the young lady who suffered that awful fit at the Maypole on Saturday."

Lisa's eyes widened. "Of course." That's why the child appeared familiar. "How are you feeling, Tessa?

That must have been a scary experience."

Lost, dark brown eyes rose to study Lisa. The child's lips quivered. She said nothing but nodded in two sharp jerks.

Angela regarded her daughter with a frown. "Under normal circumstances it's almost impossible to shut my little lady up. I don't know what's got into her. Tessa's such a curious, excitable and chatty girl."

Lisa dragged a pouffe from next to the sofa. She settled herself close to the nine-year-old. "I remember when I was her age. During winter I had a cold that turned to bronchitis. One night my saliva became viscous like jelly, while I was asleep. I woke up unable to catch my breath. The goo spread across my windpipe and I fell into a blind panic. Mum raced in but was at a loss what to do. As I started to black out, Dad made me swill some water round my mouth and spit. To this day I've no idea how he knew that might work. It's hardly an obvious action. But, that water dislodged the obstruction. For the next few minutes I spat up a clear sludge."

Angela took her seat again. "What a frightening thing to happen."

Lisa bit her lip for a moment. "That's the point I'm getting to. For the next few weeks, I was so frightened of it happening again that I couldn't get to sleep. I sat up in bed with a lamp on, too terrified to close my eyes. I was like a zombie. When the lids became heavy, I lay upright against a mountain of pillows. The idea of stretching out horizontal where that awful thick saliva might get me again, was more than I could face. In time though, the memory lessened. I began to get some rest and have nights without further incidents. With each, I found the courage to lay further down, until the whole scary affair faded into the background." She looked into the girl's dark brown eyes. "Do you find yourself thinking about Saturday and worrying it will happen again, Tessa?"

Tessa fidgeted but didn't respond.

"Answer the lady, Tessa," Angela prodded her daughter.

Lisa held up a hand halfway. "No, it's okay."

Anne leaned closer from the other sofa. "Have you taken her for a proper examination, Angela?"

"The medics couldn't find anything physically wrong with her at the festival. They advised me to get her a blood test. She has an appointment tomorrow. Our doctor will discuss any findings with me on the phone, once the results are back."

Anne hummed. "Better safe than sorry. Hang on, I've an idea what might help."

Angela watched the old lady get up. "What's that?"

The schoolteacher opened the door. "Back in a minute." Stairs creaked as the homeowner ascended to the floor above. When Anne returned, she was clutching an old rag doll with red woollen hair tied in bunches. "This is Molly. She belonged to my sister. I'm afraid I can't let you take her away, Tessa; but if you'd like to hold her for a while you're more than welcome. Molly is good at offering comfort."

Tessa reached out two trembling hands to clasp the soft material figure. She drew the doll to her chest with reverent affection. No sooner had Anne sat down again than the child sprang to her feet. Molly fell from the girl's grasp onto the rug. Tessa screwed her eyes shut tight, eyebrows knitting together across an anguish-lined nose. Her chin dropped down, mouth wide open to reveal a row of young white teeth. The scream that rang out of that dainty face sounded with breathtaking force. Its pitch and volume remained constant. A din carrying like a note of record-breaking duration, delivered by a professional wind instrument player. The kind a technique like circular breathing might produce for the skilled. On and on it went. Lisa was so taken aback she slid off the pouffe onto the floor next to the doll. Anne raised withering fingers to her ears in an attempt to alleviate discomfort. She sat square in the path of that impressive vocal assault. Angela leapt up and grabbed hold of her daughter by the shoulders. If the mother was attempting to shake her, that rigid girl must be putting up some invisible form of resistance. Tessa remained immobile, her balance and posture uninterrupted by forceful attempts at restraint.

"Tessa. Tessa." Angela strained her biceps, panting from shock and exertion. "Tessa, please." The tone softened from stern authority and embarrassment to heartsick desperation.

Tessa collapsed in a vertical line where she stood, like a limp pile of clothes from which a body has magically vanished. Her torso quivered and spasmed on the floor.

Lisa grabbed hold of the child's face, fighting to hold her still.

Anne knelt with clicking knees beside her. "No Lisa, don't restrain her."

"Won't she swallow her own tongue?"

"That's a myth. She might bite it, but we mustn't put anything in her mouth." Anne removed her cardigan. "Here. Place this underneath her head."

Angela snapped out of her momentary paralysis of shock. She moved to embrace her child.

Anne placed a soft hand against the woman's left forearm. "She needs space. Don't crowd her." The old lady caught sight of tears welling up in her ex-pupil's eyes. "I understand, Angela. You want to help. When it passes she'll need you to hold her then."

Lisa edged back. "Should I call an ambulance?"

Tessa's body tremors ceased with as little warning as they had started.

Anne glanced at the clock. "Less than five minutes. I'd rather help her recover and let her go home instead." She released Angela's arm. "Best to mention this at the doctor's."

Tessa sobbed. Angela pulled her daughter close and hugged her on the floor.

Anne scooped Molly from the rug, pressing the doll against her chest with one arm. Lisa followed her out into the hall.

"Easy to tell you're an experienced schoolteacher. I was at a loss in there. Knew I should have taken up that offer of a first aid course back in Durham, when the company sent round an invitation."

Anne drew the living room door to behind them. "If you put your fingers or anything else into a person's mouth while they're fitting, you run the risk of choking them. You can't swallow your tongue all the while it remains attached."

"Do you think she's epileptic?"

"That's for the doctors to discover. I taught for over forty years and I've seen epilepsy before. If it's a factor here, it's not the only one."

"Right - the screaming."

Anne sighed. "And the other children on Saturday. Oh, I know they didn't have fits, but-"

"They all collapsed together."

Anne stroked Molly's woollen red hair. Her face fixed into a stare without focus, eyes glazed.

Lisa frowned. "Anne?"

"Yes?"

"Do you know stuff you're not telling me?"

The old woman shook her head. "It reminded me of something that happened a long time ago, that's all. Would you fetch Tessa a glass of water?"

"Yes of course." Lisa wandered into the kitchen and ran the cold tap. When she came back, Anne had helped Angela settle her daughter in a seating position on the sofa again. Lisa lifted a small tumbler at the mother. "Would she like a drink?"

Tessa looked from her anxious parent to the woman with the water and nodded. Lisa handed the glass over, making sure the girl had a tight grip before relinquishing her own.

Anne eased down opposite again. "You take a few small sips on that, Tessa. Water works wonders in many situations, as Lisa already explained."

The nine-year-old drank in silence.

Lisa stood watching the scene near the door. "Can I get anything for you, Angela?"

"No. Thank you. We'll be off in a minute, once she's a bit better." She wrung her hands in her lap. "I'm so sorry, Anne. If I'd known this was going to happen…"

Anne put the rag doll down on the sofa cushion beside her. "How could you know? Think nothing of it. Once Tessa's on a more even keel, you must bring her round for tea. Does she like coffee and walnut cake?"

"I'm not sure. I think so. One of her classmates likes baking. It's the new big thing on TV right now. Something she talks about a lot, when-"

"When she's her usual, bubbly self," Anne completed the sentence. "Well, if she doesn't mind an older teacher, I could have her over for the afternoon and we'll bake one together."

A hesitant smile eased the strain lines creasing Angela's face. She touched Tessa on the knee. "Would you like to bake a cake with my old class teacher?"

Tessa nodded.

"Right you are then," Anne winked at the child.

Angela rose, followed by the dumbstruck girl. Anne retrieved her cardigan from the floor and put it back on. She followed her visitors to the front door, embracing Angela as they stepped out into a chilly evening. Angela rubbed the old woman's upper arms. "Thanks again, Anne. I'm sorry I didn't get more of a chance to talk with your lodger. She seems nice."

"Yes, she is. Another time. Have a restful evening, if you can. I'm sure the doctors will help. Goodbye."

From inside the hallway, Lisa caught the exchange. Anne's words sounded reassuring, but when she came back in her expression didn't support them.

Anne read the younger woman's facial aspect. "Now then. How about one of those chats I recruited you to engage in?"

Lisa let the look of concern go. "Alright. What's the topic?"

As it happened, the topic was a bit of everything. They sat in the living room discussing politics, technology, current events, the environment, religion, spirituality, education, societal changes and generational attitudes, and the list continued. Lisa almost wished she'd had time to prepare. Anne was well informed on so many subjects, the young writer/editor almost felt a fraud. A case of impostor syndrome that required her to dig deep into her memory of facts. And all without the luxury of an Internet search to remind her. By the time the clock struck eleven, Lisa had developed a new admiration for the eighty-year-old. Full of surprises as ever, Anne Weaver came from a life of learning and retaining information without the technology crutches upon which her own generation now relied.

"If you don't mind, I'll head up." Lisa stretched.

"Is that the time?" Anne caught sight of the clock. "I've made you earn your position tonight, haven't I?"

"It's a pleasure." Lisa plumped a sofa cushion as she rose. "What a great discussion."

Anne scooped Molly into her arms.

Lisa hesitated.

The old woman watched. "You want to learn what happened long ago."

"Only if it's not too painful to retell."

Anne stepped across to the old photograph of her family. She stood with her back to Lisa. "The year I was due to dance round the Maypole and Beth took my place, something similar occurred."

"You mean the kids fainted?"

"So the local stories went. As I mentioned, I was laid up in bed with chickenpox. But I heard people discuss it afterwards and my sister came home changed. A few days before Daniel suffered his accident, Beth had a screaming session right here in this room, like Tessa."

"Did she fit too?"

Anne's head nodded in a slow sweep. She remained looking away.

Lisa puffed. "Crumbs. No wonder it shook you. Did the doctors have any idea what caused it?"

"She disappeared before we ever got that far." In the dead quiet, Anne swallowed hard. "A lot of bad things happened in Wrenham Green that year, in the months before the war came to an end."

Lisa wanted to ask more but decided not to push. "Let's hope history isn't repeating itself then."

Anne hesitated. When she spoke, the tone came calm but dismissive. "Goodnight, Lisa."

"Night." Lisa slipped out the door.

As the footsteps disappeared upstairs, Anne wiped a tear from her cheek and touched the photograph with shaking fingers. Her desperate prayer slipped out in a cracking, breathless whisper. "Not again. Dear God, please not again."

6
Shattered Peace

"Okay everybody. This morning we have a special guest come to talk with us." Katie Hunt was the same age as Lisa, unmarried but with a great love of children. The teacher's semi-patronising *'happy face'* demeanour around her young charges made the incomer chuckle to herself. How had Anne managed to talk her into volunteering for an assembly at Wrenham Green County Primary? Lisa fiddled with her top in a desperate attempt to conceal the anxiety gnawing at her gut. They were only children between the ages of five and eleven. What was the big deal? A plump, middle-aged male teacher with a greasy comb-over and a brown corduroy jacket leaned closer to the school visitor.

"Nervous?" The words were soft and subtle, seeping out one corner of his upturned mouth.

Lisa chewed an imaginary cud and fidgeted in her seat. Were the fellow's inquiry not spoken with such genuine tenderness, she might have felt indignant. Instead, his honest concern added to the clenching of her stomach muscles. She replied while attempting not to move her face.

"I shouldn't be. They're kids, aren't they?"

At the front of the small, provincial assembly hall, Katie turned their way. Her hands extended to signal the obvious new face in the room. A face every curious child had remained transfixed by, ever since they filed in from their respective classrooms. Katie kept her arms outstretched but twisted to keep eye contact with the children. "Lisa Marston is a professional writer and editor. She's staying with my old retired teacher, Miss Weaver, right here in the village. Let's give her a big Wrenham Green welcome, as she comes to tell us all about her work. Over to you, Lisa."

The assembly hall filled with enthusiastic applause from around ninety pairs of young hands.

For one brief but silly moment, Lisa thought her legs were going to give way as she wobbled to her feet. Sweat glistened beneath her collar. Warm blood pulsed through her head. The pleasant, airy assembly hall now felt more like a sauna. Celebrity had never appealed to the somewhat self-contained and private young woman. Gossip mags and reality TV left her cold. She preferred to curl up with a good book or watch a decent documentary or classic film. Big socials and large groups tired her out. Now, here she stood, the centre of unblinking attention. *Oh crap, I never realised what a responsibility this is. Whatever I say, these impressionable youngsters are likely to believe and take on board. I'm shaping who they'll turn out to be.* Lisa fought down the urge to hyperventilate. *Okay, calm down girl. They want to know how you got into writing and made a career from it. Keep it simple and fun. Lots of encouragement to work at their own reading and writing skills. You can do this.* She took a long breath and smiled at the abundant faces locked onto her like a mass collection of laser beams.

"Good morning, Children. How nice it is to be invited here to meet you all." Lisa knew full well that teachers were desperate for decent assembly topics and speakers. In a strange sort of way, this lowered expectations and lessened the pressure on her.

Before she could utter another word, an eleven-year-old boy shot straight up to his feet at the back. A girl in his class further along the same row followed suit. In the next row and the next, similar pairs of youngsters sprang up like jack-in-the-boxes. Only the front row of five-year-olds remained seated.

Lisa began to look across to where Katie Hunt had taken her seat. She paused upon catching sight of a familiar nine-year-old. Tessa Hackman was one of the risen children. Each child stood like a skittle, arms clamped down at their sides as if Rigor Mortis had set in.

Katie Hunt half rose. "Children, what are you doing? Please sit down." The ebullient teacher was less comfortable asserting authority than delivering her usual fluffy rabbit act. Was this a sign of respect like a standing ovation? If so, why weren't those children applauding?

In a single, unified motion, ten young jaws lowered. Each child shut their eyes tight. Then the screaming began. Hearing one child erupt in such an outburst had been shocking at Bramley Cottage. Nothing could have prepared Lisa for five boys and five girls belting out such a continuous stream of noise in her direction. All around, the remaining seated children clamped hands over their ears. Some five-year-olds burst into tears of fright and confusion. The plump male teacher squinted at Katie Hunt, still frozen in her half sitting, half standing position. She had lost all power to act. The man grunted and ambled over to stand beside Lisa. His face dark and serious, he flapped his arms up and down in a demonstrative gesture.

"That's enough. Stop it. Ivan. Helen. Gemma. All of you. Stop this noise at once." Even shouting in a manner that exhausted his hoarse voice, it proved difficult to compete with the wall of juvenile sound.

As one unit, the ten ended their screaming and dropped to the polished parquet floor. Writhing, jerking and shaking like victims of chronic St Vitus's Dance, they rolled and twitched in a frenzy of faces and limbs.

The male teacher put one hand across his mouth. The school secretary was first to respond. She raced to her office and phoned for an ambulance.

Lisa moved to the nearest child, a six-year-old girl. Other teachers squeezed amongst the assembled children to tend to their own classes. Soon enough the synchronised violent fitting ceased. School staff and their would-be assembly speaker worked hard to comfort and reassure the victims and their upset classmates. Some semblance of order crept back into view as a Doppler effect of emergency vehicle sirens wailed to a halt in the lane outside.

* * *

"I don't care, Nicola. I'm not having our boy grow up to be a wimp." Robin Jarrett dumped a sturdy plastic bucket into the kitchen sink of their three-bedroom, sixties rural semi. He squeezed some car shampoo from a bottle into the container and ran both taps to fill it with foamy suds.

The man's wife closed the door on their washing machine. "He's not a wimp. Ivan's a quiet one. A bit shy and uncertain around new people and situations."

Robin shook his head and scowled. "You're not doing the lad any favours by mothering him all the time. It's bad enough he had to take part in that effeminate May Day dance like a bloody pansy."

"Robin, that's an old tradition. There's nothing girlie about it."

"He might have at least raised an objection, instead of taking part with such enthusiasm."

Nicola sighed. "Being chosen for the Maypole is a great honour. He put himself heart and soul into it to make you proud. Now you intend to throw it back in his face?"

"If he wants to make me proud, he can join the local junior football squad and develop some teamwork and social skills."

"For goodness' sake, he's only nine."

"All the more reason to stop his dreamy, loner behaviour before it becomes ingrained." Robin left the bucket in the sink and moved to call upstairs from the kitchen door. "Ivan. Get down here and give me a hand washing the car, please."

Nicola folded her arms. "Does he have to help you wash the car?"

"You think I'm going to let him waste his Saturday on one of those nerdy pastimes?"

"He's been through a lot in the last week. First fainting at the festival. Then that seizure in assembly yesterday. Why don't you cut him some slack? The doctors advised rest."

"Too much rest is the problem. He's so weak from lack of sport and exercise, it's affecting his physical development. A bit of exertion will do him good." Robin leaned back through the door. "Iva- Oh, there you are."

A gangly nine-year-old with dreamy but worried eyes and wire-framed glasses appeared on the staircase. He looked as though a strong gust of wind might blow him away like a leaf.

Nicola leaned around her husband to address their son. "How are you feeling now, Sweetie?"

Robin snorted. "Sweetie? For God's sake Nic, you're determined to make a sissy out him, aren't you?"

Nicola's face reddened. "I call *you* Sweetie. Am I making a sissy out of you also?"

"That's different and you know it. When Ivan grows up and gets a girlfriend - *if* Ivan grows up and gets a girlfriend - she can call him whatever the hell she likes." He looked down at his son who had now reached the bottom step. "There's a bucket of soapy water in the sink. If I lift it out, do you think you can carry it down the drive to the car?"

Ivan nodded but shuffled his feet.

Robin walked back into the kitchen. "Okay then. Here we go." He hoisted the sloshing plastic container down onto the floor.

Ivan took hold of the grip with both hands and struggled to lift it. His face turned an impressive shade of crimson. The boy puffed and hobbled across the room, the swinging receptacle less than an inch from the tiles.

Robin shook his head from side to side in slow, deliberate dismay. "This is painful to watch. My own son a five star weakling. If he spills that, he's getting a clip round the ear."

Nicola prodded her husband's stomach. "Don't you dare. If I come home and find you've laid a hand on him, Robin, so help me God I'll-"

"Okay, okay. Enough. The worst he'll get is a tongue lashing."

Nicola exhaled a long breath. "You might find he responds better if you stop berating him all the time. How about a little love instead?"

"Love won't make a man out of him, Nic."

"Are you so sure? Look, I'm going to smarten up and pop over to Rachel's for our usual get together. Would you peel the spuds when you're done with the car?"

"Yeah."

Nicola kissed him on the cheek. "Play nice, Rob. He's a good boy. Try to nurture him, will you?" She disappeared upstairs.

Ivan reached the red Audi saloon parked in their driveway and lowered the bucket. It didn't have far to descend. The journey across the kitchen, over the back step and round the side of the house had burned through five minutes of intense effort. He wiped sweat from a broad, smooth brow.

A familiar, authoritarian voice bellowed with faux encouragement. "So, you made it. Well done." Robin Jarrett sauntered along the concrete hard standing and dropped two dry, clean sponges into the water. "There we go. You take one and I'll use the other. We'll start on the car roof and work down."

Ivan found lifting a soggy sponge blessed relief from his previous exertions. The lad was tall for his age, so reaching across the roof wasn't too much of a chore. He watched his father press down on the top and slop soapy water around. The sponge squeaked against the metal bodywork as he applied pressure. Ivan attempted to mimic his performance with reasonable success.

Nicola Jarrett appeared on the front doorstep, a handbag slung across her shoulder. "You boys have fun. I'll be back soon."

Ivan's heart sank. Dad was always at his most testy and belligerent when Mum wasn't home.

Robin called out. "See you later."

Ivan paused to gaze after her down the road.

His father grunted. "Come on son, put your back into it. I didn't ask you down here to watch me do all the work."

The boy gulped and redoubled his efforts. His father stepped back a moment to observe. "Better. That's the way. Keep the pressure up. Go back over that bit, you missed a spot. Okay, now we're getting somewhere." He plunged back in, making the nine-year-old's attempts look pathetic by comparison. Ivan wondered if this was deliberate. Did his father intend to make him feel useless? Was this another attempt to drive him to compete? Dad was always doing that, and the boy hated it.

After they'd reached the wheels, Robin dropped his sponge back in the bucket. "There. Now we'll wash it off with the hose and get stuck back in for a good leathering off. Don't you feel better for having used your muscles for a change?"

Ivan shrugged. He craved intellectual and positive emotional stimulation over an endorphin release from physical activity. But intellectual and positive emotional stimulation weren't part of his father's repertoire. Not unless it was the intellectual stimulation of discussing sports statistics. Or the positive emotional stimulation of fist-pumping the air after a team goal in football, or a rugby try.

Robin studied the lad's noncommittal response. The cautionary advice of his wife floated back into memory. "So what were you doing upstairs when I called?"

"Drawing."

"Oh. What were you drawing?"

"A dragon."

"A dragon." Robin's shoulders sank. "Still into all that fantasy nonsense?"

Ivan shrugged again. "Would you like to see it?"

"Your picture?" The man bit his lip and took a breath. "Okay then. Go fetch it while I empty this bucket and hose down the car."

Ivan ran inside and stomped upstairs.

Robin stood still and engaged in a moment of thoughtful soliloquy. "Well at least something gets him fired up enough to run, I suppose."

When Ivan returned, Robin was spraying a concentrated jet of water around the wheel arches from his green garden hose. The boy held up an A3 sheet of paper for his father to examine. His drawing depicted a massive but agile black-scaled monster with fearsome claws and impressive wings. Its open mouth roared at the viewer, displaying row upon row of dagger-like teeth. Two glowing red eyes stared out with unfathomable malice atop a horned head. Below and to the right the artist had inscribed a word.

Robin leaned closer. "What's that, an artist's pen name or something?"

"No. The name of the dragon," Ivan corrected him with an uncertain voice.

"Your monsters have names too? Nid- Nidh- What's that say?"

"Nidhogg."

"What kind of name is that? Shouldn't you call a dragon 'Flame,' or 'Claw' or something menacing?"

"It's from mythology."

Robin raised his eyebrows. "Oh, I see. That interests you too, does it?"

The boy moved his head in subtle agreement. If he emoted with too much enthusiasm, his father would use it as another weapon to beat him down.

Robin swept his attention from his son's sheepish gaze to the drawing and back. Without another word, he flicked the hose in the lad's direction, drenching both artist and artwork. "Come on boy, let's see some spirit in you. Doesn't this make you angry? Fight back. Be a man. Stand up for yourself."

The sodden paper disintegrated. Ivan held up both hands to shield himself from the jet. Water dripped from his curly brown hair as he stumbled to keep his balance. A gentle nature - given to emotional reactivity - tipped him into a spiral of total overwhelm. He burst into tears and sank to squat on the driveway, shoulders heaving in a cascade of rising sobs.

Robin averted his jet of water back to the vehicle. The hose hung in one limp hand, spraying the nearside front wheel. The man gritted his teeth at the pathetic sight of his son crying in a soggy mess at his feet. "What on earth do you think you're doing?" He scanned left and right to check his neighbours weren't witnessing this embarrassing display. "Get up. Don't be such a baby. Big boys don't cry. It's only a stupid picture, for goodness' sake."

Ivan fought to crest the emotional tidal wave with bursts of strained speech, between his sobs. "I worked on that for hours. It was the best one I've ever done."

"Maybe you won't waste your time on such

foolishness in the future."

Ivan wiped his dripping nose. "You don't understand. You never understand."

Robin flushed. "Oh, get out of my sight before you make even more of a scene. I'll finish cleaning the car myself. Go back to your stupid colouring pencils. I'm done with you. Go on. GO!" The final word bellowed with such force, Ivan almost lost his footing in an attempt to stand up and leave. He stumbled, teary-eyed back down the drive.

Late afternoon sunlight gleamed off the immaculate red Audi. Two coats of fresh wax had buffed the vehicle's paintwork up to a mirror sheen. Robin Jarrett stood inside at the kitchen window, admiring his work. A potato peeler traced the contours of a Jersey Royal in his hands with unconscious muscle memory. Peelings slipped down into a bowl of water in the sink. At the lounge doorway, the man became aware of a familiar presence. He chose not to look round. "Have you finished crying yet?" There was zero empathy or concern in that voice. When the boy didn't reply, the man turned. Ivan stood there, watching him with dry eyes this time. Any hint of that earlier outburst was no longer evident on his son's face. "Have you drawn another dragon?"

Ivan stared back at him, unblinking. The taunt registered zero impact. Not breaking his stare, the lad spoke. "Why don't you like dragons?"

Robin smirked. "What? Why don't I like dragons?

There's no such thing as dragons, Ivan. They belong in fairy tales and to kids a lot younger than yourself. You've got to grow up sometime, son. In a few years you'll be meeting girls. They won't put up with a beanpole weakling who likes childish things. I know it seems hard, but you'll thank me one day."

Those words washed over the boy unnoticed.

"Dragons are real."

Robin slammed the potato peeler down on the draining board and folded his arms. "Okay, prove it. Come on."

Ivan continued to stare. "I don't need to prove it, I've seen one."

Robin threw up his hands. He shook his head and sighed. "Do you have any idea how stupid you sound right now? You've seen one. I'm raising a liar as well as a wimp, am I? Why did you even come back downstairs? Sod off back to fairyland. I'll be having a few choice words with your mother when she gets home. It's time we made some serious changes around here."

Robin turned back to the sink. The sound of a cutlery drawer rumbled open behind him.

Ivan's once timid voice deepened and filled with rage. "You will not disrespect the Master."

A thin bladed filleting knife sliced into the area around Robin Jarrett's appendix. Shock and pain dropped the man to his knees. Dark blood spilt from a narrow entry wound, staining his white shirt. He gasped, twisting back to catch a vacant expression on the boy's face. A cold light glistened in those young eyes. The body was Ivan's, but whatever gazed out from those windows of the soul didn't belong to his gentle son. The man reached to grab hold of the filleting blade's handle. Ivan's hand shot down. A grip like iron denied his father any attempt to withdraw the implement. Instead he plunged the blade deeper inside up to the hilt and pressed hard. The wooden handle snapped off, leaving the cutting edge buried within. Robin moaned in pain. His other hand stretched across to the burning incision. Ivan grabbed hold of the potato peeler and swept it up in a dramatic arc above his head. Robin reacted in time to hear the stiletto-like cutting tool hiss through the air. His head tilted back as the point gouged into his left eye socket, bursting the white orb like a poached egg. A yolk of ocular fluid and crimson spray splattered against the kitchen window, such was the frenzy of the puncture. This motion repeated on the other eye.

Did Robin Jarrett scream like a sissy? In those final agonising moments of life, it didn't seem to matter anymore. His lungs gave voice to the horror inflicted upon him, until they too were punctured by assorted cutlery items. Air escaped from his chest rather than his mouth. The strength and incessant fury of his attacker went beyond all human comprehension. In the quiet lane outside, birds tweeted at the afternoon sun in oblivious contentment.

"See you later, Rachel." Nicola Jarrett twisted to wave at her friend. From the half-open front door of a

Victorian terraced cottage, a feminine hand extended in farewell. The visitor hummed to herself, enjoying that quiet walk home. *I wonder how the boys are getting on with the car? God, I hope Robin has been easier on Ivan today. For once it would be nice to see him show an emotion other than disappointment in our son. The boy's wired different to his father. He can't help it.* Her murmured tune lessened with the ever decreasing spiral of worrying thoughts. She was at a loss how to make her husband realise he was damaging Ivan's self-esteem, not building his resilience. Tough love and aggressive challenges weren't going to work as a child-rearing tactic in this instance. She rounded a bend into their tranquil lane. The red Audi glimmered and flashed like new. *Looks like they did a good job. Hmm, did Robin remember to peel the spuds?* She glanced down at a fresh manicure Rachel had given her. *Oh please let him have remembered the spuds.* She hesitated on the doorstep to retrieve a set of keys. "Hi guys, I'm home," she called, closing the front door behind her. "Robin? Ivan? Where are you two? Robi- Oh my God!" Her heavy leather handbag thudded onto the lounge carpet. Nicola slapped both manicured hands with immaculate nails in front of her mouth. Her eyes fixed on the motionless, bloodied torso of what had once been her husband. He sprawled on the kitchen floor, covered from head to waist in a range of different sized puncture wounds. Jagged, gleaming metal shards poked at assorted angles from each hole. Scattered all about him on the blood soaked floor tiles, lay a variety of knife handles, sans blade. Both his eye sockets had become dark, empty hollows. A potato peeler hung out of the right one. The thick stench of blood filled the woman's nostrils. Her thoughts immediately flashed to her son. "Ivan? Ivan!" She wailed and ran upstairs, breaking a nail on the banister from the force of launching herself forward. There was no sign of the lad in his bedroom. All remained as neat and ordinary as he always kept it. Nicola searched the upstairs rooms, whimpering and fighting to catch her breath. No sight of the boy. She almost lost her footing on the way back down. Somehow she made it to the phone and dialled 999.

* * *

"It's a beautiful evening. I like May when the weather's fine. There's still something fresh about it." Lisa ran her hands across some tall grass as she walked. Alongside, Anne Weaver wandered with pursed lips, lost in thought or memory.

"Yes. This time of year always reminds me of being young again. I enjoy summer, but it's not quite the same once everything passes its peak, and the weather heats right up."

They turned down a residential lane behind some houses on the far side of the village school. Lisa caught sight of an array of police vehicles clustered outside a sixties semi. "Hello. What on earth is going on here?"

"Doesn't look good. We should steer clear." Anne observed a flurry of activity from forensic investigators in white coveralls.

"Let's cross over and pass by on the other side," Lisa agreed.

Some uniformed officers stood on the doorstep of the neighbouring house, talking with the occupants.

"Anne?" A calm, dignified voice cut through the din across the street. It belonged to a tall man around thirty-five. His extensive broad forehead devoid of hair might not have looked out of place on a scientist. Instead it sat beneath a buzz cut of dark brown fuzz belonging to a blazer-wearing plain clothes detective. Lisa pondered for one well-humoured moment how *'fuzz'* was an appropriate hairstyle for a police officer. Wispy brown eyebrows and watery grey/green eyes glittered far apart either side of a long nose. A firm, pronounced jaw with a slight overbite and thick neck, gave an impression of well-controlled strength beneath a polite demeanour.

Anne squinted in the fading light and stroked her chin, straining to put a name to the inquisitive face. "Good heavens. Marcus?"

The man beamed and crossed the lane. He and the old teacher exchanged a kiss on both cheeks. From the front lawn of the house at the centre of the furore, another plain-clothes officer shouted. "Inspector wants you to phone an update ASAP, Fuzz."

The blazer wearing officer gave him a thumbs up.

Lisa raised an eyebrow and smirked. "Fuzz?"

The man glanced at her. "Old nickname that stuck from childhood. Nothing to do with my profession, believe it or not." He tilted his head forward. "Nor my receding hairline."

Lisa chuckled. They hadn't been introduced but already this guy was going in her mental *'nice'* box.

Anne grabbed her arm. "Oh, I'm sorry. Lisa Marston, meet Marcus Foster."

Lisa took the hand Marcus offered her. "I see. Foster/Fuzz, right?"

He nodded as he shook. "You've got it. Pleased to meet you. Anne is-"

"Your old schoolteacher?"

Marcus let go and grinned. "Yeah. How did you guess?"

"I'm staying with her for a while. Running into old school pupils is a bit of a habit."

"I see. Not surprising. Miss Weaver was a legend. I wish I could get over to the village more often to visit. But I haven't made it back since college. My folks moved away long ago. How time flies."

"And now you're a police officer?" Anne asked.

"That's right. Detective Sergeant - for my sins."

Lisa indicated the house across the lane. "Dare I ask what's going on, if we're even allowed to know?"

"Murder, I'm afraid. No question about it. Mr Robin Jarrett, stabbed multiple times with multiple kitchen implements."

"Oh my goodness." Anne stepped back a pace.

Marcus' happy face darkened. "It seems his wife, Nicola Jarrett went out to visit a friend, leaving Robin and their nine-year-old son, Ivan washing the car. When she came home, she found her husband stabbed to death on the kitchen floor. The boy is nowhere to be found. At this stage we've no idea if he ran off in terror after witnessing the crime, or was kidnapped by the perpetrator. Whoever they are, they must be a serious beefcake. Mr Jarrett was well built. To be overpowered and attacked with such ferocity, well... Let's say I wouldn't want to run into the thug on a dark night with only my warrant card for backup."

Lisa frowned. "Any motives?"

Marcus licked his lips to disguise a faint smile. "What are you, a young Miss Marple? We've only been here a short while. Have either of you come round this way earlier today?"

"No," Anne replied.

"What about Ivan Jarrett? Have you seen him, or would you know him if you did?"

"Ivan Jarrett." A flash of realisation swept Lisa's countenance. She turned to Anne. "He was one of the boys who passed out at school yesterday."

"Another of the Maypole children?" Anne said.

"That's right."

Marcus inserted a hand between them. "Whoa, whoa, whoa, slow down. What's all this? What Maypole? You mean the village one?"

Lisa nodded. "Last week at the May Day festival, ten children dancing round the pole all collapsed together. Yesterday the same kids had a screaming fit at school and passed out again."

"Are you a teacher?"

"No. I'm a freelance writer and editor. I'd agreed to speak at a school assembly."

"I see. Has anyone looked into these blackouts or whatever they are?"

"I know at least one parent has arranged for a blood test. Mrs Jarrett might have done the same for Ivan."

Marcus jotted some lines down in his pocket notebook. "She must have been too distraught to mention it when we first spoke to her. Small wonder."

Lisa scratched her head. "Could it have anything to do with the murder?"

"Unlikely. But, worthy of note. A screaming fit, you say? Could be the children have seen something and are frightened to disclose it. Might help with our enquiries. I'll look into it. Thanks for your help."

Anne took a deep breath. "Well, if you've no further need of us now, we'll be on our way. I'm sure you've got plenty to get on with. You remember where to find me if you need any further help, Marcus?"

"Bramley Cottage?"

"Of course. And even if you don't need our sleuthing skills, it would be splendid to have you round for a cuppa."

Marcus gave her a quick hug. "Thanks, Anne. If I can catch a break from my duties, I'll try to pop over sometime soon." He shook Lisa's hand again. "Lovely to meet you. Take care now." With that the detective exchanged his pocket notebook for a mobile phone and brought up his inspector on speed dial.

As the women headed for home, they caught the last strains of him talking into the device. "Hello Sir. No, the boy hasn't shown up anywhere yet that we're aware of. Initial search has drawn a blank. Yes. Given the nature of the savagery involved, we'd appreciate a PolSA on standby to help locate the lad. Okay. Will do."

7

Vitruvian Vicar

The vicar's study at St. Mary's adjoined the main body of the church. It was an untidy, windowless room, off-limits to parishioners. All except those helping out at special events. Volunteers who might need to fetch a display board or raffle ticket book from a spacious, shabby cupboard with a broken door latch. Several dusty shelves were fixed to one wall. A portrait of a minister from Victorian times hung alongside. Across the room, the only other piece of furniture was a rough wooden decorating table used as an improvised desk. Assorted church documents, certificates, orders of service and fliers for a 'bring and buy sale' lay heaped in messy, disorganised piles either side of a desktop phone and closed laptop computer. An embroidered kneeler cushion adorned an uncomfortable plastic chair. A piece of furniture that once belonged to the school before they threw it out. This makeshift softener provided some extra posterior comfort. A white dove - symbol of The Holy Spirit - had been sewn into the cushion with great care and artistry by one of the older members of the congregation. The irony of spreading his butt across that sacred image while surrendering to his private obsession, wasn't lost on the vicar. But his faith and the many struggles he held over Biblical accuracy and interpretation were always eclipsed by a different call to worship from his flesh. When those desires arose - as they often did - no ancient threat of eternal damnation could compete.

"I'll see you tomorrow, Reverend." Leonard Harris the carpenter called from the porch door. "Is it okay if I leave my toolbox and materials here?"

Brendan Stokes hovered in the study doorway. "That's fine, Len. Thanks for your work. Janet Malcolm the cleaner will be in to open up first thing, if I'm otherwise engaged."

"Right you are. Night."

"Goodnight."

Once the main church door clunked shut, the vicar nipped back out to lock and bolt it. Janet had a key for the double-locked side door to let herself in. His steps were almost on tiptoe, like a sneak thief or petty criminal trying to avoid detection. *Why am I doing this if God is everywhere and sees everything?* It was a pointless but automatic way to move. One that heightened the excitement and arousal associated with his intended nocturnal activity. He flicked a row of switches on the wall to leave the main sanctuary in darkness. From outside, nobody would be aware that someone occupied the church. If they were, their thoughts might turn to visions of their smiley minister, engaged in a time of personal intimacy with The Almighty. He re-entered the study, illuminated by a single, shadeless sixty-watt bulb. For one doubtful moment, Brendan offered a half-hearted prayer. "Please God, let what I do in darkness never be brought into the light." Despite his sin and any post-life consequences - if such a price were levied - the thought of the church brought into disrepute still made him squirm. But it couldn't quell his raging appetites, whether engaged in fantasy or reality with those poor, unfortunate young souls who attended his one-to-one religious instruction classes.

The laptop whirred to life as Brendan opened the lid and pressed the power button. Extra light from the screen flooded into the gloomy study. He moved to close the door and kill the sixty-watt bulb. Now only the computer illuminated what would take place in the coming minutes. The minister licked his lips and got comfortable on the chair cushion. He logged on, brought up a web browser and keyed in a specific URL. It was one he always deleted from his local Internet history after each call to 'prayer.' A private website login screen appeared. The vicar typed in his details and password; information common to only a handful of select members who shared their private media with the rest of the ring. Seconds later he was in and scanning through a list of new entries. One from *'Whosyadaddy27'* caught his attention. It contained an attached video file. The subject line read: *'Big boys playing with the girl next door.'* He turned up the speaker volume and ran the clip. In that ancient room, built by the faithful for worship of the Divine, ungodly acts flickered across the weathered stone walls. Brendan stroked the bulge in his trousers and unzipped the fly. In the dancing glow, naked men robbed a young girl of her innocence. From the computer speaker, her cries of distress mixed with jeers of delight from the excited participants resonated to the rafters. Throughout it all, another silhouette played large across the walls: The frantic masturbatory beatings of a paedophile sex addict vicar, grunting and gasping for breath in the house of the Lord.

That copious cupboard with the broken door latch creaked. The voyeur was so lost in his reverie, he thought it a protestation from the mattress altar upon which the on-screen abusers were sacrificing their lamb. From inside the closet, a pair of young, female eyes twinkled out at the wild and perverse display. But it wasn't the first time those eyes had seen Brendan Stokes in all his glory, whether they wanted to or not. The door slipped open, and the girl giggled. Brendan jumped from his chair and closed the laptop screen in shock. The room darkened.

"Who's there?" Stokes stuffed his erection back inside his trousers by feel. The zip rose in a flash.

"Why put it away, vicar?" The girl stepped out of the cupboard, a familiar yet altered voice rasping in the inky blackness. Her tone he knew, but the cheeky confidence behind those words sounded foreign. A slender hand slithered across the wall to the light switch. It re-ignited the hanging bulb.

"Helen? What are you doing in here?" The minister juggled an emotional smorgasbord of relief and worry.

The study door creaked open from the main church. An eight-year-old boy's silhouette stood back-lit by flickering candlelight from the sanctuary. In his left hand he clutched the carpenter's sturdy toolbox as if it weighed nothing at all. In his right he held a hammer.

"Jimmy? What's going on here? What are you doing with Len's tools?" Brendan gasped. "How can you even lift them?"

A sinister smile crept across the pretty face of the ten-year-old girl. "It's your Calvary moment, Reverend. Time to become the propitiation for your own sins."

Brendan's brows knitted together at such a technical, theological phrase on the lips of one so young and uneducated. He stretched out a hand to the desk phone, his eyes flicking from child to child. The minister adopted a sudden air of business-like concern to quell a rising flicker of fear. "I'm calling your parents to come and get you. They must be worried sick."

Helen Taylor lifted the bottom of her dress with two seductive hands. The minister paused with the telephone receiver clasped in a sweating palm. He swallowed hard and felt the eager pressure of his personal resurrection trying to roll back the zipper 'stone' and burst from the material 'tomb' below. The figure in the doorway cast one hand forward. His hammer whistled end over end, connecting with the man's shoulder. The receiver clattered onto the table, its delay sounding a continuous tone. Brendan fell against the rear wall, clutching his injured limb with the other hand. Pain throbbed down his arm with excruciating ferocity.

"You've broken it." A salty taste of blood teased his mouth. The room span and went dark.

When blurred vision and sound filtered back into his semi-conscious senses, Brendan found himself staring at the timber vaulted ceiling of the main church. Both arms were raised above his head; each hand held by two smaller, softer ones. But the power in those appendages gripped like vices from which there was no release. His back slid along the floor, bumping across the rough stones of medieval graves. The last resting place of former parishioners interred in the aisle. The dazed man tilted his head back to observe an inverted view of where the children were taking him. All about the altar, candles burned in a semi-circle. They surrounded the nine foot, plain, oiled wooden cross that stood before the church's most ornate stained glass window. In front of the cross, someone had set a bulky brass holder adorned with St. Mary's Paschal candle with obvious precision. Its flame licked so close to the wood, it threatened to blacken the simple but beautiful Christian symbol.

Jimmy let go of one hand. It belonged to the arm with the broken shoulder. The act of being dragged through the church, inflamed Brendan's agony further. That dazed and groggy man knew he had to resist. The effort of trying to push himself up on the injured limb, made the room spin again. Helen's foot came down upon his chest and pinned him to the floor. She leaned closer and wagged an index finger in his face, like a parent offering a gentle rebuke for naughtiness to their wayward child. Brendan attempted to thrust his body upward, but the weight of that foot felt like millstones used to 'press' people accused of evil in ancient times. He remained immobile.

Jimmy re-appeared in his field of vision. He passed a handful of long nails to Helen and hoisted the hammer in a victorious gesture.

Tears rolled down Brendan's cheeks. In one helpless moment, he echoed the words of Jesus at Golgotha. "Father, forgive them, for they know not what they do."

Helen and Jimmy sneered. Half-lidded pupils pressed against their fluttering upper eyelids as if experiencing a spiritual vision. In a chant-like chorus they lifted their arms and spoke as one. "Into the Master's hands we commit this spirit."

* * *

"Bit early in the morning for gardening, isn't it?" Lisa Marston stood on the doorstep of Bramley Cottage, clutching her first cuppa of the day in both hands.

Anne Weaver knelt on the slabs between the building and its low brick wall. She put down a trowel and arranged several red blooms in an old trug next to her. "I like to tidy up after I pick tulips."

Lisa examined the flowers. "They must be coming to

an end this far into May."

"Almost."

"Thought you'd pop a few in a vase to enjoy indoors? Auntie Joan used to swear by lemonade rather than water, if you want cut flowers that last longer."

Anne clambered to her feet and brushed down her skirt. "She was right. But these aren't for indoors."

"Oh?"

Anne pointed her head across the green to the church. "It's Daniel's anniversary. Mother and I always took tulips from the garden to his grave on this day. After she and Father passed, I carried on the tradition."

Lisa shifted from foot to foot. "I'm sorry."

Anne regarded the attractive petals with their distinctive shape. "Tulips were always Daniel's favourite flower. Beth and I grew up on tales of how he loved them as a baby, before we were born. Except he couldn't pronounce tulips. It came out *'toolips'* instead."

Lisa repeated the phrase. "Toolips."

"He would insist mother take him by the hand and walk him along the flowerbeds to see them all. At each bloom he used to pause, point and demand *'more, more toolips,'* with his limited speech at that age."

"That's so sweet."

Anne picked up the trug and trowel without making eye contact. "It would be nice to have some company on this day again. It's been many a year since…"

"Of course. Did you want to go now?"

Anne and Lisa entered the churchyard. The old teacher still bore the trug dangling from one forearm. They paused at the Weaver family graves. Lisa stepped back a couple of feet to give the woman space. Anne placed the trug down in the grass and bowed her knee to retrieve the blooms. Loving hands spread them across the greensward and patted each with gentle affection. "There you go, Dan. I hope you like them this year. I love you."

Lisa choked at the tender words, delivered with such honesty and heartfelt care after all this time. In that moment she almost felt sorry. Not sorry for Anne, but sorry no man had ever enjoyed that attention and commitment in an intimate relationship. They were qualities the dedicated spinster possessed in abundance.

A plump, jolly figure of a woman waddled through the gate, swinging a plastic container of cleaning products and dusters. Lisa looked up long enough to observe her amble round the back of the church, then extended a hand to help Anne to her feet.

From a small door on the other side of the building, a blood-curdling shriek cut the still morning air. Two crows cawed and broke into the sky from a nearby tree.

Lisa went to pace forward, but realised she still held onto the old schoolteacher's arm.

"You go on, quick. I'll be right behind," Anne said.

The northerner encircled the medieval house of worship and made the side door. Her mind swam with the possibilities she might witness inside. The cleaner couldn't have been frightened by a big spider, could she? In her line of work it seemed doubtful. What else was so terrifying about an old church?

Lisa's eyes adjusted to the transition in light levels. Janet Malcolm stood halfway down the aisle, grasping the back of a pew with both hands for support. Her arms shook. Her face paled to an alabaster hue. The box of cleaning products lay on its side at her feet. Tins of beeswax polish, plastic cleaning sprays and assorted cloths scattered across the stone floor. Lisa followed her frozen gaze to a gruesome display at the altar. The naked body of Brendan Stokes hung suspended, rectally impaled upon the sturdy Paschal candle. His arms and legs were lashed in a star shape before the plain, nine foot wooden cross, like some modern art installation homage to Da Vinci's Vitruvian Man. Both eyes were missing, replaced by heavy duty, long nails. Metal spikes that were hammered through the sockets with considerable force. These connected his torso with the cross through the back of the minister's head. One final nail impaled the trunk of his genitalia. It secured a blood-soaked sheet of paper obscuring his private parts in almost sarcastic modesty. Someone had used the blood as ink to leave a message on the would-be loincloth.

"Lord have mercy," Anne appeared in the doorway a couple of feet behind Lisa. She sidled up to Janet Malcolm. The two women embraced for mutual comfort.

Lisa forced herself to approach the altar, fighting the

urge to heave but overwhelmed with curiosity.

"Hold it right there." A commanding voice barked from the open doorway.

Lisa spun to lock onto the piercing grey eyes of Martin Coleman. "There's a note."

"You mustn't disturb a crime scene." The retired police officer marched into the building.

Lisa edged a couple of paces closer. She could make out the writing from behind the altar rail, scrawled with a rough hand. *"Suffer, little children while I come over Thee."* Her face creased. "That phrase sounds familiar."

Martin reached her side. "It sounds like a sick parody of *'Suffer the little children to come unto me.'* Jesus' words from the gospels. Has anyone called this in?"

Lisa shook her head and rummaged in her pockets for a mobile phone. "No. We just got here. Hey-"

The brusque man swiped the device from her grasp, whirled on the spot and stormed back down the aisle, keying in a number.

Lisa fumed and pressed fingernails into the palms of balled fists.

From the back of the church, Martin spoke with a confident and demanding voice into the phone. "Please connect me with the FCC Duty Inspector - Police to police enquiry."

Lisa's furious stare moved to where Anne and Janet now sat in a pew halfway back. Anne caught the anger in that expression and gave the younger woman a sympathetic look. The aggrieved woman let out a snort. She stomped off in the only direction available. One that wouldn't take her closer to the grisly remains or infuriating ex-policeman. The vicar's study door hung ajar. Lisa pressed it open with her foot so as not to touch anything. The room appeared messy but unremarkable. What looked like an old plastic school chair with kneeler cushion, stood back from a decorating table on the far side. From the angle and distance, this must have been the result of someone standing in a hurry. Lisa moved to the table. A laptop connected to the mains was still running, although the lid remained closed. She glanced around to see if anyone was watching. No sign. Martin Coleman's voice rang out from the main structure, talking in some kind of acronym-filled police gobbledygook to the party on the other end of the line. The woman slipped a small handkerchief out of her pocket. She used it to prise open the computer screen at a place she thought it unlikely a normal person might touch it.

"Oh my God." She caught her breath. The vicar's computer had no lock screen time-out set. The monitor displayed the final frame of a finished video clip: four middle-aged naked men spraying their intimate seed across a terrified and weeping young girl.

"I told you not to touch anything." Martin appeared at the study door, face severe.

Lisa's discovery sapped her of any will to fight back. Shoulders slumped, she turned away from the computer.

Martin moved closer and caught sight of the screen. His harsh expression darkened and he let out a sigh.

"Not this. Please, not this." The man shook his head. He regarded the woman with easing features and handed back her phone. "Thank you. Come on, we shouldn't stay in here. The force will want statements from everyone when they arrive."

* * *

"I'll get it." Lisa called upstairs to Anne as she walked from the kitchen of Bramley Cottage into the hallway. The brass bell jangled again before she managed to open the front door. "Ah, DS Foster."

The blazer-wearing detective moved his neck from side to side, releasing some stiffness. "You can call me Marcus. Anne does. Is this a good time?"

Anne's voice sounded on the stairs. "Who is it, Lisa?" She reached the door. "Oh, hello Marcus. Come on in."

Lisa stepped aside to allow the officer across the threshold.

He wiped his feet on the doormat like a house-broken husband. "Thank you. I can't stop long. Only wanted a quick word, and to check you're both alright. That was quite a scene you stumbled upon this morning."

Lisa closed the door. "I'm wondering if we'll have nightmares. Can I get you any refreshments?"

Marcus looked back. "A glass of water, if I may. I've been buzzing around like a blue-arse fly all day long. Now to cap it all, two more children have gone missing with Ivan Jarrett: Jimmy Walter and Helen Taylor. Do you know them?"

Lisa scratched her head.

Anne stepped closer to the younger woman. "Were they-"

"From the Maypole children?" Marcus cut across their exchange. "Yes, they were. I got a list of the ten kids from the school."

Anne's chin trembled. She fingered a sweating forehead.

Marcus placed a hand on her shoulder to steady the dizzy spinster. "Are you alright, Anne? You look like you've seen a ghost."

She gulped. "I'll be okay. The shock of everything, that's all. Let me sit down."

"Of course." The officer released his hold and followed her into the living room.

Lisa entered a minute later clutching a glass of cool water. "So, another savage murder and more missing children." She handed the drink to their guest.

Martin perched alongside Anne on her sofa by the window. "Thanks. Yes, it's been a busy few days. We could have made more progress if the budget wasn't so tight. Much as I hate to say it, having three missing children in the mix now might loosen purse strings somewhere."

Lisa sat opposite as usual. "Well, that's a positive."

Martin flinched. "Not in reality. Robbing Peter to pay Paul. The money's got to come from somewhere. I don't envy the decision maker who delivers a judgement call about what we're *not* going to do as a result."

Lisa bit her lip. "I'm sorry about touching that computer. I *did* use a handkerchief."

Marcus frowned. "Hmm. I imagine Martin Coleman pulled you up on that enough for me not to have to repeat it. Listen, both of you. I know it's a horrible situation." He glanced from Anne then back to Lisa. "Especially with your discovery on the laptop. But can I ask you to please refrain from discussing it with others? Whatever the vicar was or wasn't into, we'll get to the bottom of it. Digital Forensics have the computer in for analysis now. Wild speculations and rumours circulating the village or media won't help. We also can't go making assumptions, however things appear."

"We'll keep it to ourselves," Anne said.

"Good." He gulped down some water.

Lisa sat back. "Do you know anything else about the disappearance of the new children?"

Marcus shook his head. "I sent some people over to take down the details." A mobile phone buzzed in his pocket. "Please excuse me one second." He lifted the unit to his ear. "DS Foster. Hey Vince. What?" A long pause. "They were. Both of them? Yeah. Okay, it's something to go on, I guess. Thanks for the call. Catch you back at the station." He hung up. "Speak of the devil. Jimmy and Helen had been receiving one-to-one religious instruction sessions with Reverend Stokes." He thought for a moment. "I shouldn't say any more. Comes back to my request that you keep things to yourselves."

Lisa shrugged. "Okay. So, did you get a hard time from Martin Coleman today?"

Marcus rolled his eyes. "Ugh. First, he phones the control room Duty Inspector on a police to police enquiry, as if he's still in the job. 999 would have been fine, not to mention correct. Then I get an hour of him chewing my ear off about how a DS should conduct an investigation. How it was done in his day. Moans about us not being real police officers like the old sweats he worked with. On and on."

Lisa beamed.

Marcus groaned. "There's nothing in this world more annoying to a serving copper than a retired one. And I imagine I'll be as bad myself, one of these days. Thing is, I agree with much of what he says. But there's precious little I can do about it. I wish the world hadn't sped up and moved on. Life as a bobby in his era sounds grand to a former country boy like me. These days it's all target driven statistics and scarce resources to do anything. Oh how I'd love to be able to deliver the service the public want - and deserve. But that's not realistic, I'm afraid. Not anymore." He coughed. "I should add that's not the official position of the Force."

Lisa pointed. "You should have told Martin that."

"I wanted to. What I also didn't tell him, was that he was the reason I ended up joining the job in the first place."

Anne smiled. "How so?"

"When I was at Wrenham Green County Primary, he came and took an assembly, much like your lodger here."

Lisa cut in. "Except I never got to deliver mine, thanks to the mass screaming session."

"Right. Well, Martin did. I remember he spoke with such passion about duty and keeping the community safe from crime and the fear of crime. It inspired me. Not TV shows with car chases and action, but that primary school chat. Makes me seem like a boring old bugger, but it sounded like a worthwhile thing to do with my life." He finished his water.

Anne took the glass. "Not boring at all, Marcus. I'd say you joined the police for the right reasons."

Marcus stood. "Anyway, I'd best shake a leg." He pulled a card out of his jacket and passed it to the old woman. "Here are my professional contact details with a direct dial number, in case you learn anything new. Please don't assume we already know it. We always appreciate a call, on the off chance."

"Thank you."

"If either of you suffer as a result of what you've seen, I'll see if I can sort out some help. We have volunteers trained to counsel victims of crime and the like. I'm sure I could arrange a visit, should you need it."

Lisa got up. "Let's hope we don't. I'll see you out."

8
A Head for Pastry

"Do you know what recipe you and Leslie are going to bake today?" Angela Hackman turned the wheel and looked in the rear-view mirror at her daughter.

Tessa remained quiet. She had become increasingly morose in the last week. Her mother feared that if the blood test revealed no obvious anomalies, she could be looking at some form of psychological help for Tessa. How would these issues - whatever they were - affect her daughter's schooling and future prospects?

"Tessa?" Angela spoke again.

The nine-year-old gazed out one of the rear windows, as if present only in body.

Angela let it go and signalled into the lane where the Claridge family lived. It was the same lane where Robin Jarrett was brutally slain the previous weekend. The Claridges owned a whitewashed cottage, set apart from the modern, mid-twentieth century semis that occupied the bulk of the thoroughfare. Their front door opened wide as the car came to a halt in the driveway.

"Hey Vicky," Angela got out of the vehicle and waved to a woman her own age.

A round-faced, portly nine-year-old with curly fair

hair squeezed past her mother on the doorstep and hastened to the rear car door. Tessa watched through the window, unmoving.

Angela frowned. "Come on Tessa, out you get." She opened the door and stood aside.

Tessa unfastened her seatbelt, evidencing a distinct lack of drive or urgency. She climbed out, offering no form of greeting to her hosts.

Victoria Claridge reached her friend's side. "How's she doing, Ange?"

Angela closed the car door. She watched Tessa trudge up the path. Her daughter's playmate gave the appearance of a sheep dog attempting to usher its flock into a pen, as the pair hovered around the front door. "I'm worried, Vicky. It's getting harder to provoke any response from her by the day. Like talking to a brick wall. Ever since those three kids disappeared, she's become more agitated and impatient when she does speak. Have you seen Nicky Jarrett at all?"

"From time to time. What do you say to someone in a situation like that? Her parents came to stay midweek. They wanted her to get away for a few days, but she won't leave until there's some news about Ivan."

"Yeah, what *do* you say? *'Sorry someone murdered your husband and your only child has vanished'* is one standard greeting card the shops haven't come up with yet." Angela bit her lip. "I shouldn't joke. But if I don't, I'll end up in a waking coma like my daughter. What's happening around here? First Robin and then the vicar. Have you heard any more?"

Vicky shook her head. "The police are being tight-lipped about it. I reckon they've put pressure on those who found Reverend Stokes to keep quiet."

"Who was it?"

"Janet Malcolm. Anne Weaver and that northern girl who's moved in with her also showed up, as I understand it. I haven't met her."

"Lisa? Oh, she's nice. Tried to help Tessa when she had a fit round at Anne's. Bet she's regretting her decision to come to Wrenham Green now, though. What with everything that's happened since."

"Are you sure we should leave the girls alone while we head down to Hythe?"

Angela crossed her arms and made a gentle clicking with her tongue. "We can't watch them every minute of every day. Your house is secure, isn't it?"

"We've got locks, bolts and chains the same as everyone else. About the best you can do without digging a bloody moat round the place. I've told Leslie not to answer the door to anyone while we're out. Unexpected visitors can come back another time."

"Where's Simon?"

"He's working today."

"Any idea what the girls are going to bake?"

"Jam tarts. That is, they'll be preparing the pastry. I've asked Leslie not to use the oven unsupervised. Last thing we need is a disaster involving the fire brigade. Once we get back, they can pop them in."

"Okay. Best be off then."

"Right-o. Hang on while I remind Leslie of the salient safety points, Ange."

"Sure."

Victoria went back inside the house. A couple of minutes later, she stepped out into the sunlight again and pulled her front door shut. She tugged at it a couple of times afterwards, as if to reassure herself some deranged killer couldn't waltz straight in unhindered.

At the kitchen window, Tessa and Leslie watched the car containing their mothers reverse down the drive and slip away.

On a worktop behind, an array of baking trays, jam jars, a bag of plain flour, mixing bowl and sturdy wooden rolling pin were piled up ready for use.

Leslie lifted a set of scales across from the windowsill. "Can you pour in 250 grams of flour, Tessa? I'll get the butter from the fridge. Mum and I already diced 125 grams earlier, so we can rub it straight into the flour with a pinch of salt."

Tessa crossed to where her classmate had placed the scales. She opened the bag of plain flour and lifted it.

Leslie bent down behind to open the fridge and retrieve her pre-made fat content for their pastry. "How are you feeling now? You haven't even said hello to me today. Whoa, Tessa, what are you doing? Only 250 grams, not the whole bag!"

Tessa stood holding the empty flour packaging with zombie-like indifference. The worktop now resembled an indoor blizzard. The scales overflowed with flour. Small heaps spread across the laminated surface and clumped in drifts of powder around the various utensils. The silent girl's stare remained devoid of emotion or cognition.

Leslie popped the butter to one side and retrieved a dustpan and brush from a cupboard beneath the sink. Without a further word, she swept up the excess flour. From time to time her furtive gaze fell upon the bosom companion who had once been so full of fun and mischief. "I wish I knew what's going on. We've been friends since play school, Tessa. Please tell me. If there's something you're worried about, I could help. We're all nervous over Ivan, Jimmy and Helen. Do you know where they've gone or who's taken them?"

"You wouldn't understand." They were her first words that day.

Leslie tipped the flour into a bin and stowed the pan. "You mean, you know something?" Her tone rose from wonder to excitement. "We should tell the police. Or our parents, at least. Are they okay?"

Tessa's young pink lips curled into a sneer. "Why do you need to bake tarts, flesh bag? There's room for a hundred souls inside your saggy body."

Leslie blinked back a sudden tear. The corners of her mouth turned downward. "Tessa. How could you?" Her voice cracked. "You've never teased me about my weight. You always stand up to the boys when they're rude about it."

Tessa's eyes narrowed. "Fatty, fatty, fat bitch. How about a nice lard sandwich?"

The plump girl backed away, shaking her head. Her lips quivered. "What's happened to you? Why are you talking like this?" She let out a single, involuntary sob.

Tessa mimicked the sound, twisting it into that of an animal. "Squeal piggy, squeal. Fancy a toasted bacon buttie?" She strode to one corner of the kitchen and plugged in a shiny metal toaster. Next to it sat a stoneware bread bin, from which she retrieved a pre-sliced Danish loaf.

"Tessa, no. We're supposed to be baking jam tarts." Leslie dipped a dishcloth into a washing-up bowl at the sink. She wiped down portions of the work surface not cleaned by the brush.

Tessa inserted two slices of bread and depressed the toaster spring.

Leslie washed out her cloth in the bowl. The power of her classmate's stare burned into the side of her head with such intensity, she twisted to observe her.

Those eyes were alive now. Alive and glistening with malice and intent. In her hands Tessa clutched the toaster. A long, deep-throated laugh heaved out of her mouth. "Time to visit the abattoir, little piggy."

Sound dulled to an indistinct murmur for Leslie, in a drawn out series of heartbeats. The tossed toaster gleamed and span, its lead allowing enough play to reach mid-air above the sink. The cable snapped taut, and the appliance fell into the bowl of water. Leslie shook and staggered back half a pace. Every muscle twitched at the burning fire that raced through her nervous system. Her plump body hit the floor with a quiet flop. The wannabe young baker lay unconscious but still breathing.

Tessa leaned back against the worktop, back straight. She licked her lips and turned to rummage around in wall-mounted cupboards behind. A long cardboard box bore the title '180W Electric Carving Knife.' The nine-year-old placed it on the worktop and opened the lid. An impressive power utensil rose in her hands. Its shiny, razor-sharp blade reflected a pair of wild young eyes that gazed upon it with unsettling glee. The plug clicked into a wall socket and Tessa activated the switch. With the whirring business end pointing towards the floor from one motivated hand, she stood over the figure of Leslie Claridge and giggled.

* * *

"I always feel better after some shopping, a bit of sea air and a stroll along the Royal Military Canal, don't you?" Victoria Claridge pressed her back against the passenger seat in Angela Hackman's car.

"Hythe's retained a lot of character and charm." The driver pulled off the Roman road of Stone Street at Stelling Minnis. "Soon be home. How do you think our budding bakers are getting on?"

"Let's hope my Leslie has managed to coax a few words from Tessa. She's been so worried about her, Ange."

"Best friends are everything at that age. I appreciate you allowing her over to make a mess of your kitchen."

"Shouldn't be too bad. My girl's more fastidious about tidiness than I am."

They passed the village sign for Wrenham Green.

"No obvious indicators of devastation," Victoria murmured with a grin, inserting a key in the front door of her house. As the portal swung open, she inclined her head to listen. "Is that the fan oven? Can't be."

Angela strained to filter out the birdsong from a competing low, pervasive hum. "Does sound like it. I thought you asked Leslie not to use the oven unsupervised?"

"I did. They must have got impatient." She closed the door. "At least nothings on fire."

Angela sniffed. "What is that smell? It's like a Sunday roast rather than pastry cooking."

Victoria pushed open the kitchen door. Nobody visible, but the fan oven was definitely running. The kitchen hung with a rancid odour. "She knows better than to leave an oven on and go upstairs to play. Whatever have they been doing?" The woman rounded the central island and screamed. "Oh my God. No, no, NO!" She dropped to a squat, fingers twisted like talons in the air either side of her head. Angela reached her side.

Chest facing up between the island and sink, lay the plump, headless torso of Leslie Claridge. A lake of blood flowed from the stump of her neck. The stream ran in right-angled rivulets where it connected with the base units, guided like some morbid sanguine aqueduct. Her pretty, floral print dress looked like a shop window exhibit on a toppled mannequin. Spray from the act of decapitation splattered the under-sink units, as if someone removed the head while the girl already lay on the floor. The family toaster rested in a bowl of washing up water, lead still connected to the wall socket. An electric carving knife sat discarded on top of a metal pedal bin. The blade dripped with gore, running down the sides of the waste receptacle like strawberry sauce poured on an ice cream dessert. Victoria gagged. A choking waft of sickening carnage mingled with internal emotions of shock and heartbreak. She lost the light lunch enjoyed with her friend in Hythe, adding a stench of stomach acid and vomit to the already putrid concoction.

One of Angela's hands reached down to touch the woman on her shoulder. "Vicky?"

Victoria followed the woman's petrified, open-mouthed gaze to the fan oven. Its light illuminated a roasting tray in which sat Leslie's young head. A pair of lifeless staring eyes bulged outward then burst from the effect of the heat. Their fluid ran down scorching cheeks like bloody tears, basting the cooking meat in that morbid traverse.

Angela's thoughts snapped back to her absent daughter. "Tessa?" The initial query transformed into a shriek. "Tessa?" She ran from the kitchen, thrusting open every door and cupboard within the house. The frantic search continued upstairs. "Not her too. Please, not her too. Tessa?"

* * *

Marcus Foster climbed out of his car and took a hard look down the unassuming country lane.

"Here we are again," a bald, tubby, plain clothes

colleague greeted him from the path outside the Claridge's home.

"Twice in one week, Vince. And only a few doors apart."

"Twice not including the vicar over at the church, Fuzz."

"Yeah, I know. The once sleepy village of my youth isn't doing too well. Per capita, it's about to become Kent's number one violent crime and missing person hot-spot. Can't wait for the next Intel brief. The Super is going to use my arse as a football if we don't get on top of this mess PDQ. If Inspector March doesn't nail it first." He took a deep breath. "I scanned the incident log on STORM before I left the station. Murdered child and missing friend, discovered by their mothers. What are we looking at so far?"

Vince pulled a pocket notebook from his jacket and flipped over a few pages. "The mother - Victoria Claridge - left her nine-year-old daughter Leslie preparing jam tarts with her best friend, Tessa Hackman. Tessa's mother - Angela Hackman - then drove the two women down to Hythe for a light lunch and some shopping."

"Sounds like an ordinary Saturday. Where's the father?"

"Right now, he's inside with his wife. Came home from work after she called him."

"How long were the women away?"

"Three hours, give or take. They got back to find the fan oven running in the kitchen. Victoria thought it odd, because she'd instructed Leslie not to touch it.

When they took a peek, the room appeared empty. On the far side of her central island, they discovered Leslie's decapitated torso."

Marcus blinked. "Decapitated?"

Vince nodded. "Looks like someone cut her up while she lay unconscious on the floor. We found a toaster in a bowl of water at the sink next to her body. It was still plugged into the wall."

"Wouldn't it trip the fuse panel?"

Vince rocked on the spot. "We put that to Simon Claridge, the father. It seems he was planning to have the electrics rewired this summer. There's no ground fault interrupt on the kitchen. Toaster must have shorted itself out after hitting the water. Enough juice to produce a shock though. I guess the coroner's report will tell us more. His already hysterical wife went ballistic when he let that little gem slip out. Took two female officers to calm her down."

"Ouch. Was the poor mite's head still in situ on the floor?"

"Err, no. That's what was cooking in the oven."

Marcus cleared his throat. "What?"

"Yeah. Stowed in a roasting tray, staring out the glass door. To make matters worse, the eyes popped right at the moment the women noticed it."

"Jesus. What kind of freak are we dealing with here, Vinny?"

"There aren't any words. It's a mess in there. Mrs Claridge emptied her stomach all over the scene. One of our probationers did the same about thirty minutes ago. It made me want to retch, and I've attended enough murders and sudden deaths to develop a stronger constitution."

"Okay. What about the other girl - Tessa was it?"

"Tessa Hackman. Gone missing."

"Wait a minute." Marcus pulled out his own notebook and flicked to the list of names he'd acquired from the primary school. "That's what I thought. She's one of them."

"One of who?"

"The Maypole kids who collapsed at the festival. Are we sure she didn't run off in a fit? Is she local?"

"Other side of the village. No problem for a distraught nine-year-old to get home, assuming she felt safe there. I got Vanessa Scutt to drive Mrs Hackman back and sit with her. She called to say there was no sign of the girl at their house. Angela Hackman's other half is away on business up in Manchester. If little Tessa's disappeared too, that makes four kids."

Marcus scratched his head. "A husband, a vicar potentially indulging dubious sexual preferences, and a nine-year-old girl - all murdered with inhuman brutality. Then two girls and two boys of primary school age missing, presumed kidnapped or worse. What's the motive?"

Vince shrugged. "Or connection?"

Marcus put his notebook away. "Crap. I'd better go in and have a gander, I suppose. God, there are some days I struggle to grasp how I ever got into this job. Or why I keep doing it."

Vince walked with him towards the front door. "Yeah. They didn't stick any of this on the recruitment poster."

*   *   *

"They paid. They paid." Lisa bounded into the kitchen at Bramley Cottage like an excitable schoolgirl.

Anne folded a tea towel and hung it from a rack. "I assume you're talking about that freelance work for those Gresham people?"

"Gresham Associates. The money cleared in my account this morning. They've also commissioned me for the entire series I was hoping to get. I'm a proper freelancer, Anne."

"Congratulations, that's quite an achievement."

Lisa grabbed the old woman's arm. "We should celebrate. What would you like to do?"

Anne held up a hand. "Ah, I'm afraid I need to go into Canterbury and take care of some business."

"Would you like me to drive you?"

"No, that's alright. My Corsa needs a run and there's a private legal matter to deal with. It would be a boring day, sitting in a solicitor's waiting room. This old biddy could use a turn behind the wheel for a change." She hesitated. "Why don't you buy Jeremy Lewis lunch at the pub or something?"

"The White Hart?"

"Yes. The food's not gourmet, but they serve solid pub grub. Should suit a trim, hungry man who likes to work outdoors. You haven't been there yet, have you?"

"No. No, I haven't." Lisa wagged a finger. "If I didn't know better, I'd say you were trying to fix me up."

Anne shook her head. "You're far too smart for games like that, Lisa. But it would do both you and Jeremy good to form a friendship with someone local your own age. Any romantic entanglements that do or don't ensue are between the two of you, as far as I'm concerned."

"Okay then, I'll see how he's fixed."

"Make sure you've got your key. I don't know how long I'll be. I've promised to stop by Angela Hackman's on the way back. She's sick with worry but craving familiar, friendly faces to console her."

"Poor woman. I hope they find Tessa safe and sound."

"And in one piece," Anne coughed.

"Quite. Who could do such a thing to a child?"

Anne bolted the back door. "Not the peace and quiet you'd hoped for, is it? You've arrived in Wrenham Green at an unusual time."

"Unprecedented, I should hope."

Anne examined her for a moment without a word.

Lisa's brow creased. *Why is she staring at me like that?*

The old schoolteacher moved out into the hallway. "I hope Jeremy is amenable to your offer. Have a nice time."

Lisa leaned on the kitchen door frame while Anne fetched a coat from the rack and checked for a set of car keys. "I will. Take care on the roads." It was an expression Lisa had found herself uttering to many people over the years. A talisman to ward off horrific events. Those like the day traffic police came to tell a teenage girl her parents would never be coming home again.

The bluebells were blooming at their absolute zenith now. All along the verges of that tiny rough track leading to Ashdene, the pretty, fragrant overhanging flowers nodded in a gentle breeze. Lisa unlatched Jeremy's five bar wooden gate. His workshop door stood open. Even at this angle and distance, the woman detected the rubbing of some manual paper sanding. She secured the entrance and crept towards the sound of artistic industry.

"Knock knock," her voice bore a hint of cheeky surprise.

Jeremy blew some fine sawdust from the nose of a gorgeous carved otter he was working on. As the glittering cloud settled, his eyes refocused on the visitor. "Hey."

Lisa waited for more. *Not a big one for conversation sometimes, this guy. Is he even pleased to see me?* "That's a lovely piece. Otter?"

"Well, at least you don't think it's an elephant." He carried on rubbing the exquisite animal.

"Right," Lisa muttered to herself. She snorted and spoke louder. "If this isn't a good time then, I'll clear off. Wouldn't want to be a bother." The last sentence flashed out with undisguised sarcasm. She hung on a second longer then spun on her heel.

"Wait, wait, wait." Jeremy put down his sandpaper.

Lisa couldn't decide whether he was remorseful or

annoyed.

The woodsman wiped his hands on a rag and joined her outside. "I was engrossed in my work. It throws me when people show up at a time like that, uninvited."

Lisa's cheeks reddened. "Well, if I'm not welcome..." She began to storm off.

"Hold on, hold on," Jeremy grabbed her arm. "Sorry, Lisa. I didn't mean to be rude."

"AGAIN." Lisa stressed the single word.

Jeremy looked at the ground to hide his smile. "Yes, again."

"You've got the lonely hermit act down fine, haven't you?"

His torso sagged. "I suppose. What did you want from me?"

Lisa folded her arms across her chest. "Nothing. I came to make *you* an offer, as it happens."

"Oh?" It was the first time the strapping man appeared flustered; even nervous.

"Yes. I got paid for my first freelance job and wondered if you'd like lunch at the pub? My treat."

"What about Anne?"

"She's otherwise engaged. I haven't been to The White Hart yet."

"It's not bad." He looked around the site. "Well, if the offer still stands, I'd be delighted. Thank you."

Lisa lowered her hands. "I'll overlook your ill manners and lack of charm on this occasion."

Jeremy sucked his teeth and closed the workshop. "You're all heart. Let me lock up."

The pair wandered in slow, aimless steps down the winding lane leading back to the village green. Jeremy fastened some buttons on his checked shirt, previously undone while working up a sweat.

Lisa studied his toned figure. "You don't come across as a ladies man."

Jeremy shrugged. "Should I?"

Lisa thought for a moment. *I can't say it's surprising because he's so buff, or I'll sound like a desperate tart. God, he is a bit nice though.* In that moment it amazed her to find herself missing Keith. Or rather, the days of simple intimacy and shared affection she'd taken for granted before it all fell apart. "Oh, you know - a healthy man your age."

Jeremy sighed. "When I first moved onto the site, I met a girl called Carla."

"Local?"

"Not to the village. I met her in Ashford. She was a single Mum on the rebound from a broken relationship. Anyway, she moved into Ashdene with her little boy for a while."

Lisa swallowed hard. She hadn't expected this. "Should I ask what happened?"

"Once the bloom was off the rose, she found someone else. Things got testy for a while. She threatened to shop me to the council over my living arrangements."

"Oh dear."

"Needless to say, she didn't. It was a relief to have

her out of my hair. I've always preferred my own company, so-"

"Once bitten, twice shy?"

"I suppose. Women, but especially forward, assertive women tend to put me in a defensive posture. I love the life I'm living now."

Lisa stopped and waited for him to notice.

He turned back. "What's going through that brain of yours this time?"

"Thoughts about a piece I once did on intimacy fears for a committed singles website."

"Dr Lisa now, is it?"

"No. I wrote a regurgitated jumble, cobbled together from a little research and a few personal observations. Not my best work, but the client was happy."

"And what's my diagnosis?"

Lisa waved a hand away. "It doesn't matter."

"No, I want to hear it. You started this."

"Okay. From what you've told me: fears of engulfment, loss of individual identity and the like could be an issue. What about angry attacks?"

"What about them?"

"Do you fear them? Are you nervous about conflict?"

"If I were, five minutes with you is enough to force anyone to face their fears and come out fighting."

Lisa grinned. "I deserved that one."

Jeremy stepped closer to her. "Let me ask you something."

"What?"

"Why is it that people who write articles for sites like

that, always consider someone who enjoys a quiet, single life to be in need of help or counselling?"

Lisa thought. "I guess loners scare people."

Jeremy shook his head. "The stereotype media journos have *created* about loners scare people. That and the thought of being alone itself. The very idea sends some into a blind panic. Being stuck with their own thoughts is almost as frightening as a visit from the murderous nut-case who's prowling our village, for folk like that."

"You think the murders are being committed by the same person?"

"I don't know. I hope so."

Lisa gawped. "You *hope* so? Why?"

"Because if they're not, we've got more than one sadistic psychopath stalking Wrenham Green. Even *three*, though I haven't heard much about what happened at the church."

"The cleaner found Brendan Stokes. Anne and I were also there. The police have advised us to keep quiet about it."

"If horrific gossip from the other two killings is anything to go by, I'm not surprised. I'm no prognosticator, but the cops aren't going to be able to keep a lid on this thing much longer. Three murders - including a vicar and nine-year-old girl, and four missing children? When this thing breaks, we're going to be at the centre of a media circus. I reckon it's only due to the localised nature of the dead and missing, that they haven't gone on TV already with an appeal for information. If this had happened in a town…"

"I know. Here's the pub. Find us a nice quiet table, would you? I'm bursting for a visit to the ladies room."

Inside, Lisa reappeared from the toilet as Jeremy crossed from the bar clutching a pint in each hand. "I see you got me a beer."

The woodsman flushed. "Whoops. Didn't even think. Automatic action. Is that okay?"

Lisa sat down at a small circular table near the front windows. "If it's like your home brew."

Jeremy put the glasses down. "I hope it's better than that. Otherwise I should get a duty license and have a word with Kevin Laycock the publican about supplying him."

"If you're between wood carving commissions, it might work. How *are* things since the festival?"

"Great. I made several new contacts on May Day. That otter you found me working on is for a new business client. They run a nature reserve and want it to display in their visitor centre and gift shop. I should finish it in a day or two."

From the opposite corner came the sound of gentle weeping. Lisa leaned over to learn the source. A white-haired man in his late eighties sat alone next to the dart board. His head bowed low over an empty glass, bobbing as the tears flowed.

Jeremy followed her gaze. "Oh, that's old Neville. Bless."

"What's wrong with him?"

"He lost his wife."

Lisa's eyes turned downward. "Poor soul. How long ago?"

"About twenty years."

"Huh? You're joking."

Jeremy shook his head and sipped his beer.

Kevin Laycock brought over two leather-bound lunch menus for the pair. He caught sight of the old man weeping and called across. "There now, Neville old son. You're with people who care about you in here. Sit tight and I'll refill your glass in a second. She's in a better place. I'm sure she's happy." He leaned closer to Lisa. "Weekly occurrence round here, to find Neville crying over his dead wife. Been a tradition at The White Hart going on two decades."

Neville pulled out a red handkerchief and blew his nose. "What about the children? Are they in a better place?" he sniffed.

Kevin tilted his head. "You never said you had any children."

Neville raised two reddened eyes. "The missing children."

The publican straightened. "Now then, let's keep the faith. We're all hoping those kids will show up safe and well."

Neville folded the hankie. "The others didn't."

"What others?" Kevin took a hesitant step nearer.

"The other Maypole children. They never came back. I remember it, I was there. And the deaths…" Neville noticed he had now become the centre of attention. With trembling limbs he stood and hastened to the door, eyes never deviating from his course of travel.

Kevin turned back to Lisa and Jeremy. "Poor old sod. He's harmless enough, and he means well. What can I get you?"

9
Intolerable Infamy

"Louis is sleeping like a baby," Samantha Randall plonked down on the sofa next to her husband.

"Louis *is* a baby, Sam. Let's hope he goes most of the night this time." Terry Randall yawned, put an arm round her shoulders and pulled the woman closer for a cuddle.

On a padded living room window seat of their extended Victorian terrace, a seven-year-old girl sat like a powered doll with the batteries removed.

Terry nudged his wife and pointed a subtle finger in their daughter's direction. "Things can't go on like this, love," he whispered.

Samantha bit a nail. "I know. Right now I'm thankful she hasn't gone missing like the others."

"Speaking of which." Terry caught an opening headline banner on the early local evening news: *'Triple murder and four missing children in small Kent village.'* He picked up the TV remote to increase the volume from a subdued murmur to fill the room with sound.

The picture snapped to a senior police officer standing outside his Maidstone headquarters. *"We would appeal to anyone with potential information as to the whereabouts of these children to contact us on 101, via our on-line portal or at the front counter of their local station."*

The screen faded into three photographs: Robin Jarrett, Brendan Stokes and Leslie Claridge. An announcer narrated over the imagery. *"Three brutal murders have rocked the quiet Kent village of Wrenham Green in the space of a week. One victim was a girl of nine. Police describe the killings as evidencing inhuman savagery. Also, four children, at least two of whom were connected with the victims or present during their deaths, have disappeared without a trace."* The screen altered to images of the four missing children. *"Eight-year-old Jimmy Walter, nine-year-olds Ivan Jarrett and Tessa Hackman, and ten-year-old Helen Taylor are all unaccounted for. Tonight police are stepping up their efforts and declaring this a major incident. Is there a kidnapper and serial killer at large in this quiet corner of the Garden of England? We'll be speaking with senior investigating officers."*

Samantha's eyes watered. "I hope they find them soon."

"They're not missing." Their daughter's flat statement caused both parents to stare at her.

Terry leaned forward. "What do you mean, Karen?"

The girl twisted on her seat to face them. "They're not lost, they've gone home."

Samantha joined in. "That can't be right, darling. If they went home, it would be all over the news."

A wry smile crossed the seven-year-old's face for a split second. Her eyes narrowed. "They've gone to their new home. Their real one."

Terry's face darkened. He was on his feet in an instant. "Karen, we've had enough of all this nonsense. I don't know what game you're playing, but it has to stop. If you know where those children are, you need to tell us right now."

A maniacal laugh rang out of the girl's mouth. Gleams of delight flickered in her now-bulging eyes. "Ooh, Daddy's getting angry."

Samantha recoiled at the mocking voice that cackled from her beautiful daughter. "Oh my God, Terry. What's wrong with her?"

Terry paced forward. "Nothing a good spanking won't knock out."

Samantha stumbled to her feet and grabbed hold of her husband. "No. Please don't raise a hand to her. She's not well."

Karen bounced on the window seat cushion, flicking her tongue up and down in exaggerated laps. A joyous grin stretched from ear to ear. Her vocal emissions laced with a subtle, deep gurgling. "Spank me, Daddy. Oh yes, spank me. Make it hurt so good. Is that what you do to Mummy? Does it make you hard when you give a good spanking? Are you hungry for fresher meat than Mummy's crusty old carcass?"

Samantha let out a gasp, tears stinging a face strained with anguish. "Oh, Karen." She broke down, still clinging to her husband.

Terry stood in open-mouthed disbelief, face drained of colour. His posture slumped. With one hand he stroked his wife's back. With the other he pointed towards the staircase. "Go to your room." The words floated out with lacklustre delivery.

Karen's face lowered. She bawled and rubbed her eyes. The normal, cute, girlie seven-year-old voice returned. "You both hate me. It's Louis that you love now. Why don't you want me now you've got your new plaything?"

Samantha let go and knelt to place both hands on the child's knees. "We do love you, Karen. We love both of you as much. Louis isn't our plaything, he's your brother."

The girl stopped crying and sniffed. "You used to only love me."

"There used to only *be* you. Now we're a family of four. There's enough love to go around for us all. And think: when he's a little older, Louis will be able to love you, too. Won't that be nice?"

Karen stretched out her arms to invite a hug. Samantha squeezed her tight. Terry caressed a tuft of hair on the top of his daughter's head with gentle fingers. The girl let go and looked from parent to parent. "I'm tired now. I don't feel well. Can I go to bed, please?"

Samantha touched her cheek. "Of course you can. In the morning, Daddy and I will get you an appointment with a special doctor."

Karen fidgeted. "Will they hurt me?"

Terry placed a reassuring hand on her young shoulder. "No honey. They'll ask lots of questions, but it won't hurt. They may give you some medicine too."

"Will it taste bad?"

Samantha's worry lines receded. "We can ask if they

have any nice flavoured ones."

"Like cherry?" The seven-year-old bounced again, but with all the innocence of youthful joy this time.

"Yes. Like cherry."

"Okay then. Can I say goodnight to Louis before I go to sleep?"

Samantha exchanged glances with Terry. "Okay," she said. "But be careful not to wake your brother. If we smother him with love, he'll never go back to sleep. You don't want him crying half the night, hey? We need our rest more than ever right now."

Karen kissed her on the cheek. "Night Mummy."

"Goodnight dear."

"Night Daddy."

Terry bent down to receive a kiss of his own. "Sleep well, sweetheart. Don't you worry about a thing. We'll make everything right again, you'll see."

Up in the box room converted to a boy's nursery, baby Louis Randall lay dreaming in his cot. A mobile of smiling animals dangled above. A beam of light from the landing split the darkness in two. At the half-open door, the silhouette of a young girl stood clutching a pillow. Down in the living room, the child's parents laughed at a comedy show on television. Karen Randall stepped into the nursery, chest rising and falling through rasps of laboured breath. Her baby brother looked so dinky and helpless there, sleeping peacefully. The girl lowered one side of the cot and lifted the pillow to hover above his head. A giggle of glee like some deviant cartoon villain escaped her lips. "If we smother him with love, he'll never go back to sleep." She mimicked the words of her mother. The pillow sank until the little boy's head became completely enveloped in its fabric. "But if we smother him with a pillow, we'll never have that problem again."

"Sam?" Terry stuck his head out of the back door. Cool night air woke him from a stupor induced by a bottle of wine shared with his wife. Comedy alone couldn't settle them down after the evening's events. So it was they decided to add the relaxing properties of a social lubricant.

"What's up?" Samantha appeared from the dining room.

Terry scratched his head. "Were you out in the garden?"

"No. Why?"

"The back door was open."

Both stood there for a moment. It didn't last long. Thoughts of the real and present danger posed by some lurking murderer - mentioned on the news - spurred them to action. Terry slammed the door and hurried after his wife. She was on the upstairs landing in a flash.

"Karen's not in her room." She dashed across to the nursery.

Terry made the doorway in time to hear his wife scream with heart-rending agony.

* * *

"What on earth?" Lisa Marston rubbed sleep from her eyes and folded back the sheets. Wrenham Green wasn't a place overburdened with motorised traffic under normal circumstances. A few cars and the odd clip-clopping horse were the busiest it got. In the first light of a semi-overcast day, car engines were providing an almost constant audible backdrop. She peeked around the edge of the curtains. The green was awash with vehicles. Police cars and vans occupied a third of the space. One bore a rooftop satellite dish and featured the title *'Incident Command Vehicle.'* Row upon row of officers in high-visibility jerkins lined up for an alfresco briefing. A well-managed distance apart from Kent's finest, lay a discarded swarm of television reporting vehicles and diverse cars of all descriptions. Technicians set up and tested camera and audio equipment, while sharply dressed reporters adjusted their clothing and ran through pages of notes. Between the two, a thin line of catering trucks had somehow managed to get the hottest pitches in the county at that point. Lisa caught sight of a doughnut van. She wondered how well the search team were paying attention to their briefing.

There was a knock at her bedroom door. Lisa opened it.

"Have you taken a look outside?" Anne asked.

"Yeah. Jeremy said it was only a matter of time until something like this happened."

"I heard on the radio that a fifth child went missing last night. A seven-year-old called Karen Randall. Somehow the news teams found out there was a cot death at the same household. Police are stating they're keen to avoid speculation about a fourth murder at this stage. Mr and Mrs Randall were downstairs at home when it occurred."

"Tragic accident?"

"It's what they implied. No mention of carnage like the other three."

"Odd coincidence though, isn't it? Any idea if Karen was another of the Maypole kids?"

Anne shrugged. "I'm not sure. I don't know the Randalls that well. They're recent incomers to the village. I wouldn't recognise Karen."

Downstairs, a heavy fist hammered on the front door. The brass bell jangled like a furious alarm.

Anne put a hand to her face. "Oh dear. I do hope those media people are going to leave us alone." The old schoolteacher's usually firm lips wobbled.

Hammering and ringing echoed through the hallway and up the stairs again.

Lisa pulled a cardigan over her nightwear. "They'd better not have cameras rolling when I open up in this state. Otherwise your predictions about me not living a single life forever might fall apart." She stomped down the stairs and hollered at another round of banging. "This had better be important. Otherwise I'll give you something proper to bleep out on the bloody telly!"

Lisa unbolted the cottage door and yanked it open. An immaculately groomed woman with shoulder-length blonde hair looked her up and down with disdain. Next to her stood a fat, middle-aged guy scribbling notes on a pad. The northerner latched onto the judgemental expression of the Chicky-Mickey sizing her up. Her blood rose. She poked her head through the doorway. "And I suppose you always roll out of bed looking like that?"

The blonde stepped back half a pace and grimaced. "Err, no, I-"

"Walter Sampson," the fat man cut across, extending a hand to the scruffy house occupant.

Lisa eyed the sausage-like fingers and left him hanging. "Never heard of you."

Walter adjusted a pair of thick-rimmed spectacles. "Then you might be familiar with Jennifer Lane - Invicta News?" He motioned to the awkward media location eye candy at his side.

Lisa stuck out her bottom lip and shook her head in a manner that indicated she wasn't impressed. "Nope. But then, I'm not from around here."

"Ah." Walter waved his pen with a flourish. "Name?"

Lisa frowned. "Excuse me?"

"Your name."

"Yes, I caught what you said. Why do you want my name? Did I win the lottery overnight and become hot news?"

The blonde found her voice again. "We're looking for people to interview about the Wrenham Green Disturbance."

Lisa raised one eyebrow. "The Wrenham Green

Disturbance? Catchy title. Not interested."

Walter held up a hand. "Please. All we're looking for is someone to speak on a piece to camera about normal life in the village. Did you know any of the murder victims or missing children?"

"*Did* I know the missing children? I hope you mean *DO* I know them, unless you're keeping something back."

"Yes, of course that's what I meant. Unfortunate turn of phrase. We all want to see them turn up safe and well."

"Sure you do." Lisa crossed her arms.

"Why wouldn't we?"

Jennifer chipped in. "A happy ending makes good television too."

Lisa moved the door half shut. "Can I offer you people some words of advice?"

The pair leaned closer.

Walter coughed. "Please."

"This is a quiet, friendly village. People live or move here because that's what they like. They're private, decent folk who've suffered unimaginable upset in the last week or so. Please tread carefully, lest it's you who become the Wrenham Green *Disturbance*."

Jennifer smiled to reveal a row of pristine capped and whitened teeth. "Would you be willing to say something like that about the village on camera?"

Lisa bounced her head from shoulder to shoulder and fluttered her eyelashes like a pretend beauty queen. Her voice squeaked with faux, cute, girl-next-door innocence. "No I wouldn't. But you can quote me on it if you like."

Walter shifted his body part way across the threshold. "Under what name?"

Lisa gave him a shove with both hands. "An anonymous source." She slammed the door. A second later, concern for the lovely old structure caused her to tap around the frame with remorseful fingers. She called upstairs. "Sorry about the door slam, Anne."

A warm, approving voice sailed down over the top banister. "That's alright. This old cottage is built of sterner stuff than most. A bit like you. That was wonderful, my dear. Are you sure you're not descended from Boadicea?"

Lisa snorted and grinned from ear to ear. "Bloody news vultures circling the animals in distress."

"There you go, love. Nice and fresh. Careful when you bite into them, they're piping hot." The mobile food vendor leaned over the serving hatch of his vehicle and handed Lisa a warm bag of heavily sugared mini doughnuts.

"Thanks." She passed a fiver across. Heat from the calorific parcel comforted her fingers. A spicy hint of cinnamon teased her nostrils and set saliva in motion. Ever since spying the catering van from her window earlier, she had experienced a strange hankering for a bag of the sweet, starchy holes. It was an unusual breakfast. But, if she was going to enjoy a breath of fresh air before settling down to work for the day, it seemed like a good plan. The only other people purchasing from the street vendors, were police or media personnel. Maybe if she walked around clutching doughnuts as a disguise, some journalists - ravenous for sound bites - might assume her to be one of them? Anything for a quiet life. Besides, the aroma was glorious.

"Miss Marston," a familiar voice called from behind a cordon of police tape.

Lisa took a dainty bite of the top doughnut. She squinted in the sunlight, hurrying to swallow. "Marcus?"

"In the flesh."

"I would say it's nice to see you again, but under the circumstances…"

"Agreed. How's Anne bearing up with the recent developments?" DS Foster stepped across the barrier.

Lisa offered him a doughnut.

He waved a hand to decline. "No thanks. I'm an addict in recovery from my years as a TCC in Canterbury."

"TCC?"

"Town Centre Constable. Someone who-"

"Yeah, I get the picture." A cheeky glint shimmered in her eyes. "Someone who waddles around town in a uniform eating doughnuts."

Marcus grinned. "Cynic."

Lisa flicked some sugar from her fingers. "Would I also be a cynic if I said some of this was for show, now *that* lot have turned up?" She nodded at the impromptu media camp.

Marcus sighed.

Lisa went on. "You said more missing children in the mix might move things along."

"I did, didn't I? Okay. I'm not in charge of all this. Well above my pay grade. Whatever you think, I can assure you every officer wants to find those kids and catch the killer. Many have families of their own, even if they don't live round here."

Lisa's face fell. "I didn't mean to suggest-"

Marcus waved the offence away. "It's alright. I'd be lying if I said the same thought hadn't crossed my mind. Enough time in this job would make a cynic out of anyone."

"Explains a lot about Martin Coleman."

Marcus rubbed some coarse stubble on his chin. "Years dealing with the worst aspects of humanity."

Lisa tucked into another doughnut and studied the detective's uncharacteristically unkempt appearance. *Poor guy must have been down here half the night, if not all of it.* "You were asking about Anne?"

"Yes please. She appeared quite upset when I mentioned the children who disappeared the same night Brendan Stokes was killed."

Lisa moved her gaze around the various activities on the green. Her eyes settled on Bramley Cottage in the distance beyond. "She's never recovered from the loss of her twin sister."

Marcus stepped back. "I've never heard about that. When was this?"

"May 1945. Right after her brother fell out of an upstairs window and broke his neck."

"Goodness." The officer's own gaze moved to join Lisa on the cottage.

Lisa blinked. "I'm surprised nobody ever told you. What about when you were a pupil?"

Marcus shifted on the spot. "Most of the kids knew Miss Weaver grew up in that cottage. I seem to remember somebody once saying that she lost siblings in the war. But that was it."

"Literally *lost*, in the case of her sister, Beth. They never found her."

"No wonder children going missing in the village cause her distress. I thought it was because of her vocation as a primary school teacher. She's always loved children."

"I'm sure that plays a part. Her brother, Daniel is buried in the churchyard with her parents. But there's no grave for Beth. No marker to mourn the loss at." Her eyes fell upon old Neville, attempting to pick his way across the green from his little house in the direction of The White Hart. A regular trip for morning coffee. Jennifer Lane and Walter Sampson sprang upon him like ravenous wolves. A cameraman strode across his path, adjusting the focus ring of his shoulder-mounted monstrosity. Lisa slammed the bag of doughnuts into Marcus' chest. "Shit. No way." She ran across the green, weaving between criss-crossing technical crew members. "Leave him alone," she shouted.

Jennifer Lane fidgeted with her microphone and spun one finger at the cameraman. "We'll have to go again."

Next to her, old Neville gazed around with sad and confused eyes. He gulped. "It's happened before. I keep telling people, but nobody seems to remember."

Jennifer's face brightened like a dozing cat who has woken to spy a hapless mouse scurrying past. "What's happened before, Sir? You mean kidnap and murder in Wrenham Green?"

Neville nodded. "That's right. Children. Ten children."

Jennifer stared at Walter, standing next to their cameraman. The fat man winked and pushed his hands forward in an urging gesture. The presenter switched back to the flustered old man. "And when was this?"

"1945. May 1945. They were the Maypole children."

Now, ear-wigging national news crews encircled the scene, cameras filming from assorted angles.

Lisa burst through a gathering crowd and grabbed hold of Neville's arm. "There you are, Granddad," she lied through her teeth. "I've been waiting for you at the pub. You scared me. I was worried something had happened."

The Invicta News cameraman groaned and lowered his kit, but the others rolled on.

Jennifer Lane prodded Lisa's shoulder with the sharp nail of a bony finger. "Excuse me. He was giving us an interview."

Lisa recoiled and wrinkled her nose like an angry animal. "Touch me again with those cat claws and no amount of blusher will hide the bruises. He's a lonely, confused old man. Leave him alone. Come on,

Granddad." The woman led the poor fellow away.

He scratched his head and peered into her pretty eyes. "You must have mistaken me for someone else."

Lisa squeezed his arm. "No matter. How about we sit down and have a nice cup of coffee? I'm certain I'd like to hear what you've been trying to tell everyone."

Neville's face brightened. "Would you like to share a bacon sandwich too?"

Lisa grinned. "You know how to spoil a girl, don't you? Sounds wonderful."

Back at the Invicta News van, Walter Sampson stood next to Jennifer Lane. They watched the odd couple stagger towards the pub.

Jennifer flicked back her hair. "Do you think he really was confused?"

Walter shook his head. "Haven't the foggiest. But, it's too good an angle not to look into. Got the big boys' attention." He twisted to shout at a grey van behind. "Jerry. Get the office to do an archive search for missing children in Wrenham Green around 1945." He turned back to Jennifer. "Have a stroll over to the school, Jen. See if you can turn on the charm and get a list of kids who took part in the Maypole dance this year."

"How do you know they're from the school?"

"I don't. But if they're not, some kindly head teacher will tell you where they *did* come from."

"Are you sure they still do all that round here?"

Walter pointed his arm past the police cordon. On

the far side of the green stood the old, dark Maypole. "Unless that's for show. Either way they'll have some answers. Worth a shot."

"Got it, boss. See you back here for the lunchtime broadcast. No doubt the studio will want a live update."

Walter cracked his knuckles. "Happy hunting."

* * *

Lisa escorted Neville home after their morning refreshments. No way was she taking the chance he might get pounced on again in the rising media frenzy. Martin Coleman stood talking to Anne across the low garden wall, as the northerner approached Bramley Cottage. His erect bearing presented a quasi-military appearance.

He noticed her draw near, but returned his gaze to the old schoolteacher without acknowledgement. "I'm amazed the Cold Case Review team haven't got hold of anyone on the investigation about this. Sooner or later media types will make the connection. Then you can expect all kinds of sensational conclusions from the press."

Lisa cleared her throat. "I imagine this has something to do with the 1945 Maypole children who vanished?"

Anne flushed and lowered her head. "I'm sorry, Lisa. I should have mentioned it sooner. How did you find out?"

"I prized old Neville from the clutches of a news

crew. We sat down for a little chat." She winced, a little disappointed. "Why didn't you tell me Beth wasn't the only one to disappear?"

Martin cut across. "Well, that settles it. If an outsider like her can find out, Anne, anyone can. When the story breaks, it'll blow the lid right off this thing. The remaining five kids and their families won't have a moment's peace."

Lisa put both hands on her hips. "*An outsider like her?* Thanks a lot. You know, they can do wonders with transplants now. Might be worth talking to your GP about a deceased person with a donor card who no longer requires their manners. Perhaps the vital parts are located in an organ you were born without?"

Martin studied her for a second, unfazed. "When I was a young constable back in '73, some old sweats in the job remembered the Maypole Mystery from their own probationer days. It was a legendary case, once upon a time. Ten missing children; a range of bizarre, fatal accidents and horrific murders."

"I got an in-depth description of some of it from that sweet old man. He said the police never caught anyone."

Martin sighed. "No. That's right, they didn't. Young DS Foster complains about lack of resources now. Imagine what it must have been like in the spring of '45, after nearly six years of conflict. V1 and V2 bombs had rained down on this part of England for almost a year when the kids vanished. People disappeared or turned up dead all the time. There was a war on. Only a handful of locals like Anne here still remember the events first-hand. Let's see if I can recall the names: Beth Weaver, of course. Then Margaret Watson. Err, Henry something-"

"Brooks." Anne spoke the surname, staring into space. "Emily Tate, Jeffery Barker, Phyllis Michaels, Sharon Bates, Terry Carter, Clive Mortimer and Andrew Benson." She retrieved a handkerchief and blew her nose.

Lisa leaned on the gatepost. "Weren't there any theories about what happened?"

Martin joined her on the other one. "Plenty. I heard the most popular story at the time was a psychotic, escaped prisoner of war. The line of reasoning supposed that he kidnapped and slaughtered the children (plus performing various other local murders), then succumbed to an air raid. Either that or an accidental death."

"And no-one ever recovered any bodies?"

"Not of the missing."

"So are we looking at a copycat? Some nutcase who has read an old newspaper cutting and decided to resurrect the sequence of events in modern times?"

"Whether we are or not, you can expect people to draw those conclusions. Once the link between the missing and the Maypole becomes general knowledge - and the 1945 story is re-discovered - it's all we'll hear."

Anne wiped some mild perspiration from her brow. "If you'll excuse me, Mr Coleman, I've been outdoors too long and need to sit down inside for a while."

Lisa pushed past the retired police officer at the gate.

She escorted her host by the arm.

Martin Coleman wiped a flustered hand through his white, Dracula hairdo. A flurry of activity continued on the green. He set off to accost and hassle any officer unlucky enough to linger unoccupied near the police cordon.

"I'm so sorry I didn't say anything sooner." Anne moved her face closer to Lisa than the younger woman could ever remember.

Lisa patted her hand. "I think I understand why you didn't. I know a little of what it is to carry painful memories. You were worried it was happening again to other families, weren't you?"

"Yes. I didn't want to even suggest the idea. As if by vocalising it, I'd cause those events to repeat themselves. It was such an awful time. First Daniel's death, then Beth's disappearance, and all with Father away fighting the Germans. In the midst of the horrors of war that struck Kent on a daily basis, we had to endure accidents, murder, and the sudden disappearance of our friends."

Lisa took her into the living room. "Shall we see what they're saying on the lunchtime news, or would that be too hard?"

"No. I want to know what's going on. We can't hide from it."

Lisa turned on the TV. "Not in a village this size."

Jennifer Lane filled the screen. A keen light glistened off her contact lenses. Or at least, Lisa wanted to believe she wore them. The presenter lingered on the busy green and lifted her microphone to speak.

"What started as a heart-breaking set of gruesome murders and childhood disappearances, appears to have morphed into something far more sinister. Seventy-three years ago, ten children from the quiet Kent village of Wrenham Green went missing. Different ages, different families, but with one curious thing in common: They all performed a dance at the very Maypole you can see behind me." The camera zoomed over Jennifer's shoulder to highlight the object in question. As it pulled back out, the presenter continued. "Their bodies were never found, and the case remained a wartime mystery. But someone, it seems, is keen to recreate those gory days or yore. As of this morning, five children from the village have disappeared. What is the connection between them, if any? You guessed it. We can now exclusively reveal that each of those children also danced around the Maypole during this year's May Day celebration. Is a copycat serial killer and kidnapper stalking the innocent youngsters of Wrenham Green? We'll be asking the police later what they're doing to protect the remaining five. For Invicta News, I'm Jennifer Lane."

Lisa plonked herself down next to Anne this time. "I hate it when Martin Coleman's right."

Anne picked up the remote. "Shall we see what the nationals are saying?"

"Fill your boots."

Anne changed channel and Lisa lurched forward. An offside angle freeze frame of the village green appeared. It depicted her grabbing hold of old Neville. The rich voice of a male, national news anchor delivered a voice over. *"It seems not everyone in the community was pleased to see the press. One of our local competitors discovered how much spirit still exists in Wrenham Green, when she tried to interview an elderly gentleman."* The video footage played. It showed Lisa pull back from the blonde presenter and shout: *"Touch me again with those cat claws and no amount of blusher will hide the bruises. He's a lonely, confused old man. Leave him alone. Come on, Granddad."* The image snapped to the presenter sitting at a news desk. He chuckled. *"Sorry, Invicta News. Not your best start to the day."*

Lisa put her head in her hands. "Oh no." She drummed fingers against her reddening brow.

Anne switched off the TV and gave a wry smile. "Granddad?"

Lisa sat up. "Best thing I could think of on the spur of the moment to rescue him. Sorry Anne, you're housing a liar."

The old woman laughed. "That's thinking on your feet. I haven't had this much excitement in a long time. It's just a shame about the circumstances."

Lisa gritted her teeth. "Not quite how I wanted my fifteen minutes of fame to go. Let's hope we get a breather from all this soon."

10
Shooting Stars

Lisa cruised past Canterbury Cricket ground in the Clio with Anne at her side. She hung a right onto Nackington Road, driving south. Neither woman spoke, the car radio filling their silent vacuum. Bulging bags of grocery shopping jostled on the rear seats.

"Tonight there will be clear skies. A great opportunity to catch remnants of the Eta Aquarriids meteor shower: One of two such events caused by debris from Halley's Comet. Earth crosses its orbital path in April and May. The resulting display of shooting stars should be clear, even to the naked eye this evening."

Lisa glimpsed The Chaucer Hospital pass by her driver's window. "I love shooting stars. Do you think we'll be able to spot them?"

"I don't see why not. One advantage of being out in the country is a lack of light pollution. The night sky is clearer than in town."

"That's assuming the police and media aren't up at all hours with floodlit base camps again."

Anne fiddled with her seatbelt. "I *would* suggest the ash grove. Up there on the hill, you'd be away from the hubbub and disturbances. But, I don't think wandering around after dark is such a good idea in the present climate."

"With the killer at large? Would they be daft enough to attack someone in the middle of an active police search zone?"

One corner of Anne's mouth raised. "You could take Jeremy along for safety. And company."

"Oh ho. For a spinster, you're an incurable romantic, Anne. How do we know Jeremy isn't the killer, anyway?"

Anne gasped. "Lisa, you don't honestly think-"

"No." She clicked her tongue against the roof of her mouth. "I wanted to get a rise out of you."

"It was only an idea. He's a quiet man."

Lisa winced. "Yeah. If guys are supposed to make the first move, I'd be retired myself before he ever found the gumption. Someone hurt him; I know that much. Anyway, I'm not looking to rush into anything, as I said. I know I sound like a broken record, but I'm not even sure I want another relationship right now. Wrenham Green is a small village. Not the sort of place you can disappear and avoid somebody if things fall apart."

Anne lowered her window a touch to allow a breeze of cool air into the vehicle. "I could say *'sometimes you've got to take a risk.'* But, I hardly qualify as a person to give romantic advice."

Lisa shifted up a gear as they passed a national speed limit sign. "Oh, I don't know. You're an observer; a student of human behaviour. Think I'd rather get advice on love from you than someone who's been in fifty failed couplings. To be honest, I like our handsome, neighbourhood woodsman but he also annoys me."

"Because he's not effusive?"

"There's emotion there, buried deep inside. How could anyone without some sort of spark create such beautiful carvings? I only wish I could coax a little more out of him. He's hard work. But here I am talking like I've known the guy for months, rather than a couple of weeks."

Anne sheltered her smile behind a discreet hand. "That's not such a bad sign."

Lisa accelerated along Stone Street. "I'll see how things are on the green tonight. If it's like a roadie's convention again, I'll take a solo stroll up to the grove. If anyone approaches, the cops will hear me scream from there. It's a short downhill dash through the undergrowth to Jeremy's, if I got cornered by some nutter. I know the route. That's how I met 'Mr Self-contained' in the first place."

Orange dusk blended into a clear night at Bramley Cottage. Lisa peered out from behind the thick, living room drapes. "If I didn't know better, I'd say that lot were moving in to stay."

Anne joined her at the window. "I hope they'll turn the generators off at a reasonable time tonight. I know a temporary disturbance is nothing compared to what the families of the missing are facing."

Lisa let the curtain fall back. "Makes you feel guilty,

doesn't it? I pulled the pillow over my head last night, when I couldn't get to sleep with the racket. Then I thought about the kids and their distraught loved ones. Didn't help the restlessness but stopped me swearing under my breath."

"Are you still planning to go out and watch the meteor shower?"

"Yeah." Lisa stepped into the hallway and retrieved her jacket from the coat rack.

Anne stopped in the living room doorway. "Some of the best sightings are supposed to occur right before dawn."

"Don't know if I'll be stopping out that long. On the other hand, the chances of me getting any sleep are pretty thin."

Anne fiddled with her necklace. "Be careful."

Lisa darted from the cottage door and made purposeful strides as if heading for the pub. The last thing she wanted was another news crew showdown. They'd exhausted their supply of 'experts' now. Those (often retired) psychologists, historians, criminologists, police officers and others. Anyone touting what sounded like an informed opinion, to fill the empty space between updates on the search. Now the media were back to picking on hapless villagers again. Poor souls unfortunate or foolish enough to throw the feeding frenzy a bone.

Lisa walked past The White Hart. She kept going until the uphill track to the old ash grove came into view. The Maypole stood close to this side of the green. Looking up at the dark wooden emblem rising into a starry night sky caused her to shudder. *It's only a piece of wood. Nothing to do with why those kids disappeared. Get a hold of yourself.* As if to ease the sting of self-flagellation, an encouraging thought followed. *Be careful. Keep an eye out for loonies. Someone whose tastes run to collecting children who partake in festival rituals.* She plunged into the undergrowth and immediately realised she'd forgotten to bring any source of light. The overspill from the bustling village green and star-filled, crystal clear sky had lulled her into a false sense of security. Out there, your eyes adjusted without hesitation. But under that dense canopy enshrouding the footpath, it was a different story. An earthy aroma filled Lisa's nostrils. It was the smell that might well accompany being buried alive. One foot slipped on a loose stone. She reached out and grabbed a low branch to stop herself sliding back down the track. Thorns scratched at her soft hands. "Ouch. Bloody thing." Her curse came out louder than expected. From somewhere to her left an owl hooted, as if in reply to the comment. Lisa pressed on, driving herself uphill at pace.

By the time the trees thinned out into that curious grove, the woman's legs ached. Her breath came in a series of short, rapid pants. A shaft of pale moonlight illuminated the jaunty stump she'd rested on during her first visit to this quiet spot. She eased herself onto it and gazed up at the calm night sky. Stars twinkled in the stillness like sequins. Thoughts of time-lapse imagery taken at night flooded her mind. That jewel-clad firmament appeared immobile and solid. Yet in reality, everything was circling and in motion. An unending cosmic dance of heavenly bodies. The memory of those sped-up night sequences brought on a sensation of dizziness. The ground was no longer firm, as if something broke the law of gravity. To imagine those stars in constant motion made you feel like you might fall off the edge of the planet. Fall, drift into space and keep on going.

A thin trail of light blazed across a break in the tree canopy, from somewhere off in the interstellar reaches. A shooting star flared and vanished, like an artist painting an ivory accent and wiping it away with turpentine. Another followed several seconds later. Anne had been right about this spot. Light and noise pollution from the frenetic green activity didn't seem to permeate the place. A third and fourth meteor grazed the heavens in near synchronised unison, like an intergalactic fireworks display. Lisa drew a sharp breath of awe as three more came down behind. She sat there for several minutes. If there was a divine intelligence calling the shots out there in the universe, it appeared to have placed an intermission on the show. Lisa's chest rose and fell, filling her lungs with velvety night air. Her thoughts turned to that conversation in the car with Anne and moved to Jeremy Lewis. She shuffled round on the ragged stump to face in a north-westerly direction. The same way she had once stumbled towards the lumbering sound of a man and his wheelbarrow. *Should I pay him a visit? It's gonna be a long night. Would he join me? Wish I'd brought a flask of hot tea along now. The view of the sky might be good down at Ashdene too. Okay, I've talked myself into it.* She got up from the stump and pushed through snagging branches. Her memory acted as a compass on an approximate course to that unlawful homestead at the far side of the hill. *God, I hope he's feeling more talkative this evening. If he looks at me like I'm Marley's ghost when I knock on his door, I'll scream. That's a point: How am I going to broach this? Hi Jeremy, I was wandering around in the dark and stumbled upon your hovel. Would you like to sit outside and watch some shooting stars with me? Hmm, that's naff. Screw it, I'll have to wing it. If he gives me any grief, that's his lot.*

She emerged onto the grassy downhill track. At the foot of the slope, a single light blazed in the main pole barn structure that formed Jeremy's home. *Why doesn't he have a dog? Anywhere else round here you'd get barked at by some dutiful pooch. Is a dog too much company for a loner like him? Doesn't bode well for me if that's the case.* She shook the thought aside and rounded the workshop to the barn. *What if he's got company? Don't be stupid, Lisa. Now you're chickening out.* The single light spilt out of a small window to one side of the structure. *Wouldn't hurt to take a peek first, just to be sure. Could get awkward otherwise. I'll see what I'm letting myself in for.* She crouched in knee-high grass and crept to a spot in sight of the window. A shower door opened in what appeared to be a bathroom of sorts. Nothing about that home was conventional, so the chamber's intended purpose took a second to register. A familiar, taut, muscular naked man stepped from the cubicle.

Whether from a combination of physical exertion and the effects of cascading water, or sheer libido, his own intimate 'Maypole' swayed proud upon that exit.

"Oh Jesus," Lisa clapped a hand over her mouth. She turned her head half away, but her eyeballs moved back to compensate. *Hasn't this guy ever heard of frosted glass? Or curtains for that matter?* The realisation he hadn't expected a nosey woman to scope his ablutions through the window when he built it, caused her face to flush. *Oh God, he's magnificent. Why did he have to be magnificent? I don't need this right now. You could hang a bath towel on that thing!* Lisa's head sank into her hands. From deep within, a nagging ache rocked her to the core. *Was he thinking about me in the shower?* Blood roared in her ears. Perspiration and heavy breath reminded her how long it had been since she'd last enjoyed physical intimacy with another. She swallowed hard and tried not to lick her lips with unintentional arousal.

From the bushes behind, a twig snapped. Its report caused the squatting voyeur to spin on her haunches. A pattering of several light pairs of feet strafed parallel to the building. Lisa wanted to call out "Who's there?" but her cry would also attract Jeremy's attention. She didn't have any idea how to explain that one, if he found her at the window. Some indistinct voices chattered in hushed tones. They were young. Lisa strained to make sense of the words, without success. Who on earth would let their children out in the woods at night in Wrenham Green? Could they be some of the missing kids, escaped from their captor? She edged forward with the stealth of a panther. Whoever these youngsters were, the last thing she needed to do was scare them off.

The voices moved away, ascending the hill under a thick covering of trees. Lisa darted from trunk to trunk. It was too dark to discern anything but the movement of shadowy forms in the disorienting blackness. Occasional moonlight caught a body contour here or there, but revealed little visual information. From the vocal exchanges, she counted four distinct individuals: Two boys and two girls.

"Come on, Harry. The girls know a great place to watch the shooting stars." A male tone of primary school age pulled Lisa up sharp. She'd moved faster than expected under the cloak of shadows. The result? - Considerable ground gained on her quarries. The woman pressed herself flat against a tree trunk. She wanted to reach a spot where she could see them, before making herself known. Then they could all take a trip with her to the Police cordon to find worried and relieved parents. Or so she hoped.

"Are you sure we should be doing this, Charlie? What about the killer?" A boy around the same age responded with a tremor in his voice.

"If Gemma and Sally aren't afraid, why should you be?" his friend scolded.

"Gemma's eleven," Harry insisted.

"But Sally's only eight. Two years younger than us. *And* she's a girl. Don't be such a baby or I'll tell Gemma what you said."

"No. Charlie, don't."

A ripple of laughter - the kind when someone has power over you and they enjoy wielding it - laced Charlie's next statement. "Gemma, Charlie fancies you. He said he wishes he could hold your hand. He dreams about kissing you."

"Charlie," Harry fought back a fraught whimper. One that revealed an odd, contrasting mix of defiance and defeat.

A figure beyond retraced a couple of steps. The soothing cadence of a girl's voice applied auditory balm to an emotionally charged situation. "Hush now, Charlie. I like Harry too. Harry, I *am* a bit scared. Would you hold my hand?"

A gulp cut through the stillness. "Okay."

"There we go. I feel better already." That gentle voiced lowered to a whisper. The listening woman behind angled her head to catch every word. "When we get to the top, we can play doctors and nurses. If you treat me nice, I'll let you touch it."

Lisa's legs threatened to spasm with cramp and give her position away. These were only juniors, but she also remembered playing *'doctors and nurses'* as a child. A guy called Jason Ferris had been the lucky, clueless innocent who got to touch her *'it,'* many, many years ago. Neither one of them knew what they were doing. Kids being kids. Yet something about the way Gemma made her own offer caused the woman to tremble. This was wrong; all wrong. Lisa's hands slipped warm and sweaty against the tree bark.

"Okay, Gemma." Harry's voice trembled with awe and nervous excitement. It was likely the lad didn't know what he was excited about. Curious, naughty thoughts of exploration and fumbling which sent butterflies through his tummy.

The figures eased away up the slope. Lisa crept along behind.

At last they emerged on the northern side of the ash grove. Lisa could see them moving now, bathed in an eerie, lunar glow like a desaturated colour film clip. The tallest and eldest girl held tight to the hand of one boy. Presumably these were Gemma and Harry. A couple of feet away by the stump, stood a boy of similar age and appearance - Charlie, and eight-year-old Sally. Even beneath a greater visible expanse of sky, their features remained a collection of shadow pockets and protrusions.

Gemma pulled Harry closer and leaned across to their friends. "You two wait here a minute. Doctor Harry and I are going over to the dell so he can examine me. We won't be long."

Charlie giggled. "I'll bet he's got a nasty swelling in his trousers you should look at, Nurse Gemma."

Harry bobbed on the spot like an intoxicated loon. Gemma slipped her arms around his shoulders and kissed him on the mouth with gentle lips.

"Woo," Charlie and Sally chanted.

The immature intimates frolicked hand in hand across the grove to a grassy patch of undergrowth. Once they were gone, Sally stepped up to Charlie. Her voice growled with haunting mockery. "How long should we wait?"

The boy tilted his head on one side. "Give her a few

minutes to subdue him, before we join in the sacrifice for the Master." A dull red light flashed across his face.

Lisa's breath caught in her throat. Her foot crashed across a brittle twig. It broke with the crisp delivery of a firecracker on a frosty evening. The woman's pulse raced.

"Who's there?" Charlie spun, his voice deeper than an eventual voyage into puberty would ever take it.

Lisa froze.

Sally peered back into the gloom, scanning from side to side. Her face appeared no more than a silhouette in the night, but those eye sockets pulsated with a crimson aura. Two ethereal lamps sweeping the night like searchlights. "An animal?"

Charlie crouched to rummage amongst the woodland floor for two heavy rocks, each the size of an ostrich egg. He passed one to the girl. "No matter. It's time. Soon we will earn our place in His presence."

The pair stomped off with not a care in the world for the racket they made.

Snatches from that ghastly exchange ricocheted round Lisa's brain. *'Sacrifice for the Master?' 'Soon we will earn our place in His presence.' Who is HE? My God, those children can't be planning to-.* Her thoughts collided with a brick wall of horror and disbelief. Mental reasoning might go no further, but she had to. *What are you doing, Lisa?* There wasn't time to dwell on a course of action before she had crossed the grove. From the grassy dell beyond, a young boy's scream followed a sickening thud. Two more thuds ended his wail of distress, but the dull crunch of those raining blows continued unabated.

"Stop. Stop." Whether it was wise to call out, Lisa had no idea. The sound of her voice would at least reach those children before her body was able to. She offered a silent prayer that her command might carry some weight.

Young, gleeful laughter cackled from the bushes. "Praise Nidhogg. Praise His name." One boy and two girls let their cries of worship soar like new converts to a life-affirming faith. "Praise Nidhogg. All hail the Malice Striker; Master of darkness."

Lisa broke into a tiny clearing. What she saw brought her to an abrupt halt. The loose ground laden with woodland detritus acted like rollers beneath her feet. She slipped onto her backside with a sting of pain and burning friction. Skid marks of mud stained her blue jeans. The moonlight shone clear in this secluded spot. The sight ahead made her wish it were not so. Flat on his back lay ten-year-old Harry. His trousers and Y-fronts were pulled down to his knees; lowered in a fatal game of *'I'll show you mine if you show me yours.'* A trick to sedate this innocent lamb to the slaughter before the mortal strokes fell. And fall they did. Three blood-soaked stones rested around the stoved-in skull of that poor boy. Chunks of brain scattered about his broken head, like a burst cauliflower. Only the lower part of his face remained a normal shape. The bottom of his gaping jaw hung slack in a silent scream of terror. But that mouth would never utter sound again. Lisa choked down a squeal of shock. Her knees rose to beneath her chin where she sat, clasped tight in both arms as she shivered. There were no noises from the other children; no rustling of leaves or tramp of feet. All stayed calm and peaceful in the dell. They were alone: she and Harry. She wanted to move closer; yearned to at least pull up his underpants out of some desperate care for the deceased child's modesty. Martin Coleman's warnings about disturbing a crime scene rose like a spectre from the grave of her subconscious. A crime scene. That's what it was. She fumbled around in her jacket and hooked out a mobile phone.

* * *

"Send word to the media camp and get that thing out of here. How many times have we told them: no camera drones?" Marcus Foster barked at a uniformed officer. A remote-controlled rotor platform buzzed across the treetops near the ash grove. The Detective Sergeant eyeballed Vince who stomped along beside him. "So what have we got?"

"A ten-year-old boy whose head looks like it's gone half a dozen rounds with a pile driver. And a woman who claims she knows you. Same one who called it in. One of the team said they saw her at the church when they found the vicar."

"Another murder." Marcus shook his head.

"Another kid," Vince added.

They pushed through to the dell. "So, who's this woman, Vinny? Scratch that." His eyes fell on Lisa, still sitting near the body. He halted beside her. "We need to stop meeting like this."

Lisa remained mute.

Marcus extended a hand. "Here, let me help you up."

The confused woman took his offered appendage and clambered aloft on shaky legs.

The detective stooped to steady her. "Easy." He twisted to catch a glimpse of the victim. "Another image that could keep a person up nights. Do you want to tell me about it?"

Lisa's mind was a fog. "You m-m-mean my stateme…"

Marcus took her to one side. "We'll get to the formal statement later. For now, why don't you tell me how you got here and what happened."

"Okay."

They wandered off back towards the grove as officers and forensic staff got to work.

Half an hour later the pair re-emerged. Vince ended a mobile phone call and stuffed the device into his jacket pocket. "Fuzz, you're not going to like this. There's more."

Marcus squeezed Lisa's hand and turned to his colleague. "Let me guess: missing children?"

Vince rocked on his heels. "Yep. Four of them from different families."

The former Wrenham Green pupil pulled out his pocket notebook and flipped to a well-thumbed page of names he had pored over in a mental quest for answers. "Gemma Harvey, Sally Henderson and Charlie Grant. Ages eleven, eight and ten. I would imagine the fourth is that poor lad in the dell."

Vince blinked. "How the fuck did you know that?" The sight of Lisa brought him up short. "Oh, excuse me, Miss. Yeah. The fourth missing kid is ten-year-old Harry Powell. From the clothing description our call taker got, I'd say that's our vic. Who told you the other names?"

Marcus waved his notebook. "Nobody. Not the full names, at least. It was a joint effort; a hunch. From your reaction: the right one. Lisa here saw - or rather heard - the kids talking. First names and ages. The missing three are more of the Maypole children, Vinny. I matched the first names and ages with those I wrote down at the school."

Vince slapped his forehead. "Oh, for God's sake, no. The press are going to be all over this like a rash."

Marcus frowned. "It gets worse. From what the lady told me, we could be looking at a child on child murder."

Vince staggered and nearly tumbled into a depression in the dark woodland floor. "Are you serious?"

Marcus checked to make sure they weren't overheard. "None of this gets leaked to the media, understand? If I told you half the freaky story I've just been presented with... I don't know what to believe. How much is down to the effects of shock and sensory deprivation on this unfortunate woman and how much is true, is anyone's guess. Anyway, until we have ironclad proof the murder was committed by those kids, the suggestion stays under wraps. It's circumstantial unless we know for certain to the contrary." His downcast eyes moved up to regard the woman at his side. "Though the circumstances don't look good."

* * *

"I hear you were up at the murder scene last night?" It was more statement than question. The sudden booming voice of the retired police officer stopped Lisa in her tracks near the pub.

What murder scene? It hasn't been formally announced yet. Do I deny it? Ask him what makes him think that?

He spoke the next words like a mind-reader scanning her thoughts.

"I got chatting with a nice young lad in uniform."

Lisa spun on her heel and crossed her arms. "Did you now? Perhaps he was mistaken?"

Martin Coleman smeared back his pointed white hair. "I think not. Scuttlebutt is: there's been another child murdered and more have gone missing."

"I'm sure it'll be on the news later. Half the world's press seem to be here, even if it *is* only the nationals and a few regional outfits."

Martin walked right into the woman's comfort zone, cold eyes drilling into her face. "You know something you're not telling. What is it?"

Lisa's nostrils flared. "Why don't we leave that to the professionals?"

Martin snorted. "Why you-"

The woman stepped aside and spoke in his ear. "And what was the name and number of that talkative acquaintance of yours? I imagine DS Foster will be keen to learn if the ship of their investigation has sprung a leak. When the general public like *us* need an update, I'm sure we'll be informed."

Martin's face deepened to the colour of beetroot.

A familiar, friendly male voice rang out from the lane. "Lisa? Hi. I was coming over to see if you fancied an afternoon drink. Hello Martin, how are you?"

Coleman took a deep breath and resumed something approaching his normal colour. He wheeled about and forced a smile. "Hello there, Jeremy. Fair to middling, all things considered. And yourself?"

"Tolerably well, ta." Jeremy Lewis stopped next to the duelling pair of verbal combatants. "Sorry. Am I interrupting something?"

Lisa smirked. "No, that's alright. We're done. We were discussing the importance of letting the police do their job unhindered."

Jeremy nodded. "Ah. Well, there's a big commotion at the ash grove. I went for a turn up the hill and got sent down again. Police tape everywhere. To make matters worse, those bloomin' reporters have decided to come knocking at my door every five minutes. Not the kind of publicity I want right now. Couldn't wait to get away from Ashdene today." He fidgeted. "Not that I wouldn't have come and asked you for a drink, anyway." His head sank at the fumble.

Lisa bit her lip to hide a smile. "Best save some of

that sandpaper to work on your approach."

Jeremy's eyes twinkled. "Still a bit rough around the edges?"

"Not as smooth as it could be."

Martin Coleman rolled his eyes. "I'll be off then."

Jeremy waved to him. "Nice to see you, Martin. Have a good one."

Lisa remained silent. The grumpy man glanced back over one shoulder as he wandered away.

Jeremy's face darkened. "He was giving you a hard time, wasn't he?"

Lisa's eyebrows lifted as if pulled up on strings.

The man delivered a slight nod. "I'm not completely oblivious to what's going on around me, even if I don't always join in. Now, how about that drink?"

The woman sighed. "Oh boy do I need it."

"Oh? Tough work assignment?"

"No, I was up at the ash grove last night."

"Crumbs. Do the police know? What's happened up there?"

"I called the police." Her moistening eyes fixed in an empty stare.

Jeremy leaned closer, concern streaking his forehead like a furrowed field. "What's this now? Unusual to catch Lisa Marston showing weak eyes. Are you okay?"

Lisa wanted to fling herself into his arms. She'd found some blessed relief relaying the night's events to Anne over breakfast. From the look on the old spinster's face afterwards, she felt a heel for having shared. Somehow that didn't unburden her enough though. She hooked an uncharacteristically forward and tender arm in the crook of the woodsman's. "Let's head inside the pub and I'll tell you all about it."

11
Lascivious Lines

"Glowing eyes; children sacrificing their peers? It's incredible." Jeremy leaned back in his seat at The White Hart. It hadn't taken long after Lisa sat down with him, for the whole tale to come spilling out. Well, not quite the whole tale. She omitted certain details about what she saw at his bathroom window. The biggest struggle that frantic young woman faced, was keeping her voice down. The hostelry was full of unfamiliar faces. Any number of them might be reporters hanging around for some careless disclosure to surface.

Lisa leaned closer to fix her gaze on the woodsman. "I'm not making this up, Jeremy."

Jeremy swallowed. "I'm not saying you are. It's such a fantastical story. What on earth did the detective say after you laid all that out for him?"

"Not a lot at first. He listened for the most part, until I pressed him for answers. Then he suggested that if the children committed that murder, they might have been groomed."

"Groomed? Bribed with goodies to go for a drive with strangers is one thing; but bludgeoning a school friend to death? Come on."

"I know. He said primary school children couldn't have murdered Robin Jarrett and Brendan Stokes. Both would have taken considerable strength to subdue."

"So does he think the kids lured that lad into the bushes where someone was lying in wait?"

"Since I didn't see the actual murder take place, it's one possible theory."

"And what about all their talk of sacrifices and such? Got a line on that, has he?"

Lisa took a sip of her drink. "Based on the way some of the other victims were killed, he's not ruling out a ritual element."

"Occult murders in Wrenham Green?"

"Marcus floated the idea those Maypole children could be under the influence of mass hypnosis. I suppose they'll be interviewing teachers next, in search of a culprit."

"And the glowing eyes and weird voices?"

"He didn't say anything about that."

Jeremy drummed the fingers of one hand on the small wooden table. "Probably thought that horrible discovery rattled you. The mind does weird things as a coping mechanism sometimes."

"Yeah. Weird things." The woman rubbed her opposite shoulders as if to ward off a draft. "Nidhogg could be an alias. He said he'd check for any trace of it on their records. It's a bizarre name. At first I thought I'd misheard, until they repeated it."

Jeremy wiped beads of sweat from the back of his neck and broke eye contact. He fidgeted in the seat.

Lisa waved her fingers in the air to get his attention. "What is it?"

"Oh, nothing." He rubbed his chin.

"Have you heard that name before?"

"Not since childhood."

"Huh? But you said you weren't a child round here."

"That's right."

"Then how-"

"Will you let me finish?"

"Okay, okay. Sorry." Lisa frowned.

Jeremy sighed. "Mum used to tell me old Nordic tales and legends when I was a kid. Nidhogg is a creature mentioned in ancient Norse mythology."

"What sort of creature?"

"A dragon. Or that's how it's traditionally represented. Also known as *'Malice Striker.'* A term used by the missing children in your account. That piqued my interest."

"Yes, they said that."

"The beast was supposed to inhabit Náströnd - a hellish realm reserved for oath-breakers, murderers and adulterers. A villainous being, it also gnawed at one of the three roots of Yggdrasil."

"Yggdrasil? Hang on, you mentioned that the morning of the May Day festival, didn't you?"

"Hey that's right, I did. The world tree. An immense ash that forms a backbone to the cosmos, connecting nine worlds. Its roots were said to trap Nidhogg and deny him access to *our* world."

"So what's all that got to do with schoolchildren and a Maypole in this sleepy English village? What's it got to do with the murders?"

"Nothing much, I don't suppose. These theoretical cultists could have woven some kind of belief system around the legends. Maybe their leader has adopted the name Nidhogg?"

Lisa sighed, at a loss for ideas or words.

Across the barroom, the gentle murmur rose to a commotion. A crowd gathered around someone with a sizable smart phone, streaming the latest news video. Two women and a man dashed from the pub in the direction of the parked trailers.

Jeremy stretched his neck up. "Aye, aye. Looks like the police have released an update."

Lisa pulled out her own mobile and opened a news app. Headline text announced: *'Another murder and three more missing Maypole children in Wrenham Green.'* An individual school portrait photo of a boy accompanied the wording. Gentle eyes looked out of that picture, accompanied by a shy smile. The woman stroked it with an idle thumb. *That must be young Harry.* She had never seen his face. "The murder and an announcement of the latest missing kids are out."

"How many children is that?"

"Eight of the ten. Plus five murders. Or four murders and one rather suspicious cot death they're trying to sweep under the carpet."

"You think the Randall girl smothered her baby brother?"

"If you'd asked me that this time yesterday, I'd have laughed in your face, Jeremy. I might even have stormed out in disgust. Not now. Not after last night."

The discussion caused an uncomfortable light to flicker in the woman's eyes. She pulled at her top.

"Are you okay? You've been through an unimaginable ordeal."

"I'll be alright. It was a worrying thought."

"About?"

"Never mind. Is it me or has it become stuffy in here?"

"Fancy a stroll?"

"Please. Only, let's avoid the green. One more encounter with Jennifer Lane and I'm liable to do a little bludgeoning of my own."

The pair got up and filed out into the soothing embrace of cool, zesty spring air. The peaceful sensation proved a stark contrast to a flurry of activity taking place all around them.

* * *

"We'll continue this in the morning, Class. You are dismissed for the day. Michael Bullen, you will remain behind," Katie Hunt pushed her teacher's chair away from a solid desk near the front of the schoolroom. A mix of eleven-year-old boys and girls grabbed their coats and raced for the door. The thirty-year-old teacher put on her best stern face. In the last few weeks she had suffered more than one incident that warranted a departure from her normal sugary demeanour. She walked slowly over to lean against the tiny wooden desk next to a surly boy with dark, vacant eyes. "What's all this about, Michael? I've never known you to be disruptive in class before?"

No response.

"Is it something to do with the trouble in the village? We're all worried. Is it connected with what happened at the Maypole? Why won't you talk to me? I'm here to help."

The boy refused to look at her. "Fuck off."

Katie gasped, distraught at hearing such an utterance from one so young. "Michael."

He snapped again. "Fuck off. And fuck off with your stupid traditions and stupid Maypole."

The teacher linked hands together in her lap. "Very well, if you won't talk to me. Since you don't like traditions, they'll form part of your punishment. You will go to the board and write *'I will not snatch attention from Miss Hunt, but rather set my hand to the plough'* one hundred times before I let you go home. A traditional form of correction using traditional language."

The boy sat still.

"Now." The teacher extended a straight arm at the front of the room, the gruff tone of her voice surprising even herself.

Michael Bullen slunk over to a white board with hands in his pockets. He pulled them out and uncapped a blue marker pen to write the phrase.

Katie Hunt followed his actions with the occasional vocal prompt. "That's right. Then *'set my hand to the plough.'* Keep going. If you have difficulty keeping the text straight, please use the board ruler. I know how difficult it can be to write level when you're standing up close." Her voice softened. Try as she might, Katie couldn't do 'stern' for long. She loved all her students, even when they became unruly.

A car pulled up outside. Its female driver climbed out and exchanged greetings with another woman ushering her daughter into a parked estate vehicle. Katie stood and observed from the window. The new arrival was Michael's mother. How long would she have to wait for her son to finish his lines? The teacher turned to check on the boy's progress. Breath caught in her throat as if laced with cruel barbs. After the third line of text, Michael had modified the statement to read:

'Miss Hunt wants attention and needs her snatch ploughed.'

Katie grabbed the wall-hanging radiator behind her for stability. The tone of her voice squealed like an excited young animal. "What the? Michael, what are you doing?"

The boy didn't stop scribbling with the squeaky pen. The pitch of its nib matched the vocal distress of his teacher. "Writing the truth."

"The tru-" She pushed herself away from the wall and strode forward. "Do you even understand what that means? Where did you hear language like that? Who has been influencing you?" Her eyes sloped down at the corners, nose wrinkled from tense agitation.

Michael's voice lowered to a growl. "The Master." He discarded the pen and swiped up the board ruler.

Katie let out a whimper as the wild eleven-year-old span, his eyes glowing like burning coals of fire. She collapsed against one side of her own desk, hands scrabbling for anything to resist that approaching horror. As the twisted boy drew near, her fingers found a large pair of old scissors resting in her pen pot.

* * *

Lisa and Jeremy wandered in idle and aimless steps. From the pub they passed by Bramley Cottage and followed the lane clustered with an eclectic mix of rural dwellings. Hands swinging at their sides, from time to time the pair's knuckles brushed. That glancing touch sang like a pleasant dream that becomes a wisp of smoke. One that vanishes into the ether, despite best efforts to nail it down on your journey back to consciousness. Lisa's mind reeled. *Do I want this or don't I? If I'm not sure myself, how can I give out the right signals? If I'm giving out mixed signals, how can I expect Jeremy to respond? Get a grip, Lisa. Stop over-thinking and go with the flow.* Jeremy's knuckles brushed hers again. This time he reversed the swing of his arm to maintain contact. Lisa didn't resist, allowing her fingers to loosen into an inviting gesture. Jeremy intertwined his digits with hers, while still looking straight ahead along the road. It was subtle, but a definite and deliberate act. Some of the worries and horrors lifted from the young woman's shoulders with that simple physical contact. This was nice.

On their left, an impatient lady in her late thirties paced around the primary school car park. Hers was the only vehicle, apart from two in the staff bays.

"No. No, oh my God, NO." The screams of an older female with a husky voice belted from a school window, open on the latch.

The car park lady ran for the double door entrance. Once inside, shrieks and cries of distress blended together. Jeremy and Lisa released their light hold and raced towards the school. Lisa was first to yank open one door. She slid to a halt on the mirror-like finish of a freshly polished hall floor. Ahead, one of the classroom doors stood ajar. When the pair reached it, they found the lady from the car park clutching onto a plump, female head teacher. Both women stood transfixed by the horrendous scene before them. The body of Katie Hunt lay supine on top of her desk. The woman's head hung arched over the edge at an angle. A large pair of old scissors secured it in place, their open blades splayed through both eye sockets. Blood ran down the sides and pooled near a wastepaper basket. Her legs were raised to the knee and spread apart like a woman giving birth. From beneath a savagely torn skirt, the class board ruler extended up at a forty five degree angle. It gave her lower body the appearance of a three-legged stool. But the third 'leg' had been inserted where no board ruler was ever intended to go.

Lisa cupped a hand across her mouth and looked away. An involuntary sob escaped her lungs like the yapping bark of a surprised lapdog.

"Oh my word," Jeremy grabbed hold of her round the waist. He fought conflicting urges to stare at the sight and then turn around again. The vision proved both repulsive and compelling in equal measure.

The car park lady screamed. "Where's Michael? Where's my Michael?" She pushed the head teacher aside and stumbled out into the corridor like some drunken guest at a hen party. But this intoxication was borne of revulsion and fear.

DS Foster emerged from the classroom, neat shoes clipping on the immaculate shiny floor. If the detective didn't want to resemble a Shar-Pei dog, wrinkled with worry in his old age, that guy had chosen the wrong career path. He stopped where Jeremy and Lisa rested against one wall of the main school entrance. Paintings by children in the lower classes illustrated dogs, houses and flowers in an array of gaudy colours. The woodsman still held the shivering northerner in his arms. It was so good to embrace her, but the circumstances were entirely wrong.

The detective eyed him. "How's she doing?"

Jeremy shook his head in a hesitant, non-committal motion.

Out in the car park, an ambulance crew were doing their best to calm Mrs Bullen down. One of the detective's colleagues scribbled frantic notes as he spoke to the head teacher.

Marcus leaned over to stare straight into Lisa's face. "Your gentleman here already told us you entered the school behind Mrs Bullen. Right after the head teacher found the deceased and cried out in alarm. The others have corroborated that story, so you can pop off. I'll be in touch if I need to."

Lisa swallowed. "Thank you." She turned and paused. "Marcus?"

"Yes?"

"It was another penetrative act. The ruler, I mean. Like Brendan Stokes and the candle."

The detective sighed. "Try not to think about it." This unfortunate creature had gotten too close to the business end of his disturbing investigation. And on more than one occasion.

"Have you found the woman's son?"

"Michael Bullen? No. At least he's not dead too. As far as we know, anyway."

Jeremy's eyes narrowed. "He's another of the Maypole children, isn't he?"

Marcus bit his lip. "Do you know him?"

"No. I'm right though, aren't I?"

The officer nodded. "Yes. I'm afraid so."

"Do you think he did that?" Jeremy flicked his head at the doorway.

"An eleven-year-old boy?" Marcus twisted to gaze back at the classroom. "Unlikely. Not without help. She was a thirty-year-old woman in good health." His head sank. "God, I hope not."

Jeremy shifted. "I'm no handwriting expert, but it appears the same person wrote all those lines on the white board."

"We'll look into it."

"Some consider Maypoles to have phallic symbolism," Jeremy said.

"What?" The detective frowned.

"Lisa mentioned the penetrative act. Since this series of crimes appears to revolve around the Maypole, I thought you might like to know. No idea if it's relevant."

Marcus scratched his chin. "A phallic symbol?"

"Yeah. Sounds like a lot of rubbish, even if Maypoles *are* associated with a celebration of fertility and growth in nature. I guess some people see penises everywhere."

Lisa clutched onto the woodsman. His words brought back a temporary flash of her inadvertent shower voyeurism from the night before. But haunting images of a blood-soaked Katie Hunt chased away any pleasure that might have accompanied it. She stepped away from Jeremy to stand on her own two feet.

Marcus peered over her shoulder out the window. A camera crew were setting up in the car park. Three uniformed officers corralled them away from the ambulance. "You'd best scamper off before that lot see you."

Lisa followed his line of sight. "What about the last child, Marcus?"

"What about them?"

"Are you offering some sort of protection?"

"My Inspector sent a car round on a courtesy visit. Other than keeping an eye out, there's not a lot we can do. Should we place them in some kind of custodial care? If so, for how long? Can't very well approach the parents and say, *'Excuse me, not only might your child be at risk from a murderous psychopath, but they might also BE a murderous psychopath; or in league with one.'* We're keeping the details of last night's murder out of the public eye. Though it seems your chap here has heard the story."

It was the second time the policeman had referred to Jeremy with such a personal associative term. Lisa ignored it. She got no sense that the detective was fishing. Her masculine interest radar was a finely tuned instrument. Marcus didn't register a single blip.

"Yes. I'm sorry. I had to tell a couple of people I trust."

"Anne too?"

"Yes."

"Mmm. Well, try not to let it get any further, if you would. Loose lips and all that."

Jeremy straightened. "Don't worry, I'm no gossip. And Anne-"

"I know her," Marcus cut across. "My old teacher. She'll keep it to herself. Now if you'll both excuse me, I'd better get this information back to Command. They'll want to issue a statement and an alert about the missing boy."

* * *

"Anne?" Lisa called out as she closed the cottage door behind her. Jeremy had escorted her home from the scene of carnage at the school. She gave him one last short embrace on the doorstep before they parted. Had the whirlwind cascade of the afternoon's events not overtaken them, would he have kissed her? The sight of Katie Hunt, pinned to her own desk in that final, perverse moment of mortality, made such concerns seem frivolous and irrelevant. How could she entertain these juvenile, girlish relationship fancies, when someone had butchered the saccharine sweetheart of Wrenham Green Primary in her own classroom? The cottage was still. "Anne?" Lisa called again. She leaned over the bottom of the banister and craned her neck to project the query upstairs. "Are you home?" A gentle blubbing drifted back down into the hallway. Lisa grabbed hold of the rail to propel herself upward. "Anne?" She reached the top landing in half a heartbeat.

The old woman sat on the beige upstairs carpet in a crumpled heap, outside the childhood bedroom she once shared with her twin. The natural red liner that comes from excessive weeping, streaked her puffy eyes. Those eyes lifted to meet her lodger like a pining puppy dog, fresh tears slipping down both cheeks.

Lisa stopped. "Anne, did you fall? Are you hurt?" She crouched beside the forlorn pensioner.

Anne sniffed. "No." She wiped away the tears with bony, wrinkled fingers. "This injury isn't physical in origin. Not for me, at least."

Lisa propped her back against the wall and sank down beside her host. "How do you mean?"

Anne stared at the door of the room allocated to her guest; face offering a forlorn, glazed expression.

The younger woman swallowed hard. Her thoughts strayed back to the uncomfortable idea that popped into her head at the pub with Jeremy. How to broach such a sensitive topic? "Is it something to do with your brother?"

Anne's head bowed down to her chest. "When you described what you saw and heard in the woods last night, it summoned some difficult memories. They've been running through my mind ever since."

Lisa stretched out her legs and rubbed the kneecaps. "The long suppressed kind of memories?"

Anne shut her eyes as if to ward off another replay.

Lisa hesitated over whether to give her an account of what happened at the school. The old woman would catch it on the news soon enough. Somehow that was like keeping secrets from a best friend. Lisa blinked at the realisation of how much love she already felt for this precious lady. Could it be Anne Weaver had become a surrogate Auntie Joan? Was it simply the effect of mutual aid and support in a time of need? No, there was a definite bond. The kindly spinster deserved to hear the truth, even if it added to her woes. "Jeremy and I just came from the school."

Anne looked up, mouth half open. She read the hesitancy on Lisa's face. "What's happened?"

"Someone murdered Katie Hunt. She had one of her eleven-year-old pupils in detention. The head walked in and discovered Katie slain on her own desk. She screamed. We ran in right after the boy's mother, who was waiting outside the building." Lisa screwed her eyes tight in a vain attempt to shut out the image of the slaughtered teacher. "I don't even want to tell you the state Katie was in, Anne. It's too horrible to describe. And the lines someone wrote on the class white board..." She shuddered. "Vile beyond belief."

"What about the child? Who was it?"

"Michael Bullen."

"He's disappeared, hasn't he?"

Lisa nodded.

Anne looked back down. "Poor little Katie."

Lisa studied the faraway look on the old schoolteacher's face. She was no clairvoyant, but her intuition registered a direct hit in terms of the sentiment experienced.

The old woman remembered a cute girl skipping into one of her classes long ago. A bouquet of fresh Sweet Peas in the child's hands were thrust as a gift into the bosom of her beloved teacher. That little girl adored and admired Anne Weaver in equal measure.

Anne coughed, saliva from the emotional outpouring catching in her throat. "She was the friendliest child I ever taught, you know."

Lisa rested her head back against the wall. "I saw her speak to the school that day of my aborted assembly talk. If imitation is the highest form of flattery, you should feel overwhelmed. Katie wanted to *be* you. No mistake about it. I don't know that she pulled it off, but she loved those kids."

Anne put one hand up to support her forehead on splayed fingers. Another blob of saltwater fell from her left eye. "Why is this happening again?"

Lisa kept her head pressed against the wall and stared at the closed door of her bedroom. She couldn't make eye contact for the next question. That was too much. "Anne?"

"Yes?"

"Daniel didn't fall out of his window by accident,

did he?"

Anne brought up the other hand and cupped both around her nose. A muffled reply crept out between her fingers. "No."

Lisa winced. "Beth pushed him, didn't she? She pushed him and you saw it happen."

Anne said nothing. Eyes shut fast, her whole body trembled. Lisa put an arm around the old spinster's shoulders and pulled her close for a hug. They swayed together on the carpet as Anne broke down into a fit of uncontrollable sobs. It was a pent up emotional head of steam that had waited seventy-three years for release. A cry of desperate agony rang from the old woman's delicate lungs. "Why? Why did you do that, Beth? Why did you kill Dan? Where are you? Where did you go to?" Her voice heaved and wailed.

Lisa brushed aside a mop of the trembling woman's silvery hair and kissed her crown with tender, loving lips. A talented writer she might have been, but in that moment there were no words to offer. If the pen was mightier than the sword, it delivered little to slay that monster of grief and agony: Pain seared into the soul from a long-carried secret, never disclosed. In the end Anne didn't reveal it after all; Lisa Marston discovered it. A burden shared but those heart-breaking questions remained. For many new families in Wrenham Green, such questions might form again.

* * *

The night air hung crisp and still. A haloed moon

gave the cloud-strewn sky a lustre of crumpled blue velvet. The back door of a two-up, two-down terrace cottage in the village sailed open at the ponderous pace of a moving swing bridge. A splash of cold, lunar light fell on the seven-year-old form of Patrick Collins. His innocent eyes fixed into a vacant stare, as if someone had sucked the inner playful child out through his pupils. A hollow shell like some infernal automaton stepped into the chilly back garden. His young mind swam with incomplete thoughts and recollections, like intermittent clouds passing before the eerie face of the moon. *What happened upstairs?* He could remember getting out of bed. Why had he gone into Mummy's room? Her chest rose and fell in time with the soft rhythm of her shallow breathing. She looked so beautiful laying there alone in that bed. Why had Daddy run off with that woman at work two years ago? Mummy was so lovely. In that moment he wanted to cuddle her; wanted to let her know how much she meant to him. But something else took hold inside. *What was that again?* His hands reached up to caress his mother. Fingers slid around her slender throat. The pulse of blood in her jugular vibrated against his childish fingers. What force surged into his tiny hands and where did that strength come from? The visions were foggy. Where was he? That's right, he'd been touching Mummy's neck. Then came that snapping sound like breaking twigs that cut through the silence of her bedroom. Why did the skin stop pulsing against his fingers and the neck deflate like a collapsing plasticine model? *Mummy must be in a very deep sleep. Best not to disturb her.* The woods; the woods were calling to him: 'Come and play. You've been a very good boy, Patrick. It's time to join your friends.' *I'm not supposed to go out at night. Mummy wouldn't like me playing outside at such an hour. Especially not in the woods with the bad people around. But Mummy is sleeping. She'll never know if I go out to play and come home before she wakes up.* It was like an exciting adventure. The woods called again: 'Come home, Patrick. We're waiting for you.' *Home? I'm at home.* Why did the woods feel like home, now? Home was with Mummy. But Mummy had gone away. *Gone away? No, she's sleeping. A deep sleep.* He had loved her into a deep sleep with his caring hands. He loved her with such strength it protected her from further harm. No bad men like Daddy would ever abandon Mummy again. No bad people like those hurting others in the village would ever lay a hand on his mother. They didn't have to. He laid a hand on her first.

Patrick couldn't remember putting his shoes on, but he wasn't in the back garden anymore. There were trees here. An uphill climb replaced the level lawn where he and his mother used to play ball. At the top those voices called again, beckoning him closer. Inside, something else was at the helm. He had no knowledge of where he was going or why. *Who needs to worry about such things, when 'The Helpers' are soothing your troubled mind?* The Helpers came to him at the Maypole dance. There was something magical about that May Day festival; even better than the fantasies he conjured in anticipation. The Helpers worshipped The Master.

They were the ones who woke him up and urged him to give Mummy a loving embrace. The Master would enjoy such a gift. How sweet it was to have so many special new friends. Patrick didn't make friends easily. Now he had all the company his heart could ever wish for. The Helpers were inside, somehow. Inside and out and all around. They heard his thoughts and shared their dreams with him. Oh how he longed to tell his mother all about them, but they had to keep it a secret; like a special club. There were others in the club: those dancers from school who joined him in the whirling magic. He couldn't wait to see Karen Randall again. When they were chosen as the boy and girl to represent their class, both of them leapt for joy. The Helpers said Karen gave her baby brother Louis some special love. She was waiting for him in the woods too. *Special love? Why were the adults distressed about her gift? What was the love she gave?* His mind span again. These new friends dulled the world around you. Everything that happened filtered through their whispers, as if they wrapped you in a sheet. Nothing was clear anymore. It was hard to see or hear like before. Only the things *they* wanted. Were they true friends? Would they leave him alone if he asked them to? *Mummy. I want to go home to Mummy. But what is that light ahead? It's so inviting. My friends. My friends must be waiting beyond that light. Playtime. I love playtime. I'll stop here a while to play and then go home to Mummy in the morning and tell her everything. She always makes things right. But Mummy is sleeping now. A very deep sleep.*

12

Midnight Meanderings

Lisa tossed and turned in the night watches. Aerial visions of a dual-carriageway rotated in slow circuits through her cloud of dreams. Closer. Closer came the road. Blue flashing lights sparkled like sinister sapphires. They gleamed atop a plethora of emergency vehicles from all three major services. Firemen cut away the roof of an unrecognisable red saloon. It had crossed the central reservation and collided head-on with a blue estate heading the opposite direction. Both vehicle bonnets concertinaed and collapsed, presenting a twisted composite car like some inverted 'push-me pull-you' locomotive at loggerheads with itself. A fire chief and a paramedic pulled a policeman to one side.

The fireman was first to speak. "His legs have been severed in the cabin. The dashboard and steering wheel are all that's stopping him bleeding out."

The policeman glanced over to a dazed youth around twenty-one, pinned into the driver's seat of the red car. "What are you saying?"

The paramedic picked up the vocal relay and lowered his voice to avoid any chance of being overheard. "It's a fatal. When the fire crew release him from that steel cage, he'll die in seconds. Poor lad has lost so much blood and the trauma is too severe. There's nothing we can do to save him."

The officer's radio crackled to life. "Hotel-Juliet One-Five, can you provide a status update, over?"

He keyed the push-to-talk button and turned away. "Control from Hotel-Juliet One-Five. Two confirmed fatalities. Awaiting definitive confirmation on the occupant of the second vehicle, over."

"Received. Control out." The radio bleeped and silenced.

The policeman lifted his flat, peaked cap and wiped a mop of brown hair back with the other hand. He knew the score: this was his responsibility now. He approached the crumpled red saloon. A pair of nervous eyes glimmered at him from the mangled wreck, the pupils darted from side to side, desperate for hopeful news.

The trapped boy coughed and winced. "Are they going to cut me free soon?"

"What's your name, son?" The officer avoided a specific response.

"Greg."

"Greg what?" He already knew the answer. An earlier PNC check of the vehicle registration had provided him with the keeper details. But he wasn't fishing for information.

"Greg Hinkley."

"I'm PC Keeler. But you can call me Lance."

The driver put on a brave face. "I would shake your hand, but well…"

Lance broke a smile. "Maybe later. The fire crews are making ready to cut you loose." The irony of that phrase wasn't lost on the officer. It felt like the kind of dark humour his colleagues used with each other as a coping mechanism. "So where were you off to?"

"Home for Christmas. Can't wait to see the family."

"A big one?"

"Mum, Dad and two younger sisters. They still live at home. I've been renting a flat twenty miles away. Oh, can you do something for me?"

"What's that?"

"I've got their presents in the boot. Don't know if they're still okay, but would you get them out before they haul my car away? I suppose they'll take me to hospital for a check-up."

Lance swallowed. "Yeah, that's right. Next stop hospital." It was always worse when these things happened at Christmas. "Okay, I'll take care of the gifts. It looks like you had a blowout on your front offside tyre."

Greg gulped. "I wasn't going fast. It burst and I couldn't regain control of the car. Next thing I knew I was in the oncoming lane."

The fire crew moved closer with their cutting equipment, ready for the next stage of the operation. Lance took a deep breath. They were waiting on his word. The last sands in the hourglass of this lad's life rested on him doing his job. The road was shut, traffic building, costs were mounting and the emergency crews needed elsewhere. This happy, innocent life full of promise, would be snuffed out upon command. It didn't matter that he seemed lucid, chatty and in good spirits; the boy was about to die. Blinking back moisture so as not to show Greg weak eyes, PC Keeler leaned over him. "Now then. Your dashboard has you pinned good and proper. When they release the structure, it might hurt for a second or two. Don't worry if you have to cry out. There's no shame in it. The paramedics will be on you before you know it."

Greg nodded. "I'll be brave."

Lance placed a gentle hand on his shoulder. "Good lad. I need to stand clear while they work."

"Thanks. Oh, Lance?"

"Yeah?"

"Merry Christmas."

Lance's eyebrows knitted together. "Merry Christmas, Greg." He lifted a hand to the fire crew.

Once the cutting equipment was in place, it took mere moments to prize open the crushed automotive can. Greg's face spasmed into a twisted look of agony. His mouth opened in a weak gasp for one second. Then the young driver closed his eyes, lowered his head and was still.

Lance wiped his face with the back of one hand.

The paramedic sidled up to him. "I know it looked awful, but that was only a nervous reaction. The boy was gone before he felt anything, I promise you."

The officer twisted round to the estate car. "What

about the other two?"

"They've loaded the chap and his wife for transportation to the morgue."

"Killed outright?"

"Yeah."

PC Keeler returned focus to the red saloon. He watched the emergency crews working around the deceased young man with silent, respectful professionalism. "I wonder who was luckier, in the end?"

"It's the families my heart goes out to now. That's one part of your job I don't envy."

A female police officer walked from an emergency response vehicle to stand alongside her colleague. "What a mess, Lance. We've got some details back on the others; err... Craig and Pamela Marston. They have a teenage daughter."

Lance gritted his teeth. *Poor kid. Another person's Christmas we're about to spoil.*

The scene drifted away past the crashed estate car. While none of these were events Lisa had experienced first-hand, that second vehicle became immediately familiar. Was this dream of the past a product of her imagination, pieced together from fragments of information? Or had that horrific sequence been a genuine replay, like some bizarre psychic gift. "Mum, Dad," She started in bed and sat bolt upright, panting for breath.

For a moment the room remained silent, except for the young woman's gasps.

"Lisa." A female voice called in a hushed whisper from the garden below. It radiated warmth and love, yet caused hairs to raise on the back of her neck.

It can't be. Lisa threw back the counterpane and nipped across to pull the heavy drapes aside. The lattice window latch squeaked free. She opened the antique leaded light panel and peered down. A wispy, glowing white figure stood outside the cottage, staring up at her. Cascading hair blew as if in a gentle breeze, yet the air about remained calm and still. A pair of twinkling eyes shone with affection.

Lisa grabbed hold of the wall to stop herself following Daniel Weaver's mortal flight. Her voice cracked and squeaked. "Mum?"

Her mother's face shone. The figure turned and sauntered away down the path to the lane.

"Mum," Lisa called out in a harsh whisper. Her attention was torn between the apparition and the media and police camp. She grabbed hold of a cardigan, flung it around her shoulders and slipped out onto the landing. The wooden floorboards beneath the carpet creaked at her footfalls. Lisa attempted to support most of her weight against the banister. A considerate attempt to avoid waking Anne on her descent to the hallway. At the front door she unhooked her jacket, checked for keys and darted out into the still night air. The glowing, light-footed figure resembling Pam Marston strode parallel to the green, past the pub. Lisa hurried after, fingernails digging into her palms. Would anyone at the quiet camp spy her? What might happen if they did? It must be somewhere around midnight or beyond.

At the phone box the figure vanished like vapour, melting into oblivion. Lisa came to an abrupt halt and twisted from side to side. *Where did she go? Was it a ghost or have I lost the plot?*

"Lisa." A different woman's voice arose from further south along the lane. It too sang with affection.

The northerner rubbed sleep from her eyes and squinted. "Auntie Joan?" *What is going on?*

The familiar, aged guardian moved off towards the footpath at the base of the hill. Lisa decided to keep her gaze locked on her quarry this time, whatever happened. She ran as fast as a pair of slip-on shoes she'd nabbed at the cottage would allow, without twisting her ankle.

Auntie Joan turned right onto the path. The radiant vision didn't glide *through* the snagging branches; her passing caused them to part like obedient servants on her route uphill. Lisa had no such good fortune. She snapped and fought against the scratching, spiteful undergrowth in a vain attempt to keep pace. Her foot locked in an exposed tree root near the crest. Lisa stumbled headlong into a moist patch of bracken. Her nostrils filled with its pungent, sweat-like aroma. Damp foliage soaked her legs and the bottom of her nightdress, hanging beneath cardigan and coat. "Crap. This had better not be a mere hallucination." She huffed, picked herself up and brushed nature's floral embrace from her soiled clothing. Auntie Joan was nowhere in sight. The ash grove loomed ahead, its trees silent and brooding like some powerful yet defensive foe.

"Auntie Joan?" She spoke as loud as she dared. In truth, Lisa expected no response. *I feel like a prize fool.*

"Lisa." It was a fresh female voice, but not one she recognised this time. The sound washed over her like the bubbling of many waters in a mountain spring. "Lisa."

The young woman span in a frantic attempt to attribute direction and distance to the sound. It came from everywhere and nowhere at once. The voice echoed through the clearing, but also in her head. It evidenced a total presence, similar to film footage where the ambient noise has been dialled down and replaced with an all-pervasive voice-over.

"Who's there?" Lisa took a few steps forward. She stood erect in a bright beam of moonlight stabbing down through the woodland canopy. Poise and composure were the only weapons left.

A twinkling array of lights circled around her uneasy frame. Their appearance glimmered like a will-o'-the-wisp or convocation of iridescent bugs. They ducked and weaved between her legs and over her shoulders, like fairies on a joyride. Lisa fought down a rising panic and stood her ground. The sparkling display coalesced into a rough outline. It evoked childhood memories of 'join-the-dots' books. The shape morphed into a tall, slender figure. The lights burst in a synchronised flash of luminosity. Their blinding pulse caused Lisa to turn aside and scrunch her eyes shut. Seconds later she allowed them to re-open at a cautious rate, fearful of blindness. Her mouth went dry, tongue thick like a lump of leather. With titanic effort, the woman twisted her head straight, senses aware that someone or *something* now stood where the lights had shone. Whatever it was, Pamela Marston and Joan Tanner appeared to have been lures to bring her here. Memories of the last moments in the life of young Harry Powell raced through her mind. Was some gaggle of monstrous, glowing-eyed juvenile murderers about to set upon her too?

The entity read her thoughts. "No Lisa. You are safe in my presence." The soothing, playful voice of many waters sounded again in her head and all about. Its tone stroked her emotions like a parent settling down a restless baby.

Ten feet away and the same in height, stood the radiant figure of an immense, slender woman. She gazed down at Lisa from beneath a semi-transparent veil that concealed her full features. Long blonde hair flowed over creamy shoulders and alabaster skin. A silken dress made of fabric with the sheen of spider webs laced with heavy dew, reached down to her bare feet. Behind her head, an exquisite decoration of shimmering swan feathers splayed out in a regal fan.

Lisa wrestled for control of her bladder. This bizarre creature stood almost twice her own height. Its eyes glowed with a pale mauve light, but showed no malice or evil.

"W-who are you?" The words caught in her throat. They struggled out like someone attempting to speak while choking on food.

The vocal waters tinkled again. "I am Skuld."

Lisa tried to moisten her lips with a sandpaper tongue. "How do you know me and what do you want?"

The creature remained unblinking, gaze fixed upon her. "I want you."

"What?"

"My sisters and I have observed all, since you came to the village."

"Your sisters?"

"Urd and Verdandi."

Lisa stood immobile. "Who?"

Skuld turned away. Her voice blew cold and distant. "The dragon has poisoned a branch into this world. His followers influenced your kind with it once before. They are doing so again."

"Dragon?"

"Nidhogg."

Lisa let out a blast of air at the familiar name. "A branch. You mean the Maypole?"

"Cut from this sacred grove long ago. It has power to open a doorway for the creature and his minions."

"How?"

"When someone sensitive to influence from beyond joins with it."

"What does the dragon want?"

Skuld raised her eyes to the heavens. "To enslave and destroy. It already holds captive prisoners from this realm. Their life force feeds its power. Nidhogg grows stronger with each new prisoner."

Lisa stepped back a pace. "The children."

"A score."

There were so many questions they tumbled out of Lisa's mouth in rapid succession. "Score? That's twenty. Sweet Jesus, the children from 1945 are still imprisoned somewhere too? Shouldn't it be nineteen unless we've lost another? Where is this place? How do we get them all back?" She didn't stop for breath in her bout of verbal diarrhoea.

Skuld faded into the darkness, de-materialising into a cloud of whirling lights again. Her voice boomed out of nowhere. "The dragon can now cross over, when it finds a suitable host to meld with. Once it has a foothold in both worlds, my sisters and I will be powerless to defeat it."

Lisa followed the roller coaster of lights around the clearing, arms flapping like a frantic chicken. "How do we stop that? What must we do?"

The woodland grove fell pitch black. Lisa froze.

This time the voice whispered in her ear. *"You* are our chosen champion. *You* must offer yourself as a willing sacrifice in the fight. Only then can we close the door once and for all."

An icy chill rippled through Lisa's tummy. "Sacrifice?" There was no response. *What kind of sick place do these creatures inhabit?* "No. No way. I'm not getting involved in something like that." Strength and purpose coursed back into her limbs. She ran for the footpath. In a cruel twist of fate, her foot found the same exposed tree root as before. This time, downward inertia added to the energy with which she fell. Lisa tumbled into the undergrowth. The woman's head struck a tree trunk with considerable force. Her skull vibrated like a resonant bell, before all remaining light faded into a dark tunnel.

* * *

"Lisa?" Anne's voice followed a gentle rapping of knuckles on the bedroom door.

A blurry circle of light greeted Lisa's fluttering eyelids. "Huh?" The drapes remained closed but bold daylight chased around their edges.

"Lisa, are you unwell?" Anne spoke again from the landing.

The young woman propped herself up in bed and tapped her phone to catch the time. "Oh my God." It was Ten AM. She swung her legs off the mattress and reached for the door handle. "Sorry, Anne. I've overslept like an idle teenager. Don't know what's wrong with me. Ugh, the dreams I had too."

Anne clutched a cup of tea between two bony hands. "I thought you might like a drink."

"Oh, you're such a sweetheart." She took the cup and saucer. "Remind me who is supposed to be helping whom again?"

"Sounds like your body needed the rest. Were they bad dreams?"

The mobile phone chimed a notification alert at the bedside. Lisa picked it up. "More unusual than bad. A dream within a dream. You know: one of those where you feel like you've woken up but are in fact still asleep?" She swiped the alert: a news headline. "Oh no."

"What is it?" Anne took a tentative step into the room.

"The final Maypole child disappeared last night. Patrick Collins, aged seven. They found his dead mother in bed with a crushed windpipe."

Anne put a hand across her mouth. "Mercy." The word came out muffled.

Lisa's mind returned to her dream and the mythical vision's assertion of twenty captured souls. *Coincidence. It was only a dream.* "I'd better get dressed."

Anne moved back onto the landing. "Do you have any new articles to write today?"

"No, but there are a few things I want to research. Nothing heavy. Think I'll pop over to see Jeremy later."

The old schoolteacher smiled. "Why not? Recharge your batteries. Goodness knows the horrors of recent weeks are draining us all."

"How are you bearing up?"

"As well as can be expected, all things considered." She turned away. "Last time this happened the impact was worse, of course. But I grieve for the bereaved and bereft. And my heart aches for those missing children. I'll see you downstairs."

Lisa closed the door and hauled back the bedclothes. A small clump of bracken fronds lay squashed against the sheets. She staggered against the wall, one hand lifted to her breast. *What on earth?*

The rest of the morning saw Lisa hunched over her

laptop, researching names from that dream. Had they yielded no trace, it might have relieved her. Instead, the discovery of their origin led her on a walk over to Ashdene earlier than expected.

"Yoo hoo. Jeremy?" Not finding him in the workshop, Lisa poked her head around the front door of the woodsman's curious home. "Jeremy, are you here?"

A toilet flushed in a room out back.

"Hey, how's it going?" Jeremy entered the main living area. "Come on in. Tea?"

"Yes please. Thanks." Lisa stepped inside and shut the door. "Have you heard the morning news?"

Jeremy filled a kettle at the sink. "I finished a bite to eat for lunch not long ago. Caught it on the radio. I assume you're talking about Patrick Collins and his mother, Amy?"

"Yes. How awful."

Jeremy popped the kettle on his stove. "Not that I want to sound like a heartless bastard, but does this mean the murders and abductions will stop now? If the perpetrator is a copycat, they must have run out of victims. God, I hope they find the children."

Lisa perched herself on the edge of the sofa, legs crossed. "I had a bizarre dream last night. Would you like to hear it?"

Jeremy shrugged. "Not especially." He caught a flash in her downcast eyes and noticed the pursing lips. "Sorry. Wrong answer? Okay then, shoot."

Lisa frowned. "Don't do me any bloody favours,

okay?"

The woodsman swallowed hard and leaned against a table. "It was an important dream then?"

Lisa laid out the entire sequence of night-time events, from the car crash that claimed her parents to that encounter in the ash grove with Skuld. "And then I closed the door and discovered bracken fronds in my bed."

Jeremy poured the tea and passed her a cup. "That *is* a bit freaky. Do you hang nightclothes and sheets out to air at Bramley Cottage? Could it be they brushed against some plants and picked them up?"

"Bracken?"

"Maybe it got caught in other clothing. You know, from a walk. Could have been deposited with the sheets that way, somehow."

Lisa's shoulders sank. "I've been clutching at straws like that all morning. No explanation satisfies."

Jeremy laughed. "The alternative is that you went into the woods in your nightdress and encountered one of the Norns."

"So you know who Skuld is then? Why am I not surprised?"

Jeremy raised one eyebrow. "I'm surprised *you* know who she is. Have you studied Norse mythology before?"

"No, and I didn't know who she was. I'd never heard of the Norns until I searched the Internet this morning. The names Skuld, Urd and Verdandi were also new to me."

"The Norns - as you have no doubt discovered - comprise female beings ruling the destinies of both mortals and immortals. Other regional traditions refer to them as 'The Fates,' and things of that nature. The three sisters you mention cover Yggdrasil in water from the well of fate and the sand that surrounds it. The idea being that the tree will not rot. A common superstition based on the etymology of their names holds that Urd, Verdandi and Skuld correspond to past, present and future. A tenuous link. But then we're talking about the fairy tales of ancient peoples. Stories invented to explain the uncontrollable aspects of their mortal existence. A way to reconcile the unpredictable nature of life and death."

"So, like I said at the pub, what are they doing in the woods above an English village?"

Jeremy shifted. "If the stories were more than - well stories; you could argue that the beings used names familiar to folk in this realm when addressing you. Many tribes from northern climes settled here in ancient times. Belief systems across a broad geographic area often included similar myths, characters and deities. Think of the Greeks and Romans: same gods, different names. But none of it is real."

"Why did I know their names in my dream? To be honest, it would have suited me fine if my subconscious had made the whole thing up."

"It did." Jeremy paused then gulped his tea without expression.

Lisa's muscles tensed. "So you think I'm out of my

tree?"

The man put down his empty mug. "No. You've experienced some horrific and stressful situations this past year. Especially since coming to Wrenham Green. I reckon your inner self is attempting to process and catalogue it all. If it didn't, you probably *would* go mad. But I don't think you're there yet."

Lisa snorted. "Thanks. That makes me feel so much better."

"Lisa, I have no idea how some bracken found its way into your bed. But common sense suggests it must have been through natural means. Did you read up on Nidhogg after your encounter with the Powell boy's murder? It could be you saw a link to the Norns in a related article without taking it in. It's like Déjà vu. Stuff sometimes crosses over in the brain. That creates the illusion of having experienced something or met someone before."

"But it felt so real."

"Didn't you want it to?"

"Now who's the nut job, Jeremy?"

"Stay with me here a moment. This whole situation has left everyone, including the police, helpless and impotent. Why wouldn't you want to conjure up a way to bring back those poor kids? Did you tell Anne?"

"Don't be stupid."

"Don't you two trust each other?"

"Wake up, Jeremy. Like I'd walk up to Anne and say *'Hey, your sister Beth is trapped in another realm/parallel universe/whatever the fuck it is, but I might be able to save her if I pop up to the ash grove and commit suicide.'* I love that old woman to pieces. No way would I do or say anything to hurt her. Talk about irresponsible. I came to you because I needed to tell *someone* I trust. I supposed there was a growing bond between us."

"Skuld didn't say anything in your dream about committing suicide, did she?"

"Sacrifice then. Okay, so I pop up to the ash grove and get murdered. Fabulous difference. To parody Shakespeare: A nettle by any other name would sting as fierce."

Jeremy leaned forward. "Did your parents or guardian ever put your happiness before theirs?"

"Yes, why?"

"In some fashion that meant they missed out?"

"Countless times."

"Did it kill them?"

Lisa frowned. "Are you trying to be funny?"

Jeremy sighed. "Those who loved you made a sacrifice. That's all I'm saying. Death wasn't involved. People make sacrifices every single day without a fatality. Either way, it's irrelevant here. Your subconscious invented a solution to help that it knew you wouldn't go through with. A convenient 'out' that doesn't destroy the fantasy of being *able* to do something. Takes away the powerlessness."

Lisa looked out of the window up the hill. "I see. Why won't you believe me?"

"About what?"

"About my encounter. I thought you cared."

Jeremy moved to sit next to her on the sofa. "I know it seemed real. Your total acceptance of the event is written across your face, plain as day. You're a caring woman who wants to help out in an impossible situation."

"But you still reckon it's all in my head?"

The woodsman placed a hand on her left wrist. "Children with glowing eyes, ghastly voices and superhuman strength? References to mythological creatures? Ghostly night-time wanderings after your deceased loved ones? Think about how your last few experiences all sound for a minute. If I didn't care, Lisa, I'd have laughed you out of the room or called for someone with a straight jacket."

"So to you I'm nothing more than an upset and over-emotional woman? Sounds like you *are* laughing me out of the room."

Jeremy let go of her wrist, rose and paced across the floor. One hand swept over his forehead as he faced the wall. "I haven't got time for this. Fine. Tell you what: let's go up to the ash grove. You can shout and scream and wail for the Norns to take you. If the children reappear, I'll spend the rest of my life making amends. How does that sound?"

Lisa lunged to her feet and stormed towards the door, her voice rising to a shrill pitch. "I don't care what you do with the rest of your life. I don't want any part of it." The door slammed behind her.

Jeremy wrung his hands and punched a wooden beam. "Shit."

* * *

"We've now entered one of the outer circles of hell, Fuzz." Vince frowned at his blazer wearing colleague.

"I'd say we're right in the middle, Vinny." Marcus Foster shut the car door and scanned around the village green. Under any other circumstances, a late May afternoon on such a spot would be peaceful, even idyllic. But not after visiting the home of yet another local murder victim.

Vince locked the vehicle. "We'll think we're right in the middle if the Inspector doesn't find something good to pass up the chain. Shit always flows downward."

Marcus paused. "Would you look at that?" He indicated a man around thirty years of age, stretched out on the grass beside the old Maypole. The figure attempted to sit up. His ragged mop of dark brown hair stood skyward. The head flicked from side to side, eyes misted over. One hand reached up to scratch a chin that would enjoy a shave.

Vince paused. "Some people start early. Do you think he's with the media crowd?" He nodded at a plain, white Transit van parked at the edge of the grass.

"Either that or some delivery driver with a skin full. Hold up, don't you dare." Marcus knew the scruffy drunk couldn't hear from this distance, but his reaction was automatic.

Vince ambled forward. "He's not getting behind the wheel in that state."

Marcus trotted alongside and waved at two uniformed officers loitering beside a patrol car. "Get a breathalyser for an EBA, would you?"

One of them nodded. "Skip." He opened the boot of the vehicle and retrieved an electronic meter and tube.

Vince was first to the van, warrant card in hand. "Hold up there a moment, Sir. Police."

The dazed individual paused with the commercial vehicle driver's door half open. "What's wrong?"

"My colleague and I noticed you seem a little the worse for wear. Had a liquid lunch?"

"Haven't touched a drop." He still appeared sluggish, but his speech flowed clear and solid.

Marcus came to a halt, followed by the constable with his breathalyser. "All the same, we'd like you to provide a breath specimen before getting in that van."

The man looked from one to the other. "Fine."

The uniformed officer administered the test while Marcus and Vince stepped aside.

"What do you reckon if not, Fuzz? Baked?"

Marcus shook his head. "He seems coherent. We'll do a search of the van and make him turn out his pockets. Doesn't feel like drugs. Could he have zonked out on the grass?"

"We're getting paranoid if that's it. How about a vehicle check?"

"See what he says for now. I'll jot down the reg in my PNB for reference."

The constable held up the breathalyser to the detectives and shook his head.

"That must have been one hell of a sleep. Guess we were all too busy with this morning's excitement to notice him kipping there earlier." Vince stared after the Transit van as it pulled away into the village, its driver now free to go unhindered. They had detained him twenty minutes for some questions and radio verification of a few details. "Of all the places to doze off in the present state of affairs. Do you think he's involved in any of this?"

Marcus squinted. "The vehicle trace came back as described. He was telling the truth there. We could contact the rental firm for that van. If it's load jacked, we can check out his movements. If not, they'll at least verify when he hired it. ANPR unit might fill in some blanks. If our man arrived in Kent early morning as he claims, he'll sink further down the list of suspects. Doubtful he could even have offed Amy Collins."

Vince grinned. "Since when did we assemble a list of suspects on this one?"

Marcus twitched. "Don't even get me started. What do you think the personal business he needs to take care of is?"

"Yeah, that didn't sit well with me, either. We could run an info request by Durham Constabulary to see if he's got previous for anything. No stone unturned, and all that. What was his name again?"

Marcus held up his notebook. "Molloy. Keith Molloy."

13
Abduction

"Do you want to tell me about it?" Anne Weaver sat down at the breakfast table next morning, clutching her signature, muscular coffee.

Lisa pushed cereals around a floral-patterned china bowl with a spoon, chin resting on the heel of one hand. "Mmm? Oh, no thanks. Jeremy and I had a bust up yesterday. I told him I didn't care to see him anymore."

"I thought you were quiet last night. Been playing on your mind ever since, I'll wager."

"Why do I open up and bare my soul to people who don't value it, Anne?"

Anne unfolded the morning paper. "Are you sure he doesn't value it? That's not like the quiet woodsman I've met on previous occasions."

"He practically laughed at me."

Anne placed a pair of reading glasses on her nose. "Practically isn't the same as actually, is it?"

Lisa let go of the spoon. "I *was* a bit hard on him."

The old woman turned the pages, scanning various

headlines. "Jeremy isn't a word-smith like you. Sometimes I get the feeling he would like to say things, but can't."

"You make it sound like he's got a disability."

"Because he can't talk the hind legs off a donkey? No."

"Unlike me, you mean."

Laughter lines creased the edges of Anne's eyes. "You have fire in your belly, Lisa. It doesn't take much to fan the flames. Jeremy has fire too, but of a different kind. A slow burn in his case. Like embers that appear to have gone out, but remain hot to the touch. When the right breeze blows to feed them… Well, if you're not going to see him anymore it doesn't matter. What did he *practically* laugh at you for to make you so upset?"

"Huh? Oh, nothing." Lisa rubbed her brow with firm fingers. "Problem is: I *want* to see him. Do you think I should go back round there this morning?"

"No." The paper obscured Anne's head.

"Oh."

The old woman peeked across the top of her reading material. "Why not give it a couple of days? If he doesn't come looking for you, go and see if he'll talk things out. If not, what have you lost?"

"You should have considered a second career as an agony aunt."

Anne beamed. "I already had one."

"What?"

"Don't think that because my charges were aged between five and eleven, they didn't have innocent crushes on one another. I lost count of how many broken hearts I had to tend as a schoolteacher. Funny for an old spinster."

Lisa's face softened. She couldn't hold back a grin. "I'm not between the ages of five and eleven. I only act like it."

Anne gave her a dismissive wave. "Why don't you get out of the village? Go exploring."

"My car could do with a run. Do you need anything?"

"No, I'm fine. Have a change of scene to clear your head. I'll see you later."

Lisa reversed her Renault Clio out of the drive. With the window lowered a crack to allow fresh air into the cabin, she cruised away from the village on the Bossingham road. Trees spread across the narrow lanes like Gothic arches. Lambs frolicked in a steep field to one side. "Oh, how cute." She pulled over to watch them jump, as if their tiny legs stood loaded with coiled springs. That simple rustic scene provided some welcome mental distance from the cares and worries consuming her soul. On the rise behind, a white van pulled into a hedge. Lisa snapped a shot of the darling animals with her phone camera. *Janice will love a picture like this. One for a quick e-mail attachment later.*

As the Clio rolled back out into the road, the van followed suit. Lisa clocked the commercial vehicle in her rear-view mirror, but paid it no mind. After she took a couple of detours to explore the myriad of lanes, it still surprised the young woman to find the van lingering behind. *Odd. Oh well. I wonder what's down that hill?* She turned left, one eye monitoring the mirror. The van slowed, paused and signalled to follow. "Okay weirdo, I've had enough of this spoiling my peace. Off you go." She reduced her speed to a crawl, lowered the window further and waved the van past. Instead of taking her up on the offer, the white Transit trundled to a halt several feet behind. "Fuck this." Lisa gunned the engine and peeled away at pace. The van lurched and roared after. Frantic suppositions raced through her brain. *What if the cops are right about the murders being committed by a serial killer? Is this the person?* She floored it and shifted up a gear. This was no way for someone to prove Jeremy right about her mythological dreams being nonsense. Her tyres skidded on some loose gravel near the verge. Lisa fought for control. The white van tore up her side and lunged across, forcing her to swerve. The front nearside wheel sank into a soft patch of mud. That dipping action sent the Clio sliding off down a shallow, slippery bank backed by dense, coniferous woodland. Turf flew into the air as the driving wheels fought for purchase. Lisa screamed and pushed the brake so hard it seemed her foot would tear through the foot-well floor. The car shook and bounced on the uneven surface. The Renault came to a halt near the closest tree, leaving mere inches to spare. With shaking fingers the woman released her seatbelt and opened the car door.

"Come here, bitch." An angry male voice caused

rolling waves of dread to break upon her emotional shore.

"Oh my God. Keith, what are you doing here?" She backed away, bum pressed against the cool metal side of her vehicle.

Eyes sparkling with hatred, Keith Molloy advanced from the road, a cosh raised in one hand. "Thought you could run off and leave me, did you? Thought you could treat me like shit. It's payback time, Marston."

"Get away from me." Lisa span and tumbled towards the dense conifers. Her feet slid on muddy grass, sodden by run off from a nearby spring. The tightly packed, wiry twigs of the dark forest hindered her escape. They clutched at her clothing like heinous, natural barbed wire. The familiar tug of Keith's hand yanked back her head by the hair. The last thing she saw as the cosh came down, was the inverted face of a man she once loved. One she thought had loved her in return. *How can this be happening?* Blackness.

Cold concrete chilled the young woman's back as consciousness returned. Her head throbbed. Double vision and groggy, indistinct nature sounds assaulted her adjusting senses. Her sore hands pressed together at the wrists. Something like electrical cable lashed them in place. Similar bindings held her feet immobile in like fashion. Cool fingers of air tickled her right ear. Lisa blinked and twisted to try to get some visual bearing on this new environment. She sat in a cramped structure with thick walls. The breeze blew through a slit opening like a long, narrow window without glass. About her on the floor lay an old sleeping bag and the dusty ash remains of a simple campfire. The walls seemed to break at two points into an offset passageway. It gave no direct line of sight to an obvious doorway behind.

"It's an old machine gun nest from the second world war." Keith's voice rumbled from beyond the offset. He rounded one corner and squatted down against a wall. "They were built for defence of the country in case Hitler's armies crossed the channel. Not a bad place to doss down without getting discovered."

Lisa tasted blood in her mouth. She forced out some defiant and authoritative words. "What do you think you're doing, Keith? Do you want to go to prison?"

Keith folded his arms. "There I was, sitting back at home with the family feeling sorry for myself. I'd lost the flat, and my whore of a girlfriend had done a runner. Then who should I spy on the national news, sticking up for some fake granddad down south? You should have kept a lower profile, you stupid cow. Now it's going to cost you."

Lisa bunched her legs up beneath her chin.

Keith rose and unfolded a pocket knife. With a quick sawing motion he released her ankle bindings.

The young woman didn't hesitate. One foot came up and struck him beneath the chin. She couldn't get up, but blood pouring from his mouth delivered a momentary sense of victory. Keith staggered on his feet and brought down a glancing backhander across her face. The resounding slap reverberated off the chunky walls and confined space of the old machine gun nest. Lisa fought back tears with little success.

Keith pulled himself taut. "I've gone without for far too long because of you. Time to give a man his due, Lisa. Time to meet the need."

Lisa's eyes widened. She shook her wrists in a vain attempt to free herself from the insistent bonds.

Keith stood over her, one hand reaching to his fly.

* * *

Marcus Foster sat back in his office chair at the station. It was a rare moment of quiet. Afternoon sunlight filtered through a louvered blind, striping the room. The rest of the operations team were out on enquiries or down at the Forward Command Post. He clicked through pages of intelligence reports on his computer and pulled up a GIS document. An Ordnance Survey Landranger 50K base map appeared, overlaid with symbols and crosshatched polygons depicting the various incident locations and search zones. The detective rubbed sore eyes with both hands. This investigation was not only stalling, it had made scant progress since they first set up the incident room. The desk phone warbled to life. He reached down and swiped its receiver to his ear.

"Op Janus - DS Foster speaking."

A clipped and business-like woman's voice laced with a thick northern accent responded. "Good Afternoon. This is Inspector Tracey Blackthorn from Durham Constabulary DVU. You sent us a request yesterday for information on the subject of a stop-check."

"Good afternoon, Ma'am. That's right."

"Do you mind if I ask what your request is in relation to?"

"Yes, of course. I'm attached to Op Janus, investigating the Wrenham Green murders and child disappearances. It was a routine check. We found the subject asleep near our FCP. He's not under immediate suspicion. But given the nature of this job, it seemed prudent to make follow-up enquiries."

"I see. The Maypole incidents? It's all the news talks about at the moment. You must have your hands full down there."

"To be honest, Ma'am, I wish we had more leads to follow. Another reason to go the extra mile on that guy, Keith Molloy. We found no trace of prior convictions. His story also checked out with regard to a rented van he was driving. I'm sorry, did you say you were with DVU?"

"That's correct. Mr Molloy hasn't been convicted, but he was involved in a Domestic Violence Protection Order. The victim has since moved away from the area."

Marcus clicked his pen open. "He spoke about taking care of some personal business. May I have the IP's name, in case he followed them here, and it becomes relevant?"

The inspector cleared her throat. "Yes, I should think under the circumstances that might be possible. Standby while I pull up the incident record."

Marcus sat hovering over his notebook, ready to take down the details.

The phone line clicked. "Hello?"

"Go ahead."

"Here we are. The IP was a thirty-year-old woman: Lisa Marston. Hello? DS Foster? Hello?"

The line went dead. In the Op Janus incident room, one last empty chair span from the force with which its occupant left it. Down the hallway a door banged behind a pair of clipping shoes, gathering pace on the vinyl corridor floor.

* * *

"Marcus, what an opportune surprise." Anne Weaver opened the front door at Bramley Cottage while the brass bell still jangled.

The detective leaned in. "Is Lisa about?"

"No. That's why it's opportune. She went off this morning for a drive and hasn't returned. I would've expected her back before dusk. I've tried calling her mobile phone, but it transferred straight onto voicemail. What else can I do? Won't you come in?"

"Only for a minute. I need to tell you something after I make a quick phone call." He stepped in and wiped his feet.

A cacophony of thoughts streamed through the mind of Jeremy Lewis on his evening stroll from Ashdene to the green. In the crook of one arm he held a carved wooden Kingfisher, two hands high. It resembled the larger bird Lisa had once so admired. In the day since their falling out, work on this peace offering had occupied his every waking moment. *Oh man, I hope she likes it.* Would she forgive him? That his brain could not rest with questions and endless 'what if' pondering, made clear what he already suspected: Lisa Marston had stolen his heart. She was fiery, direct, and passionate. A polar opposite of his own temperament. *God help me I love her for it.*

He encircled the green, steps becoming more hesitant as Bramley Cottage loomed ahead. If Lisa was still in a strop, this could all go wrong. He would need to watch every word out of his mouth.

The doorbell rang, and he adjusted the carving to face forward.

"Jeremy. Goodness, please come in." Anne's face appeared strained and wan.

A new worry entered the woodsman's mind. The old schoolteacher wasn't her usual calm and confident self. From the living room, the cascading notes of a mobile phone rang. Anne didn't own one, and it wasn't Lisa's ring-tone.

A man answered. "DS Foster. Vinny? Where? Uh-huh. Any sign of her nearby? What about the van? Okay, I'll be right there." Marcus appeared in the doorway and almost collided with Anne and Jeremy. "Oh, Hello." He caught sight of the worry lines streaking the old woman's forehead. "We've found her car."

Anne gasped. "Where?"

"Somewhere over towards Pett Bottom. Looks like she came off the road."

Jeremy cut in. "Are you talking about Lisa? What's going on? Has she crashed? Is she hurt? Tell me."

"They haven't found her yet." He turned to Anne. "Vince doesn't think it's an accident. He found another set of tracks on the verge."

Jeremy gawped. "Do you believe the killer has abducted her?" His voice trembled.

Marcus put a hand on his shoulder. "She might have been abducted. But I don't think by the killer. Her abusive ex-partner rocked up in Kent yesterday, driving a rental van. I came looking for Lisa when I found out the details. My money's on Mr Molloy as far as this little misadventure goes."

Jeremy rubbed his neck with the free hand. "How can you be sure?"

"I can't. But the missing have all been children so far. Anyone else - well, you know. There's no blood or visible indications of injury at the spot they found her car. It also happened a fair distance from Wrenham Green, not in the village. Those are positive indicators, if we're comparing this to the murders and abductions. I've got authority for a live trace on her phone. Comms Intel will plot any active masts triggered, but it's a vague, best guess situation. That is, if the device is still switched on. Molloy's rental van isn't fitted with a tracker, so we'll need to do this the old fashioned way."

"What about your number plate cameras?"

"ANPR? Fine if he happens to trip one. If he's smart,

he'll stay out in the sticks and keep to the back roads. Now, she might have simply had a mishap behind the wheel, got no signal on her phone and walked off for help. Could turn up wandering the lanes any time."

"But you suspect foul play?"

Marcus put his hands in his pockets. "With everything that's happened, I'd rather not take any chances. She's an intelligent woman. If nothing sinister is in play, I'd expect to hear from her soon. Molloy's out there, either way. I don't like it."

"And you're going to where they found her car?"

"That's right."

"I want to come along. Help search."

Marcus looked him up and down. "Who's the bird for?"

"Lisa. We had a row yesterday. I came over to apologise and give her this gift." Jeremy handed the kingfisher to Anne. "Please let me come. I won't get in the way. If something happens to her and I don't at least try…"

Marcus released a long but subtle exhalation. He pulled the car keys from his pocket. "You do whatever I say, alright?"

"Deal."

"Okay then. Let's see if we can find her."

* * *

Light began to fade inside the machine gun nest. Lisa sat alone, propped near the window slit. Her face hung bloodied and bruised from a severe beating. She also now suffered the indignity of a twisted cloth secured as a gag across her mouth. When Keith had come at her, she screamed, kicked and bit for all she was worth. And then his rough, insistent, bullying penetration commenced. In the gut wrenching moments that followed, he forced himself on her time and again. An action once so joyous and fulfilling when undertaken with a willing desire and requisite arousal, transformed into a painful violation. Her onetime boyfriend behaved as if he had some claim to her body and intimate treasures, like they were his legal right. She sat hunched, sore and heartbroken; used and abused in the worst possible manner. The familiar sound of the van engine burbled in the undergrowth beyond. Its driver's door opened and closed with a slam. Crunching footsteps approached the offset bunker doorway.

"I got some food." Keith's matter-of-fact statement sounded like he had popped out for groceries back at their Durham flat. He squatted in front of the trussed up woman and rummaged around in a thin, rustling plastic bag. "I even bought a bar of your favourite chocolate. 'Whole Nut,' yeah?"

Lisa blinked in disbelief. *It's 'Fruit and Nut,' Shithead. You never could get that right. Jeez, this guy has completely flipped. What's his end game? He can't mean to let me walk away alive.* She moaned into the gag in an attempt to make him remove it.

Keith eyed her and wagged a disapproving finger. "Later. If you're a good girl, we'll have a bite to eat. One noise and you can go without." A cynical grin spread across his Cheshire Catlike face. "I'll let you scream after dark, while we're having some more loving. Bet I can make it hurt so good."

Lisa trembled. Her stomach ached and contracted at the mere thought of his snake hands touching her again. *Won't someone please come and help me? Anyone must be missing me by now. Will the cops think I've been nabbed by the killer? If so, might they limit their search to Wrenham Green and its environs? I'm in a world of hurt. I've got to try to make a break for it somehow.* Beneath her wrists the electrical wiring leash moved a little. While the monster had been out bringing home the unwanted 'bacon,' Lisa managed to rub the twisted binding against a chipped section of concrete walling. It was slow going. But, with her legs lashed together again, the only hope of freeing herself.

Keith sat on the sleeping bag opposite and retrieved a six pack of lager tinnies from his shopping. Between the estranged couple, the crumpled remains of the woman's broken mobile phone lay in pieces on the ground. A fitting metaphor. The second time Keith Molloy had destroyed her personal communication device, and with it any hope of rescue. Or so it seemed. A hiss of escaping gas and the peeling of a metal ring pull followed with copious gulping noises. Muscles chugged in a throat Lisa Marston would have throttled, were her hands to come free. Her ex-partner let out a resounding belch. White teeth grinned at the internal echo from those solid chamber walls. He beamed like a naughty, satisfied schoolboy. Keith scrunched the empty can and tossed it across the cramped, dingy hole. It landed in Lisa's lap. Another ring pull heralded a repeat performance of the same. The woman watched his muscles slacken. *That's it, Tosspot. Why not finish the lot and doze off so I can get the hell out of here?*

"Any luck?" Marcus Foster watched Vince and two uniformed officers emerge from a patch of hazel thicket.

"Sorry, Fuzz." Vinny shook his head.

DS Foster cupped hands to his mouth and called into the undergrowth. "We need to move on, Jeremy."

"I'm here." The woodsman slunk out of the bushes, face downcast.

The detective's phone rang. "DS Foster. Ah, thanks for getting back to me, Ma'am. That's right, Lisa Marston is here in Kent, but missing. I wondered if you had a cell phone number for Molloy? It's a long shot, but we can try for a live trace. Comms Intel will wear this without worries about collateral intrusion, given the circumstances. Yes. Thank you, I'm jotting it down." He hung up and made a fresh call to request an extra trace.

Vince stood next to him and watched Jeremy pace about like a lost lamb. "Do you think Molloy will be dumb enough?"

Marcus stretched. "No idea. Worth a shot. Even if he does, we're talking about a possible search radius of miles in rural terrain. They could be round the next corner right now, holed up in a barn or ditch. Who knows?"

A fourth scrunched lager can clattered into Lisa's lap. Keith leaned his head back against one wall, eyes distant. Without a thought in his groggy mind, he fished a phone from his pocket on autopilot. In the growing darkness, the screen lit up his facial contours with an eerie white highlight. An e-mail notification pinged up. He swiped the screen, deleted the message and scanned social media for five minutes or so. Then he killed the device again. Dreamy clouds lifted from his squinting expression. That docile, empty face spread into a fresh, wakeful grin. He rummaged in his pocket and opened the knife. Lisa shifted against the wall, clamping her legs together. In that moment, she wished them coated in Super Glue. Anything to deny that filthy bastard access to her bruised, intimate core.

"Loving time, Lisa." He moved across, sliced the ankle restraints and pressed his weight against her. Alcohol fumes like cheap cologne forced their way into the woman's nostrils, in a similar fashion to the way Keith would soon force his way into her panties. A slobbering tongue ran up one side of her neck. "What's the matter, darling? Nothing to say?" He pulled away the gag but placed a safeguarding hand across her mouth. With the other he unfastened his trousers and withdrew a semi-aroused male salute, suffering mild effects of 'Brewer's Droop.'

Lisa's wrist cables broke under intense strain, stinging her lower arms. She grabbed onto Keith's scrotum with both hands and dug her nails in as far as they would go. Keith threw back his head to yell, releasing her mouth. He didn't get the sound out. Lisa thrust herself up and butted him full on, screaming at the top of her lungs. Her brow throbbed. The room span, but she couldn't lose this opportunity to run by passing out. It was her last chance, and she knew it. The man coughed and rolled aside in agony. She grabbed the knife and staggered aloft. Uneasy on her feet after so long trussed on the floor, Lisa pushed forward and stumbled through the offset door into the night. The white van sat parked ahead. There hadn't been time to search Keith for the keys. He lay dazed but moving, not even out for the count. That wouldn't last long. She ran on disoriented, clutching the small utility blade in both hands like a talisman.

Keith's furious tone thundered from the trees behind. "I'm going to rip your fucking head off, whore."

Lisa fought down a yelp and prayed a silent prayer not to trip on the uneven woodland floor.

Marcus Foster pulled the vehicle into a passing place on a quiet country lane to answer his phone. On the seat beside him, Jeremy Lewis watched with knitted eyebrows. A police car rolled up behind them, containing Vince and the two uniformed officers.

"DS Foster. Yes Jackie? You're joking. When? Any approximate location? Yeah, I know it. Azimuth two-three-zero. In the direction of 'The Duck' from

Bishopsbourne. Okay, I'm familiar with a few tracks off there someone could park up on. Thanks. Keep me posted on any updates. You're a treasure. Bye." He gunned the engine, and they lurched forward. The police car followed.

Jeremy's seatbelt locked him in place. "You've got something?"

Marcus span the wheel. "Molloy switched his phone on. The mast it activated faces southwest from Bishopsbourne. I did some rural anti-burglary work down there a couple of years back. There are a few good spots to take someone if you don't want to be seen. It's our best lead."

"Thank God." Jeremy wiped his brow.

"Doesn't mean they're sitting still there. But, it's better than nothing."

Lane after tiny lane flashed past in the vehicle headlights. Marcus skidded to a halt on a broad patch of flattened earth, kicking up dust. "This will be a good place to start from." He looked out his own window and muttered under quiet breath. "How's that for modern coppers not having local knowledge, Martin?"

Jeremy grinned. It was a declaration of victory aimed at an absent Martin Coleman, their resident retired policeman. He unfastened his seatbelt and climbed out.

Vince decamped from the car behind. "You shot off at a rate of knots, Fuzz. Found something?"

"Phone activation on the nominal. He's got to be in an arc like that, within two miles at most. I'd say a lot less, from the places I know." Marcus extended his arms out like the hands of a clock.

From somewhere deep in the woods, a female scream split the misty night air.

Jeremy didn't hesitate, plunging up a track with pounding limbs. The four officers ran hot on his heels. A minute later, an angry man shouted across from a nearby rise.

"I'm going to rip your fucking head off, whore."

Marcus halted to get his bearings. "Bingo. This way, lads."

Ahead of them, the crashing of branches spoke of Jeremy Lewis correcting his course mid-flight at the outburst.

Keith cursed the snagging thorns that ripped at his arms. *I'm going to finish that bitch for good. Just wait until I get my hands on her.* Was it the lager that caused his head to swim so? Had that trollop bewitched him with her potent sexuality? No, there was something more. Everything had become dreamlike now; ever since his arrival in that odd little village, early the previous morning. He'd only stopped for a leg stretch and forty winks on the green by that weird pole. Next thing he knew, it was later in the day. *Could the drive south have taken that much out of me?* Why did the loneliness of recent weeks seem not to sting anymore? Somehow he was never alone, like something else accompanied him wherever he went. And then there was a curious growing sense of power within. He felt invincible. Subduing Lisa had been easier than he'd feared. His limbs coursed with a newfound vibration of strength.

God, she was even sweeter forced than willing. If I catch her in a good spot, I'll treat myself one more time before I finish her for good. I must finish her. She can't be allowed to live. Call it intuition, but something inside is telling me to take her life. Just like it told me how to corner her. Time to go with the flow. It hasn't steered me wrong thus far.

Lisa wanted to cry out, but the thought of giving her position away kept her mouth shut fast. Keith wasn't making any effort to hide his movements, yet still her pursuer closed the distance with every pace. He was impossible to avoid, no matter which way she turned. *You would think some unseen snitch is guiding him. Where can I hide that he won't find me?* Her limbs ached and went numb. *I can't go much further. My energy is spent.*

"There you are." Keith's exclamation sapped any last strength from her body.

Lisa's legs gave way, and she collapsed onto the earth like a toppling house of cards.

"No. No, please don't." Her words were a whisper.

Keith stormed forward. In that horrific moment his eyes glowed a dull red, echoing those sinister children in the ash grove. At any moment violent hands would grab hold of the woman and finish the job.

Lisa swallowed and thought of her parents, Auntie Joan and poor old Anne. "Please God, make it quick."

One muscular hand reached for her throat. A lunging silhouette dived through the bushes and swiped it away. Her attacker tumbled into a clump of roots, assailed by another man. From off to her right, the woman caught the crashing report of more figures approaching. Torch beams swayed in the darkness, scanning like floodlights during an air raid.

One voice called out. "Over there."

Footsteps thundered closer, merging with a bone-crunching exchange of blows from the fighting men.

"Give him a hand," another voice shouted.

There was enough torchlight now for the desperate and confused young woman to make out two policemen and some familiar faces. Keith rolled over and tensed like a cornered wild animal. The other combatant - now bloodied and scarred from their frantic struggle - threw himself on top. The policemen hurried over to bring order to chaos. One torch beam fell on the woman's saviour.

"Jeremy?" Lisa's eyes watered. She raised both hands to cover her mouth.

'Uniform' bundled Keith Molloy into the rear of the police car, hands secured in rigid cuffs on his lap.

Lisa clutched tight to Jeremy as Marcus Foster opened his own vehicle. The detective eyed her with a glint. "We'd better get you checked out in Canterbury." He nodded at the woodsman. "You too. That bloke gave you quite a kicking."

Jeremy licked some salty blood from one corner of his mouth. "He's stronger than he looks. From the state of Lisa, I guess you'll be adding an aggravated assault charge to kidnapping?"

"And rape." Lisa mumbled the words with an

emotionless tone.

Jeremy and Marcus exchanged pained glances. The woodsman peered down into her heartbroken eyes.

Lisa burst into tears. "I feel so dirty."

Jeremy cradled her jerking head with one caring hand. He kissed her crown and stroked the woman's nut-brown hair with loving fingers. "Shh now. Everything's going to be okay."

14

Old Flame, New Fire

"Lisa?" Anne's voice called up the stairs. "Lisa, Marcus Foster is here to see you."

The northerner stared at her reflection in the bathroom mirror with vacant eyes. A shell of a woman stared back, the spark of life little more than an ember in its zombie-like expression. In the twenty-four hours since her rescue, she had struggled to find energy or words. Most of the morning passed curled up in bed, like a chronic depression sufferer struggling to find a reason to get up. Anne was a sweetheart, of course; tiptoeing around her with gossamer softness and motherly concern. For the most part, she let the young woman sleep and gave her some space. When the northerner summoned enough will to crawl out of her pit, showering lasted an age. No matter how hard Lisa scrubbed, that feeling of dirtiness refused to wash away. The ever-present memory of Keith's carnal assault clung to her like a limpet. A psychic sensation of his body forcing itself upon hers, lingered in the manner of a phantom limb to an amputee. Keith was absent yet present. An uninvited guest emptying her storehouse of emotional provisions. She managed little more than a bowl of soup for lunch, before retiring to her room again. There were requests for articles waiting in her e-mail. Under normal circumstances this would deliver a boost of positivity to her soul. Today, their impact registered nothing. Lisa couldn't bring herself to respond to clients or even think about writing. Trips to the bathroom happened three times an hour. Anxiety released the floodgates of her bladder; self-control but a distant memory.

As the sky faded with the setting sun, her thoughts turned to Jeremy. When he rescued her, she was almost incoherent and dazed. At lunch, Anne presented her the beautiful carved kingfisher the woodsman brought for a peace offering. Lisa needed to see him. That was how she found herself in front of the bathroom mirror, checking her appearance.

"How are you feeling?" Anne's tender voice belied a furtiveness of facial presentation as Lisa reached the bottom stair.

Lisa fidgeted and played with a strand of her hair. "I'm getting there." She moved her attention onto the detective hovering in the hallway by the deep-toned grandfather clock. "How can I help?"

Marcus rubbed his chin. Watery eyes narrowed and flitted from side to side with hasty distractedness.

The young woman caught Anne's uneasy posture. "What's happened?"

Anne squeezed her hands together, bony fingers clicking. "Oh dear."

Marcus edged closer. "I'm afraid Keith Molloy has escaped."

Lisa's mouth dropped open. "How?"

"He overpowered staff in the custody suite when they opened his cell door. One received a broken arm and fractured collar bone for their trouble. Keith got out the back into the yard before they could trip the panic alarm. He made it through the closing vehicle gate with the agility of a gazelle and disappeared."

"And you think he's coming here?"

"I don't know. When I heard, my first concern was for your safety. At least with the present operation camped out front, the job can keep an eye on the cottage. We'll have a car parked this side of the green. That way we can rotate officers *standing by to standby* at the command vehicle."

One corner of Lisa's mouth twisted into a smirk. Odd, given such worrying news. A mild, rising sarcasm at the man's police jargon brought some welcome relief to scrunched muscles contracting at the base of her neck. "Standing by to standby?"

Marcus snorted and looked at the floor. "Yeah. And no, before you ask there isn't a *standing by to be standing by to standby*."

Lisa leaned back against the wall. "You've heard that one before, then."

"I know. It's another language."

"I was off to visit Jeremy Lewis. We have a lot to talk about. I wanted to thank him for… - well a lot of things, actually."

Marcus' face darkened. "I don't like the idea of you

wandering around in the dark with that lunatic at large."

"Jeremy lives off a quiet lane the other side of the hill. Not far."

"Hmm. If I escort you over there, could he bring you back?"

"I should think so."

"Alright then. Are you ready to go?"

The pair encircled the green and took the lane to Ashdene. It was a pleasant evening for a stroll; warm with the faintest hint of a breeze.

Lisa smoothed back her hair. "I haven't thanked you and your colleagues for locating me yet. Sorry. I owe you my life, as well as Jeremy."

Marcus sighed. "Would that we could have arrived sooner. Before... Anyway, the judge will throw the book at Molloy when we catch him. I hope you won't have to confine yourself under voluntary house arrest for long. As it stands, I'd stay home for a few days if I were you. He'll turn up."

"How did Jeremy end up part of the search team?"

"He insisted on it. I made routine enquiries on Molloy after we found him stretched out asleep on the green. Any strange face is worth looking into. Op Janus has drawn a blank at every turn. It's like banging our heads against a bloomin' brick wall."

"Op Janus? Is that the name for your Maypole investigation?"

"It is. I didn't choose it. Our Ops Planning

department pick the names from a pre-selected list."

"I see."

"When we discovered Molloy hailed from Durham, I put in an info request to the force up there. An Inspector in their Domestic Violence Unit gave me your name and a little background. I rushed straight over to Wrenham Green, found you missing and Anne at a loss. Jeremy showed up right after with a carved wooden bird. Said you guys had a bust up and he'd come round to smooth things over. When he discovered you were missing, he pleaded with me to come along. I could catch a flea in my ear for lack of procedure, but I wasn't going to turn him down. I hope you two fix things up. Whatever bad words were exchanged, actions still speak louder."

Lisa punched the policeman's upper arm with a gentle prod of her knuckles. "You're quite a romantic beneath that business-like, professional facade. Is there a Mrs Foster? I never asked before."

"No."

"Married to the job?"

"God, I hope not. Whoops, that came out wrong. I love what I do. It's tough on relationships and families though. I promised myself I'd wait and see who happened along. Better than trying to make something out of nothing with a random stranger."

"Still waiting?"

Marcus coughed. "You *are* direct, aren't you?"

"Sorry."

"Don't apologise. In the short time since we left Bramley Cottage, you've perked up. Not a bad thing at all. You've been through quite an ordeal."

"So?"

"What?"

"Are you still waiting?"

"Oh, yeah. Still waiting. Beginning to think it wasn't such a smart strategy. I'm thirty-five now with no prospects in my affective life. Most of my old school friends are raising kids."

Lisa swung her arms in a playful manner. "Maybe it's time to stop *standing by to standby*."

Marcus laughed. "Or even *standing by*."

"What's the police speak for getting into the fray, Marcus?"

"Go! Go! Go!"

Lisa grinned. "I like that. Please remember it next time a nice young lady makes you look twice, would you?"

The detective clicked an imaginary radio on his lapel and spoke into it. "All received. Out."

A thick, choking smell of wood smoke hung on the air at a bend in the narrow lane.

Lisa cleared her throat and wiped smarting eyes. "Someone's got a serious bonfire."

Marcus craned his head past the apex of the curve. "It's no bonfire."

Lisa's head bobbed up beside him. A hundred yards beyond on the other side of a hedge, the sky glowed with an intense orange hue. Sparks flew upward like fireflies into a starless night sky, enshrouded with low clouds. The woman began trotting, wrists hanging limp at her sides. "That's Ashdene. That's Jeremy's place."

The pair broke into a run.

* * *

"You thought you could interfere between a man and his partner." Keith Molloy stood in the middle of the pole barn living room at Ashdene, fists clenched, knuckles whitening.

Jeremy Lewis lifted his head from where he lay spread-eagled on the wooden floor. One foot still rested on the coffee table he had tumbled across from the force of the abuser's blows. The woodsman squinted through the pain. His left eye socket puffed up and swelled into a reddening mass that half obscured his vision. Jeremy touched the bruising with a delicate hand, recoiling in an instant from the sting. His raised ankle came away from the table and crashed to the floor. At that moment he realised how bad the fall had sprained it. Forearms pushed his upper torso into a press-up position. He craned his head around to meet Keith's furious eyes. The front door at Ashdene still swung where his assailant burst through it. The strength and demeanour of the man had startled Jeremy, last time they crossed figurative swords. Tonight in his own home, the effect was amplified tenfold.

Keith Molloy threw back his head to emit a deep-throated gargling sound. It rippled like the intimidating growl of a leopard before its lunge. When the countenance lowered again, two glowing red orbs like twin setting suns replaced the man's eyes. Facial muscles contorted into a frontage of pure hatred. Air hissed between clenched teeth. The lower jaw sank into what must have been a dislocated position, lending the head an appearance of heart-stopping aggression. When the words came, they rang with resonant force.

"No-one comes between Nidhogg and his quarry."

Mouth open like a long dark tunnel, Keith swept his extending neck around like a swaying cobra preparing to strike. Those eyes blazed again as he inhaled.

Jeremy froze, paralysed by fear and disbelief. A jet of flame erupted from Keith's distended oral orifice, scorching the top of Jeremy's head and setting the wall behind ablaze.

In his stupor at the impossible sequence of events, one word chased through the woodsman's brain: *Nidhogg. But it's a myth.*

That life stealing glare locked onto him again. Head rearing up, the monster took a breath deep enough to fill cavernous lungs many times the size of a normal man's. Jeremy rolled aside, colliding with his home brew shelving. A beer bottle filled for outdoor consumption dropped into his lap. The woodsman swiped it up and hurled the receptacle end over end. Its butt struck the semi-human creature full on the forehead and shattered into a glimmering spray of brown glass. Beer hissed with splashing impact upon a head wreathed in smoke and steam. Jeremy's stomach doubled over. It was like blowing spit balls at someone sporting a Howitzer. Flames spread from the wall to the gable. Splotches of burning liquid rained down upon the trembling homeowner. One splashed on his right shoulder, burned through his shirt and scorched the flesh. More than pure fire, this oral emission sprayed, stuck and singed like napalm. The beast spun and coated the igniting building interior with a fresh jet of its devastating breath weapon. Jeremy pressed his back against the shelving. His fingers scrambled for purchase and leverage in a vain attempt to raise himself up. Half way to his feet, the weight of his own body on the damaged ankle dropped him like a stone to his starting position. A wall of heat blackened his sweating face with soot. Air became thin and smoky. Each breath strained in a desperate struggle to locate vanishing oxygen. His head throbbed. The room swayed through his clouding field of vision. A rafter crashed down into the structure and split asunder, one end crackling and glowing with an orange intensity. Billowing black smoke ascended and descended, forcing the woodsman to press his face onto the floor in one final bid to retain consciousness. The far end of the pole barn collapsed, evacuating some choking fumes into a gentle night breeze. In the closing tunnel of vision, Jeremy locked onto the figure of a familiar, sixty-year-old village resident. Short white hair receded around his temples, to form a pronounced point. Piercing grey eyes glimmered out of a square head, watching, assessing, attempting to fathom and get a handle on this crisis situation.

"What the?" Martin Coleman stepped aside to avoid another collapsing rafter. His calm gaze pierced through the heat haze to see Jeremy on the floor. Some distorted figure of a man loomed above the helpless fellow, several feet closer to where he stood. "Jeremy?" He shouted to make his voice heard above the roaring conflagration. Still the sound faded away, muffled by the thunderous flames. "Jeremy?" He bellowed with years of practised authority at projecting his voice.

The heaving figure leered with seeming indifference to the surrounding fire. It twisted its head and an inhuman, elongated neck around. Eyes like glowing rubies seared into the widening orbs of the retired police officer.

"Oh my God." Martin Coleman got a hold of his breath. Many was the time he had entered an intimidating situation during his career. No matter how scared you felt, a police officer must never show fear. One hint of weakness and you could lose control of a dangerous sequence of events. He was also no stranger to the supernatural, having once been stationed at the well-haunted Cranbrook nick. But this thing was no poltergeist. They were way beyond noisy spirits, disembodied singing maidens, spinning waste bin lids and slamming cell doors now. *What in the name of all that's holy, is that?* His mind wrestled with the picture his senses painted it, live and in vivid colour. This thing bearing the scant appearance of a man couldn't be human, despite its upright, two-legged posture. What then? *Get a hold of yourself, Coleman. Jeremy Lewis is in trouble and nobody else can help him now.* The old officer sucked in his breath and allowed his chest to swell. Muscles tightened in his face. He barked a command at the bizarre and horrific apparition. "Get away from him this instant."

The creature turned its back on the old man. One foot lifted to step closer to the injured woodsman, laying pressed against a wall. Timbers behind him caught light with the rest of the structure.

Martin hunted left and right. A plain, stiff wooden chair rested beside a refurbished sideboard with a distressed look. He grabbed the back of it in both hands. The legs came up to point at the spine of the swelling monster ahead. The checked shirt it wore split asunder. Skin beneath blistered and popped into a mass of black, scaly pustules of reptilian appearance. Martin tensed his arms, lowered his head and charged. The legs of the furniture crashed into the backbone of the heaving monstrosity. They split like matchsticks, leaving the retired police officer with a couple of bits of broken wood in his hands. The inertia sent him colliding into the thing with considerable force. It staggered and turned as Martin stumbled and lost his footing.

The wall behind Jeremy gave way. He covered his head with both arms. Burning chunks of splintered timber and clanging, corrugated roof panels fell on top of him.

"Jeremy!"

It was a woman's voice this time.

"Marcus, help me." Lisa appeared out of the darkness, ducking and bobbing through blazing panels of wood. She ran with purpose in her stride, like an angel of mercy on a rescue mission in hell.

DS Foster made her side a second later. "Go for the

roofing panel first. Easy Lisa, we don't want to drop those burning slats on him."

A huge piece of corrugated metal lifted from the woodsman's legs. Jeremy winced.

Marcus tipped the panel aside. Lisa squatted beside the injured man and flung her arms around his neck. A single gasp escaped her mouth before she withdrew. This was no time for sentiment or an emotional breakdown. "Can you stand?"

"Not unaided. I can't put any weight on one ankle."

Marcus rose with the steady, unconscious consistency of the bewildered. His astounded gaze fixed on the twisting and transforming man-beast in the middle of the flaming barn. An empty gasp and gentle head shake accompanied his ascent. "Is that Molloy? But…"

Lisa followed his line of sight. "Wha…?"

Jeremy let out a choking rasp, desperate for fresh air. Much of the smoke had dissipated with his disintegrating home, but sooty fumes still caked his throat. "It *was* him."

The beast staggered where it stood. A burning wooden beam shattered across its back with a shower of sparks. Martin Coleman had found his feet again and another improvised weapon. A claw-like hand with fingers bursting into talons, whipped across his face. He flew backwards, reeled and crashed into the yard outside Jeremy's workshop.

Marcus Foster clenched a fist and reached down to slip the other hand beneath one of Jeremy's armpits. He pulled the spluttering man aloft. "See if you can support him enough to evacuate, Lisa."

The woman wrapped Jeremy's free arm around her shoulders and placed a hand in the small of his back. "Okay Marcus, let go."

The officer complied. Lisa's legs almost gave way at the sudden burden, but she fought back and held the injured fellow fast. "Okay. Okay, I think I can do it. What about you?"

The conflagration raged with almost deafening noise and power.

Marcus ripped off the blue blazer and rolled up his shirt sleeves. "I'm going to help Martin and buy you some time. If you find a quiet spot, call for help as soon as you can."

"Will do. If Jeremy has his phone." Her stinging eyes reddened and watered. "Good luck." She hesitated.

Marcus frowned at them both. "Go. Now."

Lisa and Jeremy hobbled back towards the gate. Toppling walls had fallen into the hedge bordering the lane, igniting its dry twigs. A barrier of fire prevented further egress, encircling three quarters of the site in a roaring arc. Waves of heat beat them back, as if in service to the supernatural creature.

Jeremy pointed his head in the opposite direction. "Up the track. It's our only chance."

Lisa helped him turn around. They skirted what remained of the barn exterior and struggled towards the uphill path.

Martin Coleman propped himself on one arm. He panted, winded and shaken from a blow of such force. In a mirror replay of his last attempt to engage the creature, another burning beam broke across the scaly hide of its morphing shape. Marcus Foster stood, bottom lip curled over his teeth in rage, clutching the smoking remains of the shattered club. The hideous thing roared; a sound that caused ripples of fear to quiver across all within earshot. Another taloned hand jabbed out and connected with the detective's body. He toppled backwards into a burning bookcase. The tall unit fell on top of him. Marcus struggled, pinned in situ and half buried beneath a pile of smouldering, vintage hardback volumes.

The growling monster continued to swell. Twin horns pierced the scalp of its enlarged head, sliding skyward. The long neck slithered left and right, fiery eyes scanning the site in search of something. It halted with that mangled, once-human visage fixed on a pathetic pair of figures: A man and woman limping through a gap in the flames to an uphill path.

The fire spread to Jeremy's workshop. Martin picked himself up and threw his body against the door like a human battering ram. It caved on the third attempt, dropping him onto an iron-bound chest. At the rear of the structure beyond a group of carved wooden animals, sat a workbench. A flickering glow of firelight gleamed off the metal of Jeremy's chainsaw. Martin pressed on, hands outstretched. "I hope he keeps that thing filled."

The beast strode with echoing footsteps that shook the ground between the buildings. From one structure, a motor starter cord ripped. The revving of a small petrol engine pierced the general cacophony of burning destruction. Martin lumbered from the workshop and brought Jeremy's buzzing chainsaw blade down upon the creature's left shoulder. Dark blood sprayed out in the manner of molten mud from a geyser. The monster wailed like a bear in pain, twisted and stepped back. Its other taloned hand lifted to hold the wound together. Glowing eyes narrowed to slits. It sucked in a deep breath, fang-like teeth clenched at the audacity of this pathetic mortal challenger. A ball of fire blasted from its mouth between the two combatants, igniting the chainsaw petrol tank with a sharp explosion. Martin let the shredded power tool fall with a dull clatter. He shook and writhed in screaming agony, body awash with the burning accelerant.

Marcus Foster reached out a trembling hand in anguish from beneath the pile of books. The toppled shelving still held him prisoner, rigid and immobile.

Martin Coleman leapt and pirouetted with an almost balletic grace outside his years or character, in a horrid dance of pain.

Marcus ground his teeth. Tears stung the trapped detective's blackened cheeks in cleansing trails. "No. Martin." A blur of childhood memories flooded back: the faithful police officer talking about dedication and service to the community in their school assembly. A day that changed his life forever. He snapped back to the present. The burning, retired officer's movements became more robotic and unnatural. His old, white hair erupted like a roman candle. He hesitated on one spot, swayed then toppled back into the collapsing workshop.

The creature lifted its wounded shoulder and blew a short, concentrated burst of fire to sear and cauterise the chainsaw incision. Its pulsating red eyes caught the heartbroken expression on the pinned man's face. Fangs poking through a gradually elongating face spread into a satisfied grin. The beast turned and marched with forceful steps toward the woodland track. The footfalls seemed to grow in power and impact, contrary to its widening distance from the former homestead.

A thick, musky coating of blood agitated Marcus' dry palate. What little remained of the room span. He blacked out.

* * *

"Lisa?" Jeremy choked and spluttered, almost overcome with pain, smoke and exertion. They were ascending the narrow dirt path at an agonising snail's pace.

Whenever she dared, Lisa stole a glimpse back over their shoulders. "What is it?"

"I came to apologise." He gagged. "The day Keith abducted you, I mean."

"Marcus told me."

An ear-splitting howl of some beast in agony rang out from down below. Its infernal report seemed to shake the very roots of the trees about them.

Lisa stumbled. She caught herself a split second before they would have both fallen into the undergrowth. "Look. Do we have to do this now?"

The crack of a limited explosion like a powerful gunshot, filled the cool night air. Distant screams of a human man in convulsive agony replaced it.

Even though Ashdene lay out of sight, Lisa still strained her eyes into the darkness of the tree-lined slope behind. "Oh God."

Jeremy staggered, putting more weight on his struggling helper. "I also came to tell you how I felt about you. How I feel."

"Jeremy, this isn't the time. We need-"

"Please. If I don't get this out now and that thing catches up with us, I may never get the chance."

It was the most vulnerable and open she had ever seen him. "I know. Believe me, I know. I feel the same way. Come on."

Jeremy eyed the approaching, familiar boughs of the old ash grove. "That creature referred to itself as Nidhogg when it spoke to me. Seems your dream was something more after all. Remind me not to doubt you in the future. If any of us *have* a future."

Twigs and earth jumped and jostled as if stirred by some seismic tremor. The couple rested against a broad trunk, facing back down the path from which they entered the clearing.

Jeremy's back slid along the rough bark, sinking him into a squat. "What are we going to do? How do you kill that thing?"

Lisa shut her eyes and took a deep breath through her nose. With every step that brought the bizarre, melded apparition of Keith Molloy and Nidhogg closer, the air about her sizzled with electricity. Fine hairs rose on her lower arms, as if awoken by static. Was Keith even still alive, or had that evil entity from some fairy tale netherworld consumed him without a trace?

The ground shook with greater ferocity. Two horns protruding through a once human head appeared near the brow of the hill. But the head was human no longer. Now the size of a small car, its long snout and rows of dagger-like teeth squeezed between the dense canopy.

Lisa's entire frame shook, but not from fear. The realisation of what she must do settled the matter in her inner being before words were ever spoken. A silent vow and offering of unconditional surrender sealed a contract within. This may have been a living nightmare, but it was no dream. They were real: the Norns, Nidhogg, the whole mythical party. Or spirit beings that identified themselves to this realm under those monikers.

A pair of red eyes, grown to the size of traffic lights, seared into her face from beyond the grove. Spiteful, menacing thoughts projected out of the creature into her brain. *You will not vanquish me. The children are mine. My transition to your world has come. This is my dominion now.*

Jeremy rummaged on the ground for a broken branch to use as a temporary crutch. Tears of shock and pain welled up in his eyes. He levered himself vertical to stand beside the woman he loved.

Lisa stepped in front with her back to him. Calm

resolve left her brow unblemished by any lines of concern. She flung both arms wide and threw back her head. The cry of the northerner's furious and passionate heart formed her internal sacrifice of devotion into words. In the cold light of day she would never dream of making such an utterance. It came from somewhere deep in her soul; a hidden place she never knew existed. "I offer myself to the fight. Take me, Skuld. I am your handmaiden. Take me now."

15

Malice Striker

The ash grove transformed into something not of this world. Its normal backdrop of rolling countryside beyond the trees vanished. A canvas of galactic wonder replaced it, like some deep space NASA photo imagery. Stars, solar systems, colourful planets and racing comets encircled the scene. The trees shone with a brilliant radiance, their roots visible and connected in a living web. Beyond the grove, an immense tree trunk reached up to touch countless realms above and down to many more beneath.

Jeremy lost his balance, disoriented by the spinning spray of stars and other heavenly bodies all about them. He fell into a patch of gleaming grass that glowed with emerald luminosity. Its touch caressed his arms and soothed the swelling ankle. Sweet fragrances calmed his shocked and shaking form.

A voice like a mountain spring tinkled down from the branches of the trees. "I knew you would come, child."

Lisa turned to meet the radiant mauve eyes of Skuld, peering through her delicate veil. The giant Norn floated to touch bare feet down on the lush grass.

A flash of forked blue lightning arced overhead. Its crack tore the peaceful scene apart. A whiff of ozone mixed with an aroma of putrid decay, descended upon the figures. Pitch black clouds formed about them, spreading out to cover the starry backdrop like ink droplets in water.

Another fork of lightning exploded, a strobing sapphire flare. Lisa covered her head and ducked. "What must I do?"

Skuld reduced in stature, like some character in a children's story after drinking a magic potion. She offered both hands to Lisa. "You have already done it. Let us be one now. There is not much time. Nidhogg comes. His power grows with every beat of your heart. Together we can bridge the worlds and banish him from your realm. We must drive the dragon back to Náströnd and imprison him once again beneath the roots of Yggdrasil."

Lisa extended her own hands to clasp Skuld's. Their fingers entwined. A ball of white light burst around them.

Jeremy shielded his eyes and found himself alone in the transformed grove. The encircling ash trees shook. Red light seared up from the ground, splitting their trunks in jagged fracture lines. The wood broke apart and dropped away. On an outer ring of trees, enough of the bark remained to form gnarled, ragged cages. They gave the appearance of organic gibbet irons, twisted but firm. Inside each, children between the ages of seven and eleven cried out for help. Some shook the spiritual, wooden bars. The youngest sat huddled and crying in balls of wailing terror. The woodsman recognised them at once from the Mayday festival. He wanted to speak, but no words came. Another thunderclap shook the grove. This time the trees of the inner ring followed the action of their neighbours. More children cried and trembled from within them. Jeremy looked from face to face. No features were familiar, but something about their clothing jolted his memory. "It cannot be." He pushed himself up and found his ankle strong as new. "The 1945 children are still here too?"

The ground shuddered with rhythmic frequency. A knot of dread grew in the woodsman's stomach like a fetid, gnawing tumour. *Where is Lisa? I've got to try to free those kids before Nidhogg comes.* He ran to the nearest tree, containing a girl of about seven. Memories of news reports and missing person posters brought her name straight to his lips. "Karen Randall?"

A slender, trembling hand poked through the gap. Jeremy took hold of it and clasped the lithe fingers in both palms. *Should I tell her we've come to take them home? What if I can't get them out?*

A deafening roar followed by some sort of impact burst from behind the huge, distant tree trunk.

Jeremy gazed in that direction. *Can that be Yggdrasil? Am I seeing this because that's how childhood stories conditioned my mind to understand the spirit realm?* He cast the idea aside. *No. Lisa has no background in all this, and we're here together. Or we were.* He rubbed his chin and scanned the grove for anything that might be of help. Several chunks of the split bark rested in the grass at his feet. He crouched and rummaged to find a piece strong enough to use as a lever. "Get as far back as you can, Karen. I'm going to try to break the bars."

The girl flattened herself against the opposite side of her cramped hutch.

Jeremy inserted the wood through one gap and pushed all his weight against it. Sweat poured down his face, but the prison remained firm. "Come on. Oh please, come on."

Beyond the outer trees, indistinct shadows clustered and flitted between the inky backdrop obscuring the rotating heavens. Beady pairs of red eyes the size of rose hips, gathered and drew closer. The ground shook with renewed vigour. Something massive also approached, beyond the range of vision. Every few steps the pounding ceased, interrupted by a clashing of blows. A roar followed each impact, accompanied by another sound: Pure, with crystal-like clarity and fervent, righteous anger. It was the battle cry of some inhuman female.

Those beady eyes swarmed into the grove. Dark, formless imps flitted about the woodsman. Tiny, claw-like hands ripped at his arms and legs, tearing the flesh. Jeremy let go of the lever and tugged at the shifting shapes. Every time his hands caught hold of one, it slipped through his fingers like elusive sand. Two more took its place, now jumping on his shoulders, tearing at his head and neck. He tumbled into the fragrant grass, its brilliance darkened by the raging storm. To and fro his body rolled, each change of direction an attempt to fight off the relentless assault of Nidhogg's minions.

Chattering, savage voices swirled from the mass of attackers. "Protect the Master's prize. They must not get away."

Jeremy shouted, kicked and punched for all he was worth. It was like wrestling with air that fought back. Another series of thunderous footfalls set the imprisoned children to screaming. A vast, menacing black shadow loomed overhead. Its size obscured what little light remained. The imps ceased their assault enough for Jeremy to turn and peer into the blackness. His eyes struggled to discern any kind of outline or shape.

A collective hiss of awe carried across the grove from the evil underlings. "He has come."

* * *

"Fuzz? Easy, Mate." Vince reached down to touch his colleague's shoulder where he lay beneath a fallen bookcase. "KFRS will have this off you in a jiff."

Marcus Foster blinked through blurred eyes. "Vinny?" A rush of sound like hissing steam greeted his woolly ears. His head tingled; a fragile eggshell that threatened to crack at any moment. All about him a busy fire crew hosed down the smoking remains of Ashdene under halogen lamps. Not a single building remained standing. His hands splayed out on drenched wooden floorboards. A whiff of charred and soaked fabrications acted like smelling salts, slapping him round the face. "Martin Coleman." He waved one aching arm. "He's over there. You've got to…"

An ambulance crew lifted a zipped body bag from the remnants of Jeremy's workshop.

"No." He screwed up his eyes, lips crinkled.

Two firemen pulled the bookcase off the flattened detective. Vince tossed some fallen books aside and helped his tensing colleague up. "Whoa there. We need to get you looked at by SECAMB. The paramedics are-"

"How long since Lisa and Jeremy called you?"

"Lisa and Jeremy? You mean the Marston girl? I thought you were visiting the old lady's place to tell her to stay put?"

"I did. She wanted to see her fella, so I walked her over here. That's when we found the place on fire and Jeremy under attack from Molloy." The last word caught in his throat. How was he ever going to relay any of what he'd seen during the blaze?

"Molloy was here? Shit. Well, that explains a few things."

Marcus ran a hand through his hair. "Sort of. Jeremy suffered a damaged ankle. Lisa helped him out. She was going to call you when they reached safety."

Vince shook his head. "Don't know anything about that. We showed up when things started going bang. Could've sworn it sounded like a roar myself. Must have been gas canisters for the stove. Where's Molloy?"

"He killed Martin Coleman." It was the truth, if not the *whole* truth.

"The old copper?"

"Yeah."

"That who's in the bag?"

Marcus nodded.

Vince bit his lip. "Poor bloke. He was burned so bad I had no idea who it was. What happened next?"

"Molloy went after Lisa and Jeremy. Up into the woods."

"Crap. Do you think they made it back to the village?"

"She'd have rung."

Vince pulled his mobile phone out and eyed his battered friend. "Let me check with the FCC Duty Inspector. If the girl didn't call in, we'd better ask his authority to launch QH99. Otherwise we're gonna end up with two more dead bodies to deal with."

At Boreham in Essex across the Thames Estuary, blades from a two-toned dark blue and yellow Police Euro-copter span up on its base pad. The 145mph vehicle lifted into a still night sky. It turned and climbed in a southerly direction, strobes winking in visual accompaniment to the whining engine. On board, the pilot stared out across the rippling body of water separating them from the North Kent coast. His observer ran a systems check and surveyed a moving map at his operation station in the rear. A radio transmission reached out across the airwaves to their inbound force.

"Quebec-Hotel-Nine-Nine airborne. Estimated time en route: twenty minutes. Over."

* * *

Jeremy froze. The inky clouds were rent asunder by a ray of ivory light. In the illumination provided by re-exposed whirling stars, the beast became visible in all his monstrous glory: Four muscular legs, a thick, long tail, black rugged scales and that viciously spiked and horned head. Childhood stories about dragons didn't come close to the terror evoked by gazing upon the fear-inducing form of Nidhogg. How could any of this be real? The woodsman found enough courage to tear his stare away from the cavernous maw of that enormous, black-winged creature of legend. The pillar-like tree of Yggdrasil connected with countless worlds. Were there endless realities too? Endless realms and parallel astral planes in which dwelt heavenly figures from a myriad of belief systems? Jeremy had no faith to speak of. He was suspicious of all religions and considered each one's claim to have a handle on truth as bunk. He swallowed hard, questions whirling through his mind like colliding spinning tops. *What if they're all true? Unlimited possibilities and outcomes based on the paths we choose in our hearts.* The concept almost blew his mind. *Does this place exist because some ancient, primitive people collectively dreamt it? Or was it always here, and they connected to it with their culture? Am I dead?* What was he doing? This was no time for philosophical introspection. Real or imagined, created or eternal, alive or dead, he was still cowering in front of a bloody great dragon!

All about him the shadowy servants of darkness bowed down to their master. An awe-filled chant of reverence added a disturbing arcane soundtrack to an already devastating scene.

Bursts of light struck the dragon between his shoulders. The creature lifted its massive, spiny horned head and swung a sinuous, long, scaled neck about. A well-armoured warrior maiden strode forth into the grove and raised a round shield in her left hand. In her right, a glowing white sword swooshed back and forth in the air. The woman must have been twice Jeremy's height. She stood clad in a figure-hugging leather breastplate with golden metal greaves, vambraces and pauldrons to match a long shining mane of yellow hair. A pair of white feathered wings protruded from her back. Nidhogg lowered his neck and blew out a broad jet of thunderous flame. His challenger took flight. She soared over the beast to land in the middle of the inner ring of prison trees. Nidhogg stamped all four of his gargantuan, taloned feet in rapid succession. A heart-stopping bellow of rage shook the grove.

Jeremy eyed the impressive shield maiden. *Lisa? Can it be you?* He watched from the outer ring, fingers clutching the base of Karen Randall's cage.

The warrior knelt as if genuflecting at an altar. She jammed the sword into the earth. Rivulets of pure light ran out in all directions. Streams of shimmering radiance connected with the inner cages. The wood on each split and shattered like the crack of a whip. Ten shaking, crying children pushed themselves clear of their cramped cells.

Nidhogg raised his head and inhaled. Broad, leathery cheeks puffed. The warrior pulled her blade from the ground and held it aloft. A curtain of translucent energy - liquid, living marble - stretched to cover the inner circle. Flames licked and choking smoke bounced off the swirling cover, deflecting back into the air. The winged maiden turned to where the children clustered together. Her mauve eyes blazed in a rhythmic pulse. She spoke with a firm but gentle voice, crisp and clear as ice. "This gift I give you. Be not afraid and help your brethren." The children ceased their shivering and rose in a calm unison of common intent. As one, they radiated out to the cages containing their age and gender peers across a multi-generational time span. A seven-year-old girl with fair hair approached Karen Randall's prison. Jeremy let go of the trunk, at once recognising her face from an old black-and-white photograph at Bramley Cottage. "Beth?" The word came out as a whisper.

Nidhogg's tail walloped into the earth. The warrior leapt aside and delivered a lacerating flick of the glowing sword. Howls rose as the dragon stumbled and swept its injured appendage about, spraying ebony blood like molten tar.

The freed children grabbed hold of the bars imprisoning the others. A cry of outrage rippled from the surrounding shadow minions. Clouds of biting, tearing imps hurled themselves at the would-be liberators. Jeremy scrambled to his feet and retrieved the lever. He swung and struck the branch at the throng of heaving shapes landing on Beth Weaver. At every strike they came back with greater ferocity; more numerous and vicious than before. All about the outer circle, the rescuers seemed to pulse and hum. With each fresh attack from the dragon's servants, a corresponding surge of light grew within the children. On the far side, a deafening explosion shook the grove. Jeremy whirled about, his hands still swinging the club. One of the outer cages lay in tatters, its prisoner freed. But the child rescuer no longer glowed. Instead, a wispy form lingered for one brief moment to watch its grateful peer. Without a further word, the shape rose into the air and ascended Yggdrasil to another plane of existence. A second explosion ripped open the next tree, obliterating nearby attackers. Jeremy watched again as the same, heart-breaking result played out before him. The kids from his own time were being freed. But at what cost? He whirled back to Beth. She wasn't pulsing and humming like the rest. Were his attempts to keep the assailants at bay keeping her from the same fate?

More explosions tore across the grove. Rescue by rescue caused Nidhogg to stagger and stumble. His power appeared to flounder and diminish. The warrior maiden charged at him, shield lowered, sword set forward. The blade dug into the dragon's scaly belly. He batted the woman aside. She crashed to the ground, dazed and shaken. Sword and shield scattered across the grass.

The ninth tree burst with a further, cataclysmic eruption and that same fatal consequence for the rescuer. Only Karen Randall remained trapped now.

Jeremy swiped at the imps again. They fought back, but their morale had waned with each delivered prisoner.

The warrior raised her piercing mauve gaze to the final struggle at the outer ring. Nidhogg threw back his head, sucking in air for another blast of flame. The woman leapt to her feet, grabbed the sword and ran for the prison tree. It seemed to Jeremy that as she approached, this Valkyrie was herself one moment and then Lisa the next. The transformation continued with each step, shrinking and morphing to a familiar height and shape. The voice ringing out on that frantic sprint, was that of the passionate Lancashire lass. "Stand clear. Karen, get down."

A wall of flame poured from the dragon's mouth, giving chase to the charging woman. The sword struck that final tree and stuck fast. Bark split apart, sending Karen Randall toppling into Jeremy's arms. Lisa dived and grabbed Beth from the scattering servants of darkness. Blistering flames seared into the grove, igniting what remained of the wooden soul cages.

Nidhogg yelled with ear-splitting frustration. But something else accompanied the racket this time: fear. There was fear in that note; intimidating as the cry sounded. The prisoners were released. The dragon's power base had been destroyed.

Massive, shimmering roots tore through the earth like tendrils of Yggdrasil. A luminous serpent; one wrapped itself around the dragon's body. The beast fought and writhed, but the root tightened and held fast. The captive Malice Striker swung overhead and disappeared into the earth, dragged down to its ancient prison.

Lisa and Jeremy squatted with the girls in their arms. The remaining Maypole children from present day Wrenham Green huddled about them. A howling wind whistled past their ears, rising to a deafening crescendo. Lisa squinted through the whipping storm. The galactic backdrop faded into a more familiar canvas of the Kent countryside. A ghostly figure turned, looked over its shoulder and faded away. "Keith." The woman closed her eyes and let him go with a breath of release.

Then came the fiery explosions.

* * *

"Quebec-Hotel-Nine-Nine on station. Commencing FLIR sweep of the target area. Over." The police Eurocopter pilot spoke into the cockpit radio. His blue and yellow whirlybird circled the village green and climbed to begin a circuit of the western hill. The pilot tilted a shiny helmet towards his rear operator. "Anything yet?"

"A couple of deer on the infra-red. Not much else down there with body heat so far."

"Keep looking. I'll bring us around for a comprehensive pass."

The helicopter banked and came about. Ahead, a jet of flame soared up above the woodland canopy, illuminating the night sky. A powerful explosion shook the metal frame of the aircraft. The pilot fought against a surging shock wave and sudden thermal updraft. He checked his manifold pressure for warning signs. Clear so far. A second blast shook them again. Trees lit up like candles on a birthday cake, each trunk and branch engulfed with flames.

The pilot trimmed his aircraft and side-slipped to rotate back to the source of the disturbance. "Flippin' 'eck. Are you getting anything now, Mike?"

His observer threw up both hands before a screen almost a total whiteout with heat signatures. "Are you trying to be funny, Paul?"

Their radio bleeped. "QH99 are you seeing the explosions? Over."

The pilot added more collective to gain extra altitude from the heat source. He spoke into his cabin intercom. "Are *they* trying to be funny?" He keyed the push-to-talk. "QH99 assessing the situation. Standby. Over."

Mike hunched forward across his computer screen. "What the? Paul, we've got people down there. Two-legged figures moving in and out amongst the burning trees."

"How many?"

"Difficult to distinguish with all that ancillary heat." He keyed his radio. "Control, this in QH99. We have movement in the burning forest-" Mike's mouth hung limp at a collection of diminutive white shapes picked up by the forward looking infra-red camera. With the channel held open he continued. "I estimate two adults and about a dozen children. Over."

Paul whipped around to stare at his colleague.

Down on the village green, the Scene Commander burst out of his control van. He intended to alert awaiting officers about the helicopter discovery, but everyone had caught the transmission. Eight uniformed officers, plus Vince and a sore and shaky Marcus sprinted towards the burning, wooded hill. The Commander stuck his head back into the van operations cabin and called to his information officer. "Get Fire and Rescue back over here, plus a cadre of ambulances. Put out a general request for all available officers in the vicinity to attend Wrenham Green. When those kids arrive, we're going to need help reining in the TV crews."

"Sir." A man sitting before a bank of computer screens picked up his phone.

The commander went on. "And pull up a list of contact details for the families of the missing children. If it *is* them coming down, I'd rather their folks heard it from us than on the ten o'clock news."

Another tree exploded like a bomb. The helicopter pilot tugged on his cyclic control stick, raising the nose and backing them away.

Mike shouted at the confusing camera screen, like a football supporter cheering for his favourite team. "Come on kids. You can do it."

Fire leapt from tree to tree, all about the crest of the hill.

Paul struggled with a trembling airframe. The Euro-copter couldn't stay in the thick of this heat much longer. He peered down into the flames. "I hope they can run like the wind."

The next eruption span the chopper a hundred and eighty degrees. A panel of warning lights flashed in the manner of an out-of-sequence disco. An internal siren blared, its note strained as if by the effect of g-forces on the aircraft. Paul fought with the pedals to right the flailing vehicle. The tail shook. "Hang on Mike. Anti-torque rotor's taken a knock." He climbed away from the flames, the helicopter swinging like a metronome. "Control, this is QH99. Mayday. Mayday. Have sustained a hit. We're going down. Over."

A burning blanket of treetops flashed by underneath. Paul danced on the pedals again, fighting to keep their course true. A manifold pressure light winked on. The main rotor blades ground to a halt. "Shit. We've lost the engine. Brace for impact, Mike. Let's see if I can still auto-rotate, like they taught me in the army." He disengaged the rotor from the drive train and dipped the nose forward. The blades span a little again, steadying their descent. "This isn't going to be pretty. Here we go."

The Euro-copter grazed a tree on the periphery of the lane that skirted the western edge of the village green. Smoke poured from the engine housing. Flames lapped at the tail rotor. Another wooden trunk without branches loomed ahead. Paul saw it too late to react in the darkness. "Oh crap." The aircraft smashed through the old Maypole, shredding it like a balsa wood toy. With one last effort, the pilot span them back around to avoid connecting with the police Incident Control Vehicle. Skids ploughed into the earth, jarring the helicopter's occupants. Fire from the tail licked at the last spike of Maypole wood sticking out of the grass.

From along the lane, blue strobes flashed. A procession of vehicles from all three principal emergency services raced to the scene, sirens blaring.

Paul kicked open the cockpit door to decamp. Mike tumbled out of the rear. Both crewmen staggered clear as the first fire engine pulled up.

"Is everyone with us?" Jeremy raced down the steep, uneven slope. His right hand held tight to young Karen Randall. Fire crackled at their heels; a predator in pursuit of its prey.

"I think so." Lisa span left and right, dragging Beth along behind.

All about, the other Maypole children ran for all they were worth, coughing and panting. Eleven-year-old Gemma Harvey tumbled with a yell. Her classmate, Michael Bullen stopped to help her up.

Lisa was about to reverse course, when another voice hurrying the other way startled her.

"I'll get them." The burly figure of Vince bundled past, followed by Marcus and their uniformed companions.

Youngsters in hand, the entire group made the last stretch of trees to the lane and village green beyond.

A smoking police helicopter lay at a jaunty angle

where the Maypole once stood. Fire crews doused it with extinguishers. Another group from Kent Fire and Rescue made steps to tackle the woodland blaze. Camera flashes sparkled: A shimmering pond held back by a hastily erected and policed cordon to keep the media in check. The exhausted runners came to an abrupt halt. Jeremy bent forward, hands resting on his knee caps. Chill night air made him want to gag in an attempt to catch his breath. As he straightened, the woodsman caught sight of Beth Weaver staring in terrified disbelief at the scene all about her. She wore drab, plain clothing. A simple turquoise skirt and woollen cardigan. Over her shoulder, a thin string supported a square cardboard box hanging near her waist. *Of course. A gas mask. Last thing the poor kid knew, it was 1945. The nation was still at war. Or about to finish it.*

Beth's darting eyes moved from the bright blue flashing lights, to modern vehicles filled with computer screens, and the strange machine like a flying windmill crashed nearby. She was an eighty-year-old child, held in limbo for seventy three of them.

Jeremy watched in silence. How long had her agony endured? Or did it seem like yesterday that she was back home in her now irrevocably altered community? The girl clutched tight to Lisa. The northerner stroked her hair.

Marcus staggered over to them.

Jeremy extended his hand. "I owe you a debt of gratitude I shall never be able to repay. You saved my life."

The detective shook it. "Thank Martin Coleman."

The woodsman looked around. "Where is he?"

Marcus lowered his eyes. "He didn't make it."

Lisa stooped to kiss Beth on her crown.

Vince ambled over from the Incident Control Vehicle. "Commander's arranged for the kids to be taken to Kent and Canterbury for a proper check-up. They're going to secure the waiting area outside X-ray and some examination rooms. Nice and quiet out of hours. Easy to block off and control from prying eyes. Emergency social workers and counsellors are being notified to attend. The job will inform the families to meet us there." He motioned to Beth. "Which one's this?"

At that moment, Beth glimpsed a black and white, timber framed Tudor house with high-pitched roof. It sat on the other side of the green, surrounded by a tiny, wraparound garden. She cried out, extending splayed fingers. "Mother."

Lisa hugged her close. "Easy Beth. Easy. I know it's confusing, but I'll explain everything. We'll go home soon, I promise. But first we have to visit the hospital."

Vince frowned. "Beth? I don't remember a girl by that name on the missing list. This one makes eleven, doesn't it? Was she abducted too?"

Lisa nodded.

The stocky detective blinked. "We can't have overlooked an abducted child. The parents would've reported her missing. Is she an orphan?"

Lisa's eyes watered. "Yes. She's an orphan."

Vince surveyed the child up and down. "What's

with the get up? She looks like a juvenile extra from 'Dad's Army' or something."

Marcus stared from Lisa to the girl and back again. Cogs whirred in his brain.

The woman met his eyes but remained silent. She shifted to address Jeremy. "Would you go with Beth in the ambulance while I bring Anne along?"

The child lifted her head at the sound of that familiar name.

Jeremy edged closer to the young girl. "Of course."

16

A Family Reunion

"Why are we going to the hospital?" Anne shifted in the front passenger seat of Lisa's car. Apart from some minor scratches, a recovery vehicle had retrieved the faithful Clio undamaged from where Keith ran it off the road.

"The missing Maypole children escaped the fire with Jeremy and I. They're being taken to Kent and Canterbury for a check-up."

"And you think Tessa and her mother might draw strength from having me there?"

Lisa rocked her head. "It couldn't hurt."

"But why did you ask me to bring Molly? I can't let the girl have her. I simply can't." The old woman clutched tight to the rag doll in her lap.

Lisa placed a steadying hand on the schoolteacher's leg. "I wouldn't even think of suggesting it."

"Then why?"

Lisa sighed. "I don't know where to begin. But it might be easier to explain if you see what we've got to show you first. Do you trust me?"

"Yes." Anne paused. "I'm glad you're safe. When I saw the fire and heard the commotion, I was worried that horrid man had come back for you."

"He did. Actually, he came for Jeremy to begin with. Were it not for Martin Coleman, he'd be dead. Marcus and I could never have pulled him alive from the burning wreckage of his home."

Anne lifted the back of one hand to her mouth. "Goodness. Is Martin alright?"

Lisa's eyes reddened. "No. He died in the blaze."

"And Marcus?"

"Bruised and battered, but okay."

"Did he arrest Keith again?"

Lisa shook her head. "Keith died too. Up in the ash grove."

"How did the children escape? Do you know who took them?"

Lisa signalled to pull into the hospital car park off Ethelbert Road in Canterbury. "We'll get to that in a little while. Let's head down to X-Ray first."

Inner and outer checkpoints had been set up. Temporary security to prevent unwanted visitors to the hospital holding area. Families arrived in dribs and drabs, faces drawn but eyes sparkling with tentative hope. The phone calls they received sounded too good to be true. Now, intermittent squeals of delight, sobs and shrieks of emotional release provided evidence to the contrary. All about, children cuddled tight to one or more astounded parents. Widowed Nicola Jarrett sat on a chair in stunned silence, Ivan's head resting against her shoulder. Even Patrick Collins' estranged father stepped up at a moment's notice upon receiving news his boy was alive.

Lisa stood on tiptoe to scan the throng. Doctors, nurses, psychologists and social workers milled about the busy space. She caught sight of Jeremy holding tight to Beth's hand on a far row of seats. "This way, Anne."

The old woman glanced from side to side, mind awhirl at the hustle and bustle. She waved to Angela Hackman. Her former pupil rocked with Tessa in her arms and husband standing over. The new arrivals crossed the waiting area. Lisa stepped aside and Anne stopped dead. Incessant noise from the surrounding hubbub dulled to a woolly blur. A doctor with a clipboard passed in front of some seats where a man and young girl sat motionless. Jeremy Lewis raised his head in recognition of the women. At his side, a girl played with the sleeves of her cardigan; eyes wide, face streaked with intense furrows. An old gas mask box rested in her lap.

Anne shook. She clasped the doll tight to her chest. "Oh my God." Her face ran with a waterfall of immediate tears.

Lisa stood close by, suddenly aware that such a shock might prove dangerous to the kindly old spinster. At least they were in the right place for a medical emergency.

Beth's attention fixed on the crying, silver haired woman and the doll she held. "Molly?" Her face brightened a little.

Anne edged closer and squatted before the seated

child. "Beth." The word came out with hushed fragility. She held out the rag doll.

Beth clutched it to her neck, squeezing tight to at least one familiar thing from the world she had been torn out of. Something about the old woman seemed familiar. "Why is everything different? Is this a nightmare? How do you know my name? Are you friends with my parents?"

Anne rose to sit alongside. She fiddled with her chunky necklace of coloured stones. "You mean William and Doris Weaver?"

The girl nodded. Her legs swung a little upon receiving some comfort from her favourite toy.

Anne wiped her sodden eyes. She looked at Lisa for help.

The northerner stepped forward. Jeremy vacated his seat to allow her a prime spot. Lisa sat and touched the girl's wrist. "How much do you remember, Beth? What's the last thing?"

"I remember the Maypole dance. My sister Anne couldn't do it because she caught chickenpox. I took her place. Dan, our brother stayed home to keep an eye on her."

"Anything else?"

Beth's face darkened. "I remember passing out. Teacher said it must have been the heat and excitement. All the other dancers were watching me."

"When was this?"

"The other day."

Anne leaned closer. "Can you recall the date?"

"Yes of course. It was Saturday the fifth. We didn't

have the festival on Mayday because it was a Tuesday. That was the day we heard Hitler was dead. The war should be over soon. Then Father can come home." She hesitated. "No wait. I remember more. The war *did* end the following week. In Europe anyway. We had a big party. Then some of my friends went missing. I don't remember much about it. Everything feels foggy. Still no news on Father. Have I been ill and in a fever? Is Father here? Has he been injured?"

Anne blubbed. She lifted a small handkerchief to her face.

Lisa picked up the questioning. "Is there anything else you remember? Think hard."

Beth shuddered. She buried her nose into the doll.

Lisa slipped an arm around her shoulders. "It's alright. You're safe now."

The child lifted two tiny, terrified eyes. "There were dreams. Endless bad dreams. Then you came and woke me up. I don't even know your name. Have we met before? The woods were on fire. You helped me downhill to the green. How did I get up to the grove? Nothing is how it was." Saltwater brimmed over and trickled down her pale face.

A nurse sidled up to them. She addressed the seven-year-old with a sympathetic, down-turned mouth. "Aw bless. Hello there. The doctor is ready to have a look at you."

Beth stared at Lisa. "Do I have to? When will Mother get here?"

Lisa lifted one of the girl's hands and passed it to the old school teacher. "Now then. My name is Lisa. That man is Jeremy. This lady who looked after your doll is called Anne."

"Like my twin sister?"

"Yes. Exactly like your twin sister."

"How did she get Molly?"

Lisa grimaced. "Why don't you let Anne here go with you to see the doctor? Then she can hold Molly so she doesn't get lost. We'll talk more afterwards." Lisa looked at Anne. "Is that okay?"

Anne nodded.

The old woman and young girl followed the nurse into an examination room.

Lisa hung her head in her hands. "How are we going to do this, Jeremy?"

The woodsman placed a warm hand on her leg. "It's the saddest happy outcome you could ever imagine. Even for these present day kids." He watched families posing similar questions to their children across the waiting area. "Some of those youngsters have lost parents, friends and siblings. At their own hands too, after a fashion. If there's a merciful God or any kindness in the universe, they'll be as clueless about it as Beth."

"But they'll still need to learn of their bereavement."

"Yes they will."

"Beth killed her own brother. I hope she never finds out."

"She'll have to be told he's dead though. Her parents too."

A sharp male cough interrupted them. Marcus Foster stood nearby, flexing his fingers. "Is Beth in with the doctor now?"

Lisa lifted her sunken head. "Yes. Anne accompanied her."

"Does she know Anne?"

"You could say that."

"That's good. Do you have any contact details for the home she came from?"

Lisa shook her head. "She won't know either."

"Beth, you mean?"

"Uh huh."

"I see. Trauma, amnesia or shock, I suppose. I'll be surprised if Anne doesn't know. Well, we can refer the child to social services for care." The detective examined Jeremy. "Your ankle healed fast."

"Yeah. Took me by surprise too."

Marcus turned to leave then pivoted round. "The child is something to do with that thing in the fire, isn't she?"

Lisa and Jeremy gazed at him.

The detective ran one hand through his short hair. "How am I going to report all this? Don't suppose you have any idea where the missing kids came from, or who took them?"

A flash of discomfort exchanged between Lisa and Jeremy, like discovered criminals grasping for an alibi.

The woodsman spoke. "We found them in the ash grove."

"What, wandering around?"

"After the fire took hold."

"What happened to Molloy, or whatever that deformed creature was?"

Lisa stared into space. "Perished."

Marcus put his hands on his hips. "We need to sit down and have a proper chat about this, sometime soon. Not tonight though."

Lisa frowned. "Are you sure you want to do that?"

"No, I'm not. Especially in a formal, professional setting."

"Why don't you pop over to the cottage in a few days to get the story straight? Or decide how best to - err... translate it, so others can understand."

"Sounds like I'm going to need a masterclass in embroidering the truth." He lowered his voice. "Tell me I'm not the only one who saw a man turn into a fire-breathing demon or something."

Jeremy shrugged. "You're not the only one. But unless we all want to become neighbours in adjoining padded cells, your factual needlework better be impressive."

Marcus blinked. "Thanks. That doesn't help at all."

Fifty minutes later, Anne reappeared with Beth.

"Everything alright?" Lisa said. "Where's Molly?"

Beth lifted the cardboard box lid to reveal the doll tucked inside like a child in a papoose. "I haven't carried that gas mask around for ages. But the box was always useful for things. Is Mother here yet? What about Dan and my sister?"

Lisa got up. "It's late. Why don't we take you home to Bramley Cottage? We'll talk about everything in the morning."

Beth's lips pursed. She may have only been seven years old, but the girl could spot an avoided question. *What's happened to Mother and Father? What about Anne and Daniel? Home. Get home first and maybe everything will be fine.* "Yes please."

"Miss Weaver?" The nurse poked her head back through the door. "Could you and Beth pop over to room seven. Social Services would like a word."

Beth looked up at the old lady. "Is your name Weaver too? Anne Weaver? Are you a long lost auntie?"

Anne took her by the hand. "We *are* family. One thing at a time though."

Another thirty minutes passed before a loud wailing and crying erupted from room seven. Anne reappeared with Beth clinging onto her leg. "I don't want to leave with them. I want to go home to Bramley Cottage."

Marcus Foster stood up from where he had been chatting with the Bullen family. The word 'home' from Beth's outburst rang in his ears. A male social worker attempted to prise the girl away from Anne. Marcus raised a hand. "Hold up there." He jogged over to intercept before the tension could escalate. "What's your name?"

"Rick Filmore - Social Services."

Marcus flashed his warrant card. "DS Foster. Can we all step back inside for a word?"

Filmore motioned to the door. They filed into the room with the Weaver girls.

When the door opened again, Beth appeared calm. Marcus shook the social worker's hand and escorted the girls back to Lisa and Jeremy.

"What was all that about?" Lisa said.

"Social Services wanted to take Beth away, due to her supposed confusion," Anne replied. "And because we're not her legal guardians. She has a missing identity."

Marcus chipped in. "We don't know who she is. Beth claims to live at Bramley Cottage. She also thinks it's 1945."

Jeremy folded his arms. He raised one sarcastic eyebrow at the detective. "Dresses like it too, doesn't she?"

Marcus paused. He looked from Jeremy to Lisa, to the seven-year-old girl. If this was a joke, nobody laughed. When he met Anne's furtive eyes again, his heart skipped a beat. "It can't be." His mouth opened a crack for the phrase to slip out.

Anne's head bounced in one slow, tiny nod. "I don't understand it either, Marcus. I'm hoping Lisa and Jeremy can explain more when we get home."

"I should *cocoa*."

"So what about Beth and Social Services?" Lisa said.

"Oh. I told them I could vouch for Anne's impeccable character. I've accepted responsibility for Beth's welfare, should anything go awry. She'll have to be processed through the system when her - err... memory returns. They'll send other social workers round on regular home visits to check up on her. But for now she can stay at Bramley Cottage. Poor kid's been through enough tonight. I know she couldn't be in safer hands until all this gets sorted."

Lisa kissed the detective on the cheek. "Thank you."

"Whatever for?"

The woman's face softened. "For acting like a decent human being and not a jobs-worth. Martin Coleman would be proud."

Marcus swallowed. "I couldn't ask for more than that. You'd better get the young lady home. I'll be round tomorrow afternoon, if that's okay? My Inspector is going to be crying out for answers. I can stall things until then with procedure, but not much beyond it."

"Drop by anytime. But I warn you now: it's going to sound like some unbelievable, twisted fairy tale."

"If what happened at Ashdene is any kind of foretaste, I can well imagine." Marcus lifted one hand to his mouth and coughed. "Take care."

* * *

"What time is it? Crumbs. I'd better get back to what's left of my home, if anything." Jeremy stretched on the doormat in the hallway at Bramley Cottage.

Upstairs, Anne settled her exhausted twin sister down in their old bedroom.

Lisa craned her neck and listened. All quiet. "I never want to face a family chat like that again, Jeremy."

One corner of the woodsman's mouth rose. "Would you say that's likely?"

The woman wrung her hands. "No. I suppose not."

"Do you think the poor little mite believed us?"

"Either that or she's so exhausted, she's hoping to wake up in the morning and find it's all been a bad dream."

Jeremy frowned. "Hmm. I hope not. If there's another screaming and crying fit like the one after we got back and dropped the bomb on her…"

"Yeah." Lisa bit her lip. "I was hoping it could all wait until tomorrow. But nobody would have slept a wink in the meantime."

"What about the way she was happy one minute then distressed the next?"

"The familiar and unfamiliar side by side. She saw her old home, furniture, the grandfather clock here; but lots of new-fangled appliances she didn't recognise. And no family. None that looked the way she remembered, anyway. I suppose it's one mercy Anne hasn't remodelled the place."

Jeremy scratched a patch of rough stubble on his chin. "Imagine it: Going to sleep or in a daze as a seven-year-old one day. Next thing when your head clears, it's seventy-three years later. The world you knew has changed beyond measure. Your twin sister is an old woman and the rest of your family have passed away. Yet you remain the same. Talk about culture shock. I don't know any adults who'd take that without cracking under the strain."

"Exactly."

"I would say look after her. But with you and Anne, that's a given. One glimmer of hope for the child."

"You're all heart. God, I'm tired. Sure you don't

want to crash here? Anne would be happy for you to sleep on the sofa."

"Nah. I need to survey the damage at Ashdene. Otherwise I won't be getting any sleep either. If my van hasn't incinerated, I'll bed down in the back tonight."

"Okay." Lisa yawned.

Jeremy tweaked her nose. "Off to bed." He turned and opened the door. On the step he paused and looked back. "Lisa?"

"Yeah?" She rubbed her eyes.

"Perhaps this isn't the time, but… I love you."

Lisa stopped, her face deadpan. "Maybe it's just right. We've seen the love and loss of a lifetime compressed into one tiny package this evening. If ever there was a spot to seize the moment, this might be it."

Jeremy clicked his neck and winced. "Stop being such a fancy bloody writer. What are you trying to say?"

The girl grinned. "I love you too." She kissed him on the mouth for one lingering moment, then shut the door.

* * *

When Lisa opened her bedroom door late the next morning, she found Beth standing there, eyes transfixed on the portal. The child's bottom lip quivered upon seeing her. Without a word, the seven-year-old turned and tramped downstairs with soft, slow steps. Anne's door opened wide from a mere crack.

"She's been standing there for an hour, Lisa. I didn't dare disturb her."

"Has she noticed you since she got up?"

"No."

"She was waiting to see who would walk out of Daniel's room, wasn't she? Me or your brother."

"That's why I didn't dare disturb her. If she saw the same old woman as last night emerge from where Mother and Father used to sleep... Well, it would-"

"Dispel the illusion. I get it."

"Silly, aren't I?"

"No. Kind. How do you adjust to a situation like the one she's found herself in? It's going to take time, if she ever manages to cope."

The old woman hobbled along the landing to rest beside her lodger. "Time is one thing I can't give her. Not much, at least."

"Don't say that, Anne. You're a strong woman. No reason you won't get your telegram from the monarch. Time to see Beth grow into a mature woman."

Anne peered over the banister, clutching it with two arthritic bony hands. "No Lisa, I won't."

"What do you mean?"

The old schoolteacher didn't look up. "I'm dying."

Lisa gasped. "What? How do you know?"

"I've spoken with the doctors."

"When?"

"Right before I posted my advertisement for a companion." This time she peered into Lisa's dilating pupils. "I wasn't so much seeking someone to help me, as someone I could help. I had no children or blood relatives left. Or so I thought until last night. When we spoke on the phone and you came to stay, I realised I'd found the one. Someone I could leave my home to. Someone worthy, who would appreciate it."

"Anne, I'm speechless."

"Do you remember the day I went out alone to settle some legal matters?"

Lisa's mouth dropped open. "You were amending your will, weren't you?"

"That's right. Bramley Cottage will be yours when I'm gone, along with a few savings."

"But what about Beth? That must change everything. She's your twin sister."

"But only a child. She can't inherit at her age. If someone sold the property, and kept the money in trust, Beth would still need to go into care."

"This is her home, Anne."

"Yes it is. And the thought of her leaving it and being passed around pains my heart."

"I wonder if Social Services would let me foster?"

A twinkle shimmered in the spinster's eye. "If you found a nice young man to settle down with, they might even let you adopt."

Lisa flushed. "There's another person without a home." She shook her head. "What am I doing? Did the doctor's give you any timescales? They've been wrong before. You might-"

"No. It won't be long now."

Lisa wrapped her arms around the silver-haired lady. "Why do I always lose the people I love?"

Anne kissed her cheek. "Be a good mother to my sister, Lisa. She's still very young, even if she *is* fifty years older than you."

Lisa laughed and cried at the same time.

After dressing, Anne pushed open the living room door with slow, shaking fingers. "Beth?"

The seven-year-old stood locked onto the old family portrait photograph. "Where are they buried, Anne? Where did you bury Mother, Father and Daniel?"

"In the churchyard. They're in a quiet corner of St. Mary's. Mum and I used to take Dan tulips every year on the anniversary of his death. I still do."

Beth rotated to gaze up at her sister with pleading eyes. "Will you show me?"

"Of course." The old lady offered her hand.

Lisa stuck her head round the door.

Anne and Beth crossed the room. The old woman tilted her head. "We're going to visit the family plot at the church, Lisa. Would you like to come along?"

"This time it should be a private moment between sisters. Besides, Marcus Foster will be popping over in search of answers."

"Dear Marcus. However will he explain such a fantastic tale to his superiors?"

Lisa shrugged. "I don't know that he can. Not in a way that won't end his career, if he wants to be truthful."

"There's the rub. Marcus was always an honest boy. He won't like telling lies."

"No he won't. But either he gets economical with the truth, or pleads ignorance until the investigation runs out of steam. Neither option is ideal."

When the cottage door opened a couple of hours later, DS Marcus Foster stepped from inside to squint at the afternoon sun with a perplexed expression. Anne and Beth's visit to the churchyard had turned into an extended stroll. They remained out and about. Beyond the village, the old wooded hill crest still smoked. Its top appeared flat, where the ash grove used to grow. The whole resembled a bald spot on a once virile man: hair but a memory, as the trees of that ancient, sacred grove were too.

Lisa leaned out behind the detective. "Are you okay?"

Marcus coughed. "What a question."

"Think I'm making it up?"

"If I hadn't been with you when we found Jeremy..."

"What are you going to do?"

"Report what I have in a way that works. There's a domestic violence abuser, escaped from custody after abducting and raping his ex-partner. He then tries to murder one local man and succeeds in murdering another. After that, he's toasted in a forest fire at the same time our missing children show up."

"But you know he wasn't here when the murders and child disappearances happened. They can't have been his doing."

"True enough. I didn't say I'd cracked the case; only that I've got some factual events to report. What they do with it all is their business."

"What do you *think* they'll do with it?"

"Unless you're yanking my chain about all this, they'll chase a few more dead ends before giving up. It'll go into the cold case bin for periodic review."

"Like the disappearances in '45?"

"Yeah."

"What about Beth?"

"A confused, delusional child appears with the other missing kids. Nobody can find any trace of her background. But, she has an affinity for this cottage. As a fortunate bonus, its responsible owners want to care for her. We can make that stick with Social Services, once someone has made the requisite checks. I've got a contact to lean on. In the present financial climate, they'll be delighted to have another child off their books. Once they're satisfied the girl's in safe hands, everything will work out. Don't worry."

"Was I right to tell you about Anne? She only gave me the news this morning."

Marcus rubbed one side of his nose. "I'm not sure, but I'm glad you did. For what it's worth, I'd say she's made the right decision. Choosing you, I mean."

"Thanks." Lisa propped herself against the open door. "So what's next for you?"

"Long term? No idea. For now, I'm going to pay a visit to Martin Coleman's widow. Once upon a time the police were like a big family. We looked after each other, even beyond retirement. It's one tradition we've let go. That's wrong and I intend to change it. I owe Martin that much."

"Don't forget what I said about attractive women, should you bump into any while you're busy being an all-round decent bloke."

Marcus offered up a half smile. "Go! Go! Go!" He extended his hand.

Lisa shook it. "Look after yourself, Fuzz."

"You too, Lisa. Be a good Mum."

"I'll do my best. I've had some great role models. Goodbye."

17
Just a Number

"What a mess. Did you sleep in the van?"

Jeremy swivelled on his haunches at the sound of Lisa's voice. All about him, the waterlogged remains of blackened timber lay scattered behind the now burnt out hedge at Ashdene. Metal or enamel items like his stove and bathtub rested on piles of ash. A gentle breeze whipped the dusty remnants into tiny, whirling clouds. Only his van remained untouched by the blaze. No walls still stood on what had once been his home. "I did." He rose, body stiff from an uncomfortable couple of nights in the vehicle.

Lisa closed the five-bar gate which, though darkened, had survived thanks to the fire service. "How does this affect your scheme for retrospective planning permission?"

Jeremy cleared his throat. "I need to get a non-mobile structure back in situ, as soon as possible."

"And your work?"

"I have a little cash in the bank. First order of business is a new chainsaw and some fresh timber. I'll have to put up a workshop and live in it for now. Without that, I can't earn any money."

Lisa sauntered over to him.

Jeremy pulled her close. They cuddled. "How's Beth coping?"

"Better than we'd hoped, all things considered. She wanted to visit the family graves yesterday, so Anne took her."

"Brave girl. What about DS Foster? Did he come round for his explanation?"

Lisa rolled her eyes. "Oh yeah."

Jeremy smirked. "And how is he going to explain children possessed and abducted by murderous servants of a dragon from a parallel dimension? Jeez, I'd love to read the police report for that one."

The woman grinned. "If he hadn't been with me when we found you under attack, I reckon I'd have been looking at a drugs test."

Jeremy threw back his head to laugh at the absurdity of it all. Somehow a release of pent-up anxiety and tension came with it. "You've got to admit, it does make you sound like someone on an acid trip."

Lisa rested her head against his shoulder, then twisted to stare back up the hill. "Have you been to the top again?"

"Only near the edge to check on the trees bordering my property. Thanks to the fire crew, the flames never reached down that side. The old ash grove is gone though. It's an empty clearing now." He paused in thought. "Lisa?"

"Yeah?"

"Do you think it was me fighting off those shadowy creatures that kept Beth from the same fate as her peers? I've been mulling it over. Sure, I put up a frantic fight, but they were still on her like a pack of rabid dogs."

"I don't know. There are more questions than answers in all this. I keep thinking about both Maypole incidents taking place on Saturday, 5th May. The same day in 1945 and 2018. Was that coincidence too? There have been other dances on that day and date, so it could be nothing. Who knows?"

"What was it like?"

"What?"

"Being merged with Skuld, or whatever she did to transform you into that warrior?"

"Like a dream. I was aware what was going on. Deep inside I remained myself, but a part of me connected with something bigger: An intelligence, a power - I don't know. One thing struck me most of all."

"What's that?"

"A total absence of fear. It was euphoric, Jeremy. I mean, when was the last time you didn't have some kind of worry, concern or all out fear tucked away in the corner of your mind? I know I always do. But in that transformation, fear no longer existed for me; only purpose. I faced Nidhogg not because I'm brave. I'm not. Not really. I faced that creature because fear couldn't hold me captive. I wish I'd brought that experience back, but I didn't. When I grabbed Beth, she felt like the Norns' gift to me for my service. Might answer your question about her survival."

"At least she's with her sister again."

Lisa's eyes watered. She clutched onto the startled woodsman.

"Hey now. What's wrong?" he said.

The woman sniffed. "Hold me, Jeremy."

* * *

"Anne?" Lisa knocked on the spinster's bedroom door next morning. Cup of tea in hand, she was delighted to have made it downstairs first. Time to wait on the old lady for a change. "Anne? Are you awake?"

From inside, a gentle sobbing greeted her ears.

"Are you sick?"

The sound of grief intensified, but something about the pitch felt wrong.

Lisa twisted the wrought iron ring handle and slipped the varnished dark timber door open. The master was a dual aspect chamber flooded with sunlight, dappled through the leaves of nearby trees. An old oak-framed double bed rested against the far wall. A bulge from one of the cottage's two chimneys formed a natural place on which to display an embroidery sampler. The simple phrase: *'Home Sweet Home'* hung decorated with stitched flowers. Two figures lay in the bed. The first, a silver haired old lady in a long, white nightdress. Her eyes were closed, complexion pale and waxy but with a simple smile that spoke of peace. The other was a seven-year-old, fair-haired girl. She lay on her side, clutching at the unresponsive pensioner's torso. On the pillow between them lay Molly the rag doll. Lisa stood in the doorway, a faint tinkling of a china cup on saucer announcing the most delicate trembling in her hands.

Beth sobbed again, squeezing and pulling the old woman closer. "Anne. Anne, please come back. Don't leave me here all alone. You're my sister, Anne. I love you. Molly loves you too."

Lisa rested the tea on top of a chest of drawers. She edged closer to Beth and perched on her side of the mattress. Anne Weaver looked more radiant and beautiful in her sleep of death than the northerner could ever remember. She reached over to stroke her silken, silvery hair. One silent tear dropping from her face, Lisa eased forward and kissed the woman on her forehead.

Beth rolled over and clutched her rescuer tight. "Everybody's dead. What's going to happen, Lisa?"

The woman swept the child into a deep embrace. "Everything will be alright, Beth. Anne made sure of it. I'm going to take care of you now. I love you."

* * *

"You look amazing." Janice Gange stepped back from the vision before her, fiddling with a flower that adorned her bridesmaid dress. The master bedroom at Bramley Cottage appeared much the same as the day Anne Weaver passed away in it. Seated at a dressing table, Lisa lifted the two silver combs Auntie Joan left her from a box. They slid into her hair; a final element completing the picture of bridal beauty that stared back from the mirror.

"Is she almost ready?" Beth Weaver poked her head around the door, face aglow with excitement. "Wow. Lisa, you're so beautiful."

Warm traces of a subtle smile melted across the bride's face. It was the happiest she had seen that disoriented orphan since they met. "Are you all set, darling?"

"Yes. I love this dress. Auntie Janice helped me into it."

Lisa cocked an eyebrow at her old colleague. "That was nice of her."

Janice beamed. "It was no trouble. Beth is a sweetheart." She looked at the girl. "Get yourself downstairs now. We'll be along in a minute." She ushered the child back onto the landing, closed the door and turned to Lisa. "So who is she?"

Lisa hesitated. "Beth? An orphan from the village."

"Not one from those God awful murders?"

"Not quite."

"That's a relief. When you invited me down to stay for the wedding, I was in two minds. Story seems to have blown over now."

"Yeah. Peace has returned to Wrenham Green at last."

"The media were banging on about it being some violent paedophile ring that imploded. Seems the vicar who got topped was part of it. They reckon he grew a conscience and was going to blow the whistle. That's why they did for him."

"It's one account."

"Supposedly the other victims came between them and their targets. Whole group made it appear like a lone psycho. The papers even mentioned Keith in one report. Thank God the kids survived. Wonder if any of the sickos did? Best left to the police, I reckon."

"Quite."

"So did the old lady know Beth?"

"Anne? Yes, very well. It's one reason Jeremy and I are adopting her."

"You kept him a secret. Can't wait to meet this new man of yours. Got to be an improvement on the last. He was a right monster."

Lisa licked her lips. "He could be sometimes."

"Good riddance to the bastard in that fire."

"I won't have to glance back over my shoulder anymore. That's one relief."

"Beth is so polite and well behaved. Blimey, if I didn't know better, I'd say you built a time machine and kidnapped her from the forties or something. Well then. A wife and mother all at once? You never did things by halves, Lis'. Glad something is going right for you at last. And nice to see you taking in an orphan. No surprise, given your history."

Lisa winked. "No surprise."

Lisa and Jeremy glided out of the porch at St. Mary's, Wrenham Green into glorious sunshine and an azure sky. Clouds of confetti and rose petals filled the air about them. Behind, Janice and Beth joined the crowd of well-wishers, heaping handfuls of fluttering luck upon the happy couple.

Astrid Lewis shook back a mane of blonde hair, the faintest hints of colour disguising early signs of grey. The stocky but toned Norwegian woman embraced her new daughter-in-law. "I am so happy with the girl my son has chosen to wed. You are a female of spirit, Lisa. I can tell this." She may have lived in England for many years, but her Scandinavian accent had lost none of its potency.

Lisa kissed the woman. "Jeremy has a quiet strength all his own. It's one of the things that attracted me to him."

Astrid stepped back. "I'm glad a nice girl finally drew him out of his shy shell."

Jeremy leaned close to whisper in his wife's ear. "I thought you two might hit it off. Her name 'Astrid' means 'Divine Strength' in English, you know."

"Serious?"

"Yep. She knows you're a special girl. I haven't even told her you're a part-time Valkyrie."

Lisa smirked. "I wasn't intending to stick it on my CV. Where did Beth go? Ah. Keep the crowds busy a minute, would you?"

Jeremy followed her gaze around the churchyard to where the seven-year-old girl stood alone before the graves of her family.

Lisa excused herself and slipped away, arrested en route with hugs and kisses from wedding guests.

Beth noticed the approach of gentle steps in ivory wedding shoes. "I'm sorry, Lisa. I didn't mean to-"

"Hush now. What's to be sorry about?" Lisa stood side by side with her before the quiet spot. A mound of earth still rose above the greensward where they'd buried Anne not long before. Behind them across the village green, Bramley Cottage appeared to keep watch. The green itself no longer played host to a plethora of emergency and media vehicles. They had long since departed. Today, the hustle and bustle were of a happier nature: a large marquee erected for the bride and groom to hold their reception among the community they loved. Kevin Laycock at The White Hart laid on the catering. Elsewhere among the tombs, several other tell-tale mounds of earth spoke of a busy time for funerals. Martin Coleman slept among them, his vigilant spirit almost as present in death as it was in life. Even old Neville joined his wife in the great beyond. But not before the astonishment of recognising the returned Beth Weaver. Nobody at the pub believed him, though everyone missed the sweet man now he was gone.

Beth took hold of Lisa's hand. "I didn't mean to interrupt your wedding. I'm not a great bridesmaid, am I?"

"Yes you are." The bride waved one palm across the graves in an open gesture. "Without *them*, none of us would be here. I wouldn't be marrying Jeremy. I might not even be alive. They'll always be a part of us, darling. This day is theirs too, even if we can't see them."

"Will Jeremy be moving in now?"

"Yes." She hesitated. "Beth. We're not trying to take

the place of your parents. Nobody can ever do that."

"It's okay. I like Jeremy. I'm so glad you'll both be with me."

"Bless your heart."

The child's face lightened. "Will we be safe in Germany?"

Lisa laughed with a musical trill. "Of course."

"Don't you and Jeremy need a honeymoon alone?"

"No Beth. We want one with our family."

The girl gulped. "I'm scared."

"What of? The plane?"

"No. I'm excited about the plane. I've never flown. It's just…"

"Not so long ago your world was at war with Germany?"

"I suppose."

"That's one reason we're taking you walking in Bavaria. Not big hikes too tough for your young legs, but pretty, short little routes with wonderful views. The people there are wonderful too. I want you to see for yourself that we're all friends now. There will be mountains, lakes, and forests to explore. Plus fairy tale castles-"

"There won't be any dragons, will there?"

Lisa gawped, eyebrows raised in unison. "You remember some of what happened then?"

Beth shuddered. "Only as a nightmare. Sometimes I wake up with bad dreams. But now Molly is there to help me sleep again."

Lisa pinched her little lady's cheek. "The nightmares are over. That I promise you."

* * *

"Well, that was an awesome break in Bavaria, but it's good to be home." Jeremy sat down on a chair in the garden at Bramley Cottage. "Is she asleep?"

Lisa handed across an open bottle of beer and joined him on the other seat. A starry, crystal clear night sky unfolded like a giant dark blanket of diamonds above. "Worn out, but happy. I'll look in on her later to make sure she's okay. Cheers." She chinked her own bottle against her husband's.

Jeremy took a gulp, savouring the cool slaking action upon his parched throat. "Beth's engaging with this new world around her now. That trip gave her a boost. All the same: seven years old. Should be playing bloody hopscotch or something; not adjusting to time travel and bereavement. Poor child has had to find strength and maturity beyond her years. Beyond anyone's years. Crumbs, our kid's a fighter." He grinned. "Takes after her new mum."

Lisa sipped her beer and swallowed hard. "Better watch your step then."

Jeremy placed the bottle on the table between them. He reclined and knitted his fingers together behind his head. "Dear old Anne would be so pleased if she could see how things worked out."

"She *foresaw* them. Helped get us here."

"For certain."

"A few months ago I was living in a rented Durham flat, a victim of domestic violence and a psychotic boss.

Now I'm down south, married and living in a lovely, paid for old cottage with a seven-year-old daughter."

Jeremy inclined his head her way. "Correction. With an *eighty*-year-old daughter."

Lisa nodded. "If ever there was an example of how age is just a number, it's sleeping upstairs. I'm glad they're going to let us home-school her."

"Yeah. Until she learns to live under a legend we can create, it's for the best. She'll need kids her own age to play with though."

"True. But we can limit the chances of her being stressed about explaining where she comes from. Play dates are easy to end. They're not a mandatory part of day-to-day life, like socialising at school. Are you going to work tomorrow?"

Jeremy stretched. "For a bit. Thought I'd ease myself back in a little at a time. Now there's only a workshop to build and I haven't got to live there… Well, Ashdene is my work site now. Nothing more."

Lisa sniffed. "That's good. The cottage could do with a dust and polish. You're up."

"Did I say I was going to work for a bit? What I meant was, I should get right back in the saddle and give it my all. Lots of building to do."

Lisa punched his shoulder with a playful fist. She stared across the silent, empty green to where the Maypole once stood. "Do you think they'll erect another?"

"Maypole? I doubt it. It amazes me they kept the blasted thing after 1945. What with the war ending, it seems other things eclipsed the tragedy. That or nobody made a serious connection to it as a source of what happened. Can't blame them. It's bizarre."

"If they'd demolished it, we wouldn't have a daughter. She'd still be imprisoned in that awful place, Jeremy. Her and her old schoolmates."

"I didn't think of it that way. You're right, of course. No, I imagine Maypoles are one tradition this village will eschew from here on out. The association with tragedy and death is too strong."

"Good." Lisa drained her bottle. "Don't sit out here too long. I'm going to have a peek at our little miracle."

Jeremy blew her a kiss.

Lisa opened the door to Beth's room with a faint creak. A triangle of light flooded in from the landing. The child lay fast asleep, snuggling close to Molly in bed. The woman crept in and brushed clumping fair hair away from her daughter's eyes. "Goodnight angel. Sweet dreams." Her lips brushed two tiny rose cheeks. She retreated to the doorway again.

In some alternate reality, Lisa had closed a spiritual door on an infernal beast bent on death and destruction in her own. Now in this present reality she closed a physical door, safe in the knowledge that the treasure within was home to stay. Safe and well for however long the sands of time kept her alive on this good, green earth.

ABOUT THE AUTHOR

Devon De'Ath was born in the county of Kent, 'The Garden of England.' Raised a Roman Catholic in a small, ancient country market community famously documented as 'the most haunted TOWN in England,' he grew up in an atmosphere replete with spiritual, psychic, and supernatural energy. Hauntings were commonplace and you couldn't swing a cat without hitting three spectres, to the extent that he never needed question the validity of such manifestations. As to the explanations behind them?

At the age of twenty, his earnest search for spiritual truth led the young man to leave Catholicism and become heavily involved in Charismatic Evangelicalism. After serving as a part-time youth pastor while working in the corporate world, he eventually took voluntary redundancy to study at a Bible College in the USA. Missions in the Caribbean and sub-Saharan Africa followed, but a growing dissatisfaction with aspects of the theology and ministerial abuse by church leadership eventually caused him to break with organised religion and pursue a Post-Evangelical existence. One open to all manner of spiritual and human experiences his 'holy' life would never have allowed.

After church life, De'Ath served fifteen years with the police, lectured at colleges and universities, and acted as a consultant to public safety agencies both foreign and domestic.

A writer since he first learned the alphabet, Devon De'Ath has authored works in many genres under various names, from Children's literature to self-help books, through screenplays for video production and all manner of articles.

Printed in Great Britain
by Amazon

Printed in Great Britain
by Amazon